PRAISE FOR
THE CAVANAUGH BROTHERS

Brash

"Wright once again delivers her signature mix of dramatic tension and delectable passion."
—*Publishers Weekly*

"With quick pacing, snarky humor, and plenty of steamy details, this is an installment that is certain to thrill fans." —*RT Book Reviews* (top pick)

Broken

"Fans of Wright's Cavanaugh brothers will delight in this passionate family and the fascinating small-town characters. The emotional barriers that separate her main couple are remarkably understandable and refreshingly genuine, making their journey a compelling and touching one."
—*RT Book Reviews*

"Explosive chemistry between James and Sheridan. . . . The steamy sex between them was so wonderfully done . . . a fantastic, sexy romance."
—The Reading Cafe

"I love this series so much . . . sexy cowboy romance. . . . I fell in love with James, the sexy horse whisperer."
—Reading in Pajamas

"If you're a sucker for a tortured hero, James Cavanaugh will have your heart melting . . . a great contemporary romance with a Western slant."
—Debbie's Book Bag

continued . . .

Branded

"A sexy hero, a sassy heroine, and a compelling story line, *Branded* is all that and more—I loved it!"
  —Lorelei James, *New York Times* bestselling author of *Wrapped and Strapped*

"Secrets, sins, and spurs—Laura Wright's Cavanaugh brothers will brand your heart!"
  —Skye Jordan, *New York Times* bestselling author of *Reckless*

"Deacon and Mackenzie . . . are strong and passionate, and the chemistry between them sizzles. Wright tells a story filled with heart, genuine characters, and natural dialogue. Add good pacing and a well-developed plot, and Wright's latest is one that will not disappoint."
  —*RT Book Reviews*

"Saddle up for a sexy and thrilling ride! Laura Wright's cowboys are sinfully hot."
  —*New York Times* bestselling author Elisabeth Naughton

"Deadly secrets, explosive sex, four brothers in a fight over a sprawling Texas ranch. . . . Ms. Wright has penned a real page-turner."
  —Kaki Warner, bestselling author of the Heroes of Heartbreak Creek Novels

"Saddle up for a sexy, intensely emotional ride with cowboys who put the 'wild' in Wild West. Laura Wright never disappoints!"
  —*New York Times* bestselling author Alexandra Ivy

ALSO BY LAURA WRIGHT

BONDED

THE CAVANAUGH BROTHERS

Laura Wright

A SIGNET ECLIPSE BOOK

SIGNET ECLIPSE
Published by New American Library,
an imprint of Penguin Random House LLC
· 375 Hudson Street, New York, New York 10014

This book is an original publication of New American Library.

First Printing, September 2015

For more information about Penguin Random House, visit penguin.com.

ISBN 978-0-451-46509-2

Printed in the United States of America
10 9 8 7 6 5 4 3 2 1

Penguin
Random
House

One

Some people might call it the hots, but if you asked Emily Shiver directly what her feelings regarding Blue Perez were, she'd probably say it was more like an . . . appreciation.

Especially seated on that barstool like he was.

She righted the flower tucked behind her ear and headed back into the Bull's Eye kitchen. She didn't do "hots." It sounded so junior high school—which was when she'd seen Blue for the first time. Of course, back then he hadn't been all that much to look at. Tall; super skinny; shy; huge, nervous blue eyes. Not that she could blame him on the nervous thing. He'd just come to town with his mother, hadn't known anyone—moved into the Triple C to take care of the house and Everett Cavanaugh. The older man was alone. Wife had passed on, all three of his boys gone. For Blue, it couldn't have been a happy place to come to.

From the outside looking in, doom and gloom coated that ranch like thick, hungry fog.

But truly, what did anyone expect? From Everett or from those boys? Well . . . especially the boys. They'd lost their girl. Cass. In the most painful way imaginable. Taken from the movie theater bathroom when they were only a few feet away. Those poor kids. They'd just wanted to do what every brother would've wanted to do: watch the darn movie. Not take their annoying kid sis to the bathroom. To them, she was old enough to do that on her own—and grab some Skittles and popcorn on the return trip. But there'd been no return. She'd gone missing.

Christ, the terror that family must have felt. And the horror that followed when her body had turned up in the meadow out past Lake Tonka. The world as they'd all known it, over.

Emily remembered those days well. Seemed like the whole town of River Black was just watching and praying and hoping. Their breaths held. But it was no use. No coming back from pain that all consuming. The Cavanaughs had been irrevocably destroyed. Their mama gone mad. Seemed like no light would ever find its way to them. Then in came Elena Perez and her son, Blue. Moved in, cleaned up and out. A hope for comfort and peace, and maybe things returning to some new sense of normal. Which they had. For a while. Until Everett passed . . . and the truth of his affair with Elena, long before she'd moved into the Triple C, and the child they'd created came to light.

"Emily, hon," came a voice near her right shoulder. "That's my Coke you're manhandling there."

The kitchen of the Bull's Eye came into focus like someone was fiddling with the lens of a microscope. Emily looked up into the gentle dark eyes of Rae, the Eye's longest-serving employee, then back down to her hands wrapped around a large red tumbler filled to the brim with black liquid. She instantly released the glass and stepped back from the soda machine.

"Sorry, Rae," she stumbled. "My brain isn't working well tonight."

"Least it's just the one night. Mine hasn't been firing on all cylinders for a while now." With a soft laugh, the older woman placed the bubbling Coke on her tray. "You only have 'bout fifteen minutes left, ain't that right?"

Emily glanced up at the clock on the wall. Quarter of nine. "Can't come soon enough. Along with my addled brain, my feet are pretty much done in."

"Give it a few years and a layer of calluses, honey," Rae said before pulling out and heading back into the dining room.

A few years, Emily thought. She was hoping for one at the most. Just enough time to save up for the down payment on that abandoned storefront on Main and Kettler. Granted, there was nothing wrong with serving up drinks and good food, if that was your choice, but she had a dream of opening her own flower shop she was looking to fulfill.

After filling up another glass with Coke and placing it on her tray alongside the two whiskeys, she too headed for the dining room. It was a slow night, and she had only one table still occupied. A couple of guys she guessed were traveling through, because she'd never seen them around River Black before, and one tended to see the same people over and over. They'd ordered food and several rounds of drinks. Pretty standard. Easy-peasy. She'd serve them up and get herself out, home, and to bed.

And would not—repeat, *would not*—stare in the direction of the bar while she did it.

As if the silent promise were really an enticement to do just that, Emily's brown eyes—which her father called doe eyes, or can't-say-no-to-my-baby-girl eyes—tracked left. Seated at the bar, his back to her, Stetson riding low, was the very object of her . . . what word had she resorted to again? Hots? No. Not hots. Oh yeah, *appreciation*. And boy oh boy, could she appreciate him tonight. His long, lean, hard body was showcased in nothing special: standard cowboy gear, jeans and a black T-shirt. But her eyes moved covetously over him anyway, from tanned neck to broad shoulders, trim waist, and . . . a denim-clad butt that made her heart kick up and certain unmentionable lady parts quiver.

Sigh. She'd worked at the Bull's Eye for a year and a half now, and the man had an irritating and—she was pretty sure—random habit of coming in when she was on duty. Not that he was much of a drinker or a socializer. He never sat at the bar, like he was now. Usually at a table eating lunch or dinner with Mackenzie Byrd. The pair worked at the Triple C together and seemed like pretty close friends. Or they had been. Emily hadn't seen them in the Eye together all that often lately. Since Mac had gone and married the eldest Cavanaugh, in fact.

Emily continued to stare at what God and his parents had granted him. *What the heck had brought him in here tonight? So late? And straight to the bar?* He'd been tossing back one—

"Goddammit, girl!"

Emily whipped around just as one of her customers shot to his feet, hands going instantly to his crotch. *Crap.* Emily glanced first at her tray and the now-empty glass on its side, then back at the man—and the denim that was sporting a spattering or two of whiskey. *That's what appreciating does, flower girl—makes for some pretty wet and pissed-off customers. Not to mention the no-tip factor.*

As quick as she could, she set the tray down on the empty tabletop behind her and grabbed some napkins. "I am so sorry," she began, holding out the napkins for him. No way was she offering to clean up his crotch. "Here. Please take these."

The man's head jerked up, and venom fairly bled from those two pale brown eyes. "What the fuck are you?" he ground out. "Blind? Or just clumsy?"

Perfect. No forgiveness here. She ignored the grunt of humor from the man's heavily bearded friend, who was leaning back in his chair, arms folded over his chest. "I really am sorry. Let me get you another, on the house. And some club soda."

For anyone in River Black, this would've been enough. Hell, a free drink would've probably garnered a begrudging smile from one of the locals. But for this out-of-towner, blood and humiliation were all he was after now.

"So you can spill that on me too?" he snarled at her, swiping at his crotch with the cloth napkin near his plate of nachos. "Pass." He turned to his friend. "Should've known. Stopping in these tiny towns, all you get are stupid, clumsy bitches with big racks."

Wow. Okay. Heat spread through Emily's neck and jaw, and she felt her lip curl against her top teeth. Truth was, assholes came and went. They were part of the job. Maybe not as much in River Black as in the bigger cities, but it happened. For the most part it was always better to walk away from the table or let Dean handle it. But Emily had never been able to suffer insults or blatant misogyny well. Shoot, she'd grown up with two brothers and had schooled them early and often. In fact, they'd stopped thinking they could get away with sexist bullshit at about the age of five.

She eyed the men before her. She supposed Jerkweed One and Two here were going to have to learn that hard fact a little later than most.

"I don't think I caught all of that, sir," she began, her tone low and cool as she locked eyes with him. "What did you call me?"

The bearded friend made a low whistling sound, his smile wide with delight, before Jerkweed One muttered, "No eyes, but she's sure got ears."

"I absolutely do," she agreed. "And they're almost as big as my rack."

Both heads came up. Both sets of eyes widened.

Pressing the flower deeper behind her ear, she continued undaunted. "So I'm surprised I didn't hear all of the degrading and insulting things you just said to me." Her eyebrow lifted. "Things I'm sure your mothers, sisters, daughters, girlfriends, and/or wives wouldn't be so proud of—am I right?"

They both just stared at her.

"Now," she said, easing back just a touch, giving them room to rethink their attitudes and drop their crap. She wasn't looking to have a problem in the Bull's Eye tonight, and hell, her shift was almost over. Getting home and putting her feet up was a priority. "I sure didn't mean to splatter you with the whiskey. I'm offering to bring you another. On me. Be done with this. What do you say?"

For one brief, shiny moment, Emily thought the jerkweeds had heard what she'd said and were going to act like civilized human beings about it. But jerkweeds were called jerkweeds and not jerkflowers for a reason.

Number One opened his big mouth and let it rip. "You're a feisty one, darlin'," he drawled, dropping into his chair and spreading his legs wide apart so the whiskey stain could be seen by the few people who were still in the Bull's Eye. "But a man only likes his women feisty in the bedroom."

"Is that right?" she returned. Oh, this wasn't going to end well.

He nodded, all slow and thoughtful, his eyes taking on a glitter of malevolence. "I think someone should teach you some manners."

She rolled her eyes just as Jerkweed Two offered, "I'll do it."

"Okay," Emily said on a sigh, her patience pretty much worn down to the nub. "I'll get you guys the check. Or, better yet, leave now and I'll take care of it."

Jerkweed One laughed. "She thinks she has a say over what we do, Tim." The man snorted and leaned back even farther in his chair. "Oh, honey, get a clue. Big tits and a nice ass only sway a man—"

"How we doin' over here?" came a welcome interruption behind Emily. It was a low, masculine, unyielding voice. One that drove both cattle and the cowboys who herded them.

Where, seconds before, the fire of tightly held anger had raged through Emily's body, now a different kind of heat coursed through her blood. The kind that blanketed her with warmth and curiosity, and she instantly turned toward it, like one of her beloved flowers to the sun. Blue Perez Cavanaugh was standing beside her. He was a good foot taller than her, strong and handsome, with eyes so fierce and so piercing they near took her breath away.

"What do you want, cowboy?" Jerkweed One called out, ruining Emily's moment of intense perusal.

She wanted to club him.

A muscle flickered in Blue's jaw, but he kept his voice calm and cool and his eyes on Emily. "You all right?"

"Fine," she said, her voice a little too breathy.

"That's right," Jerkweed One chimed in. "She can handle herself. Get lost, cowboy."

Emily turned to glare at the man. He was killing the mood. She wanted Blue's eyes back on her. They were so intense. Forget appreciation. "Hots" might indeed be the word for what was running through her right now.

"I'm not speaking to you," Blue assured the Jerkweed Twins in a voice so cold it sent a shiver up her back. "Did you think I was speaking to you?"

Jerkweed One's lip curled and he pushed forward.

"Okay," Emily broke in. Last thing she wanted to do was watch a fight break out. Or hell, be in the middle of one. Best thing she could do was get the Jerks out of the Bull's Eye, and Blue back to his barstool. "It's all good here. Just wrapping things up." She turned to Blue and gave him an encouraging nod. "Seriously, nothing I haven't seen, dealt with, or kicked to the curb before."

"Or got down on your knees for, right, honey?" Jerkweed One tossed in with a chuffed grin, elbowing his friend in the side.

Shit.

"That's how we shut her up, right, Tim?" Jerkweed Two said. "Stick something in her mouth."

Emily felt Blue go rigid beside her.

"You bet," Tim answered thickly. "While I stick something in her—"

Not surprisingly, that was as far as Tim got. Blue reached out, grabbed the idiot by the collar, hauled him to his feet, and slammed his fist into the man's smug face. The guy went flying back and hit a chair at the empty table behind him. In seconds, Jerkweed Two was up and coming after Blue. But the ranch hand was more than ready. No doubt he'd taken on cows five times the man's size before. While Rae and Dean were rushing over to a mumbling on-his-ass Tim, Blue had Jerkweed Two in a chokehold and was dragging his ass across the Bull's Eye and toward the front door.

Emily turned to stare at the man on the ground. Tim. Poor, stupid Tim. She sighed. He could've just accepted the drink. *Asswipe.*

Suddenly he too was being hauled to his feet, given a good shake. Blue had returned. Controlled ire sizzled around him. As if the man weighed close to nothing, Blue dragged him over to Emily.

"What do you say?" Blue ground out, giving the jerkweed another molar-cracking shake. "What do you say to her?"

The man blinked several times in succession, no doubt trying to get his full range of vision back. Then he locked eyes with Emily. "Sorry."

Blue shook him again. "Again. Like you mean it this time."

"I'm sorry," he said through clenched teeth. "Ma'am."

"Yeah, okay," she returned. "Just, you know, don't ever come back."

Blue roughly handed the man off to Dean, who had a few choice words to spill before he escorted Jerkweed out to his waiting and possibly unconscious friend. Emily glanced over at Rae, who just shrugged, then went back to clearing a table. It wasn't as though they hadn't seen this kind of thing before. Rae probably more than a few times in her years. Emily turned back to Blue. It was then that she noticed he was bleeding. A small gash on his lip—and his chin was bruised. Must've happened outside with Jerkweed Two. Dammit . . . Last thing she wanted was someone getting hurt because of her. Especially someone with such a beautiful face. That hard, sexy jawline . . .

This time when she rolled her eyes it was internal and at herself.

She reached for a napkin on the table behind her. "Your lip . . . Let me clean it up for you."

"Naw, it's nothing."

"You're bleeding," she said.

He swiped at his lip and the blood with the back of his hand. "All gone."

"Well, that wasn't very sanitary," she said.

His eyes, those incredible blue eyes, warmed with momentary humor. Then he touched the brim of his hat and turned to head back to the bar. "Ma'am."

Emily stared after him, confused. What was that? Saves the day and on his way? "Hey, hold on a sec," she called out. "I didn't thank you."

"There's no need," he called back, sliding onto the same barstool he'd occupied earlier.

Well, that's not very neighborly, she mused. She followed him. "Maybe not," she said, coming up to stand beside him. "But I'm going to do it anyway."

He turned to look at her but didn't say anything. Good night, nurse, he was handsome.

She inclined her head formally. "Thank you."

Those incredible eyes moved over her face then. So probing, so thoughtful. They made her toes curl inside her shoes. "Something tells me you could've taken those men out yourself."

"What tells you that?" she asked.

He ran a hand over his jaw, which was darkening by the minute. "Just a guess."

Her gaze flickered to the bruise, to his mouth, and she frowned. "Are you in pain?"

"Constantly," he said, then turned back to his drink.

The strange, almost morose response made her pause. But before she could ask him anything about it, Dean slid back behind the bar and asked, "You want something, Em? After having to deal with those assholes I'd say you're done for the night. But first, a drink."

"And it's on me," Blue said, then tossed back his tequila.

Dean gave the cowboy a broad grin. "After what you did for our girl here, it's me who's buying."

"Well, thank you kindly." Blue held up his empty glass. "Another, if you please. And what would you like . . . ?" He turned to Emily and arched a brow at her. "Em, is it?"

The soft masculine growl in his voice made her insides warm. "Emily," she told him. "Emily Shiver."

"Right." He cocked his head to one side and studied her. "The girl with the flowers in her hair," he said, his gaze catching on the yellow one behind her ear.

Emily smiled. Couldn't help it. She liked that he'd noticed. "Started when I was little," she told him. "Stole flowers from my grandmother's garden every time I was over there. I'd put them everywhere. My room, the tables here, in my hair." She shrugged. "It became kind of an obsession."

His gaze flickered to the flower in her hair again, then returned to her face. "Pretty."

Heat instantly spread through Emily's insides. Granted, plenty of men came into the Bull's Eye and looked at her with eyes heavy on the hungry—either for food or for her. Hell, sometimes both. But no one had ever looked at her like Blue was now. Curious, frustrated, interested . . .

"Drink, Em?"

Swallowing hard, she turned to see a waiting and mildly curious Dean. "Just a Coke for me, boss. Thanks."

Blue groaned as Dean filled a glass with ice.

"What's wrong?" Emily asked him, wondering if his jaw was paining him.

But the man just chuckled softly. "Come on, now. Have something a little stronger than that. You're gonna make me feel bad. Or worse." Under his breath he added, "If that's even possible tonight."

Curiosity coiled within her at his words. The way he looked at her, spoke, acted . . . clearly he was working through some heavy feelings tonight. Was it about the fight with the jerkweeds? Or something that came before it? She bit her lip. Did she ask? Or did she wait for him to tell her? But why would he tell her? They barely knew each other.

Maybe she should just ignore it . . .

Dean set the Coke before her and poured another round of tequila for Blue, which the cowboy drained in about five seconds flat; then he tapped the bar top to indicate he wanted another.

Oh yeah. Definitely dealing with something. She'd worked at the Bull's Eye long enough to know that drinking like he was doing had nothing to do with relaxing after a long day. Dark feelings were running through Blue Perez's blood. And maybe some demons to go along with them.

"Everything all right tonight, cowboy?" she asked.

"Yep." He turned to look at her again, his gaze not all that sharp or engaged now. The liquor was starting to do its thing. "I remember you. Flowers, and a ton of strawberry blond curls."

Emily's breath caught inside her lungs. What a strange and very suggestive thing to say. Not that she minded. Just wished he'd have said it before the double shot. And the way he was staring at her . . . like he was trying to memorize her features or something. Then suddenly, he reached out and touched her hair, fingered one of those curls caught up in a ponytail.

A hot, powerful shiver moved up her spine.

"Here you go," Dean interrupted, filling Blue's glass once again.

"Thanks," Blue said, though his eyes were still on Emily. Even when his fingers curled around the glass, his eyes remained locked with hers. "Sure you don't want something stronger, Em?" he asked.

Emily's brows shot up, and her belly clenched with awareness. "I think you're doing fine for the both of us," she said, reaching for her Coke and taking a sip. Her mouth was incredibly dry. "And I'm going to assume that you'll be walking home."

He downed the contents of the glass and chuckled. "Not to worry, darlin'. I got my truck."

Oh jeez. Not to worry? She shook her head. People could be so stupid sometimes. So reckless. Even gorgeous cowboys with eyes the color of a cloudless Texas sky—and a pair of lips that kept calling to her own.

Like the meddlesome gal she was, she reached

over and grabbed his keys off the bar top. Blue's gaze turned sharply to hers, and under the heat of that electric stare, Emily tried not to melt. Well, outwardly at any rate.

Yes, you're hot and sexy and annoyed at my ass now. But I'm not going to let you be a shit for brains.

She held up the keys. "No rush, cowboy. I got my Coke here, and nowhere to get to. I'm going to take you home when you've sufficiently drowned yourself."

Blue didn't like that one bit. He released a breath and ground out, "Not necessary."

"I say it is," she returned.

"You don't want to do that, darlin'. I'm not fit to be around tonight."

"Maybe not. But there's no use arguing the matter. I always win arguments. Right, Dean?"

The bartender chuckled. "Don't even try anymore."

"If you're really going to push this, I can call someone—" Blue started, then stopped. His eyes came up and met hers, and it was impossible to miss the heavy, pulsing pain that echoed there.

This wasn't about the jerks or a bad day. This was deep and long lasting. Emily knew some of what had happened to him in the past couple of months. Finding out—along with the whole town—that his daddy was Everett Cavanaugh. That he had part claim to the Triple C. Along with a set of three new brothers. But clearly there was more that was weighing on him. So much more, she'd venture to guess.

She slipped the keys into her jeans pocket and settled back in front of her Coke. This wasn't how she'd wanted the night to go. Watching over a hot, drunk cowboy. She'd had visions of a bathtub, a great book, and some buttered noodles afterward. But tonight this man had offered up his protection, and she couldn't help but do the same.

She tasted like heaven, her mouth so warm and hungry he fell easily in lust with it. His mind was clouded, unusable. But his limbs, his muscles, his tongue, his dick, and his will were all alive with feeling.

She was sitting on top of him. Strawberry blond curls falling down past her shoulders, the tips licking her nipples. His mouth watered. That was what he wanted to be doing. Licking those dark raspberries. Tugging at them. Biting.

If he just knew where he was. What he was . . .

No. He didn't want any of that.

This was his heaven. In the real world, real life, he didn't get to go to heaven. She was it.

The angel.

His angel.

She smelled like flowers.

Where was that flower?

Yellow. Fragrant.

He groaned as her warm, soft fingers glided up and down his shaft. "I need to take you. Be inside you. Can I, darlin'?"

There was a moment's hesitation as if she was thinking. *Don't think. Don't think. It's bad.*

Painful.

Problematic.

"Blue . . . ," she whispered, her voice urgent.

Was he Blue? Blue Perez? Blue Cavanaugh? The tequila wasn't talking.

Clasping her soft, small waist in his hands, he lifted her up and placed her down on his shaft.

White, brilliant, healing heat surged into him.

Yes.

This.

Her.

"Wait," she uttered. Breathy. "We need—"

But his mouth was on hers and his fingers were playing in her hot, slick sex. And all that remained were the sounds of ecstasy and his cock working inside her. It was the only sound that mattered. Only music that should ever fill his ears.

"Oh, Blue . . . God, yes."

"I need to shut it out, angel," he rasped. "Them, all of them. And her. The pain. Please."

And then he was falling. No. No. Not done. Not over.

Heat and tightness, and a rush of moisture fisted around his cock.

Hated this. He wanted more. Her. Only her. She fit him.

Idiot. Fool. No one fits.

Only hurts.

He came in a growl of madness, pumping wildly into her—his hands cupping her breasts, his ears filled with her moans. He should . . . should let her go. Now. But he couldn't. Not until she ran. Or lied. Or deceived. That would be all too soon. This woman was from hell. Had to be. And yet she felt like heaven.

Still inside her, he wrapped his body around her.

She was an angel.

Dark and addicting.

His angel.

Blackness spread through his worried mind, and in the muddled seconds before sleep took him, he felt her disentangle herself from his grasp, heard her pull on her clothes and whisper a pained, "Oh God," as she hurried from the bedroom of the Triple C's river cottage.

Two

Three weeks later

"It's still small," Aubrey said in that disapproving voice she used every time they looked at the Main Street storefront property.

The Realtor wanted to go big.

It was Texas, after all.

"I think it's perfect," Emily told her, sighing with appreciation. It really was perfect. Just what she needed and wanted to get her business up and running. It even had a small apartment above it if her mother ever let her move out of the house. The thought made her grin. Mama Shiver had a hard time letting go of her babies.

Aubrey crossed her arms over her chest, which sported just the barest of cleavage in her tasteful pale pink suit. "Clearly, I will never talk you out of this mouse house, so you want to put in an offer?"

Oh, hell, yes, she did. More than anything. Problem was, she was about five thousand shy of what she needed. "You think Mrs. Tambrick would change her mind about the lease?"

Aubrey's bright pink lips thinned and she shook her head. "She wants to sell, leave clean, honey. Her son lives in Key West now. She doesn't want any ties, you understand."

Despite the feelings of disappointment running through her, Emily nodded. Hell, if anyone understood the close binds of family, it was her. She couldn't imagine not living in the same town as her brothers and parents. She'd just keep working toward her goal and hoping no one snatched the property up in the meantime.

"You're not showing it to anyone else, right?" she asked with that Girl Scout look of enthusiasm. It was the same expression she wore every time Aubrey showed her 16½ Main Street. And every time, the agent just laughed at her as if that question was just about the silliest thing she'd ever heard. Like, *Come on now, darlin'. Who would want this tiny closet posing as a storefront?*

But strangely, Aubrey wasn't laughing today. In fact, she looked a little sheepish.

"What?" Emily asked.

"It seems that mouse houses are growing in popularity," she explained. "Because there is someone else who's interested."

Emily felt the blood rush from her face. "No."

"Honey, I'm as surprised as you are."

"When did you show it to this . . . this . . . person?" Emily pressed as George Goss's "Ain't No Honky Tonks in Jail" erupted from Aubrey's very fancy snow-white purse.

The woman reached in, grabbed her cell phone, and, after a quick look at who was calling, dropped it back in her bag. "About a week or so ago."

Anger rushed over Emily like a fierce November wind across the Texas prairie lands. Holding back the urge to growl, *And you didn't tell me?!*, she asked, "Who is it, Aubrey?"

"You know I can't tell you that, honey."

Emily snorted and glanced around the small, charming space that had already, in her mind, become the home to River Black's first flower shop, Petal Pushers. "Well, you could," she pushed the Realtor. "Maybe a little hint? Hair color? Married?"

"Nope. Not going to budge. I took a vow, you know." The woman laughed and slung her purse over her shoulder. "I understand your anger and frustration, hon. But you have options here. If it's money you need, can I say it again? Suggest it . . . again?"

Emily knew right where this was going, and she cut it off at the knees. "I'm not taking money from my parents."

"Is it really taking, Emily?" Aubrey argued. "I mean, I'm talking about a loan. I've known your parents since I was a teenager. Don't know two more caring and supportive people in the world. They'd do this for you in a heartbeat."

"'Course they would," Emily agreed. "Hell,

they'd buy me the place if I asked." She sighed. "But I'm not asking."

Emily had the most wonderful family in the world. They were all real close. Honest with each other. Had each other's backs. Did their best not to judge when one or more of them screwed up. But as much as Ben and Susie Shiver wanted more than anything to help their children, they'd also raised them to stand on their own feet. Reach for their dreams and work hard to land them. Wasn't anyone else's job, now was it? No favors were owed. Nope. This shop would come to her. She just had to work a little harder, a little longer, maybe take a few extra shifts at the Bull's Eye. It was like her grandma Gypsy used to say: *Dreams ain't like milk, honey. They don't come with an expiration date.*

Of course, she mused slyly, in the meantime, there was nothing wrong with a little sniffing around. If Aubrey wasn't going to tell her who was interested in the mouse house, then maybe she'd just have to find out on her own. And if it was someone she knew . . . maybe they could have a little chat.

The plan instantly revived her, and Emily straightened her shoulders and headed for the front door. "Thanks, Aubrey. I'll keep you updated, and hopefully you can do the same with me."

"Sure thing," the woman agreed, following her out onto the sidewalk. "Sorry for being the bearer of bad news."

"Not bad yet." Emily gave the woman a quick

wave before she could ask what that meant, then hurried down the street. Her shift started in fifteen minutes, and it wouldn't do for her to be late. Not now. Not when she was going to be asking for more shifts.

She was slightly breathless when she sailed through the front door of the Bull's Eye and passed her manager, Dean, behind the bar. Dean was such a good guy. Maybe five years older than her. He had a wife and three-month-old baby and was looking to buy them a nice single-family home just outside town. Seemed everyone at the Bull's Eye was working toward something. Or for something. Grabbing her uniform out of her locker, she stole into the bathroom and locked the door. The bar wasn't extraordinarily busy at the moment, but she hurried anyway.

After she dressed, she opened her purse and felt around for her hairbrush and makeup bag. She didn't do anything special with herself for work, but she liked to look nice and put together. Maybe she'd steal one of the roses off the table for her hair, as she'd forgotten to "plant" one in her hair this morning. But the second her fingers wrapped around a box at the bottom of her bag, all thoughts of mouse houses and flowers went right out the window. Gut tight, she pulled it out, blanched when she saw the letters *EPT* on the side, and set it down on the back of the toilet. She had put the thing in her purse not that morning, but three days ago. When her period had been officially two days late.

She placed her hands on either side of the sink and inhaled deeply through her nose. She was never, ever late. Twenty-eight days like clockwork.

Then, this month—nothing.

Lord, she'd panicked something fierce, then driven all the way out to Brunsville so no one would see her at the River Black market or the drugstore.

Her stomach clenched painfully and her mouth felt very dry. She'd hoped she was just late. But every day that passed without Aunt Flo coming to town sent a new rush of terror through her heart.

Stupid. Stupid, stupid, stupid.

How could you have let that happen?

No. How could you have let that happen without a condom?

Heart slamming fiercely against her ribs, Emily turned and stared at the box. She needed to be dressed and on the floor in ten minutes.

What you need to do is this. Just get it done and over. Odds are it's nothing but stress.

Five. Days. Late.

Stupid.

Maybe she should do it later. Like tonight. At home. Hell, maybe she should stick it back in her purse and conveniently forget about it again.

Like you've forgotten that night? And him? His eyes? His hands on your skin? The way he moved inside of you like he couldn't get close enough? The way you come into work every day hoping he'll be here? Sitting at a table? At the bar? Hoping he wasn't as

*drunk as you thought he was? Hoping he can't get you
out of his mind either?*

On a curse, she pushed away from the sink and
swiped a hand across her face. *It was a mistake, Emily. One stupid night. Where he mentioned wanting to
forget his ex-girlfriend while he was inside of you.*

"Oh God," she groaned. *Please let this not be happening.*

A knock on the door of the bathroom jolted her.

"Hey? You okay in there, Em?" Rae called.

No. "Yes, I'm fine," she called back quickly.
"Just taking my time. And I . . ." *What? What do
you have? A pregnancy test?* "I have a run in my
panty hose." She rolled her eyes at herself.

"Well, I have an extra pair if you need it."

"No. Thanks. I have one too."

"All right, then. See you out there."

"Yep. See you."

Emily waited for the sound of the waitress's retreating footsteps, then turned to the box on the
back of the toilet. Oh God. Oh shit! It was now
or . . . later. And she couldn't do this at home. Not
with her family around.

She grabbed the box and with shaky fingers
tore it open and pulled out one of the tests. The
toilet felt cold against her backside, but she followed the directions and placed the white strip of
plastic on the sink counter when she was done. As
she waited, she stared at herself in the mirror and
picked up where she'd left off in the chastising department. She wasn't one of those girls who believed that a night of incredible, mind-blowing,

still-could-feel-his-lips-and-tongue-and-hands-on-her sex couldn't end in a full belly. Oh, she'd known. She'd known and she'd let it happen anyway.

No. She'd reveled in it.

Because the man had made her feel things she hadn't even known existed. It had been like a damn awakening.

Hot Blue.

Drunk Blue.

Blue who hasn't sought you out since. Hasn't called or come into the Bull's Eye. Who probably doesn't even remember anything beyond throwing those assholes out the barroom door.

Or he remembers it all but wishes he didn't.

Slowly, she let her gaze fall. *Please. Please don't be . . .* "Oh damn," she uttered on an exhalation, staring at the readout. God in heaven, how had she let this happen?

Stupid.

And pregnant.

With Blue Perez Cavanaugh's baby.

Cutting his horse left, then right, and calling out, Blue came around the twelve or so stragglers, driving them toward the fresh pasture. Stubborn females. *Got your whole herd over there taking down the green stuff, and look at you.*

In reply, the flink moved like damn snails toward their final destination. Wanted him pissed. Appreciated his frustration—his lack of control. Like most females he knew. Well, maybe not most. There was the one . . . But he wasn't thinking about her. She wasn't real. He'd decided. She was a dream. A dream that had up and left his drunk and sorry ass in the middle of the night.

"Oh no, you don't," Blue muttered, then gave a loud "Yip" as he came up on the shoulder of one of the cows. His horse, Barbarella, had an easy way with the girls, unless she felt they weren't obliging. Then she just liked to use her breath on the backs of their necks to get them moving.

Suddenly, the cow startled and took off toward the rest of the group. But it wasn't Barbarella that had gotten her going. A rider was coming—kicking up dirt, barreling toward them on a young brown-and-white paint. Behind Blue, the cows scattered in anticipation, like dogs at bath time.

"Hey," Mac called, coming up, circling him. "Where's the fire, cowboy?"

The mare the Triple C foreman, Mackenzie Byrd, was training looked as pleased as a pig in shit to be out and about. She eyed Barbarella, who gave the new girl a friendly whicker.

"I should be asking you the same thing," he returned, his tone cool. Something his foreman, and the woman who used to be his closest friend, was accustomed to now. "Barreling up like that. I'm trying to get the rest of these cows to the west pasture."

"I see that," she said, taking a quick glance around. "What I don't understand is why you didn't wait for the others. This is at least a two-person job."

"I managed fine."

She tipped her hat back so he could see her face. Confusion, frustration, worry . . . they were all there. As usual. "Sure, but it's not how we do things here and you know it."

He shrugged. "Maybe things need to change."

"Maybe," she agreed. "But not today."

"Understood," he said tightly, then added, "Foreman."

She released a breath. "Come on, Blue." She eyed him, the deep blue Texas sky stretching out behind her.

He circled Rella. "Come on what, Foreman?"

"Don't call me that. Not that way."

"It's what you are. My boss." He placed his hat back on his head. "Until maybe you ain't."

Her jaw tightened.

"Until maybe you go home to your own ranch."

"You're being a jackass," she ground out.

He couldn't argue with that. Hell, he didn't want to argue with that. Just wanted to go about his business. "If there's nothing else, I got a dozen head—"

"How long is this going to continue?" she interrupted. Her paint was starting to get antsy. "Seriously."

"Seconds, if you'd like."

"Oh, I'd like," she returned.

"Well, I can make that jumpy mare of yours take off with one click of my tongue."

Her blue eyes flashed. "I meant how long till you stop acting like you hate me, or don't know me, or like we weren't best friends for a damn decade." She sat back in the saddle, hand over the horn. She took another deep breath and blew it out all pensive-like. "I'm worried about you."

A month ago, her words would've penetrated his armor. Would've cut him, made him think back on their relationship and confide his troubles to her. But his skin had grown armadillo-thick these past weeks; her words just bounced right off. Besides, there was no heat, no passion, inside him anymore to get to anyway. He was cold all through. Everett's death had started it—bringing on the icy rain within him. Then finding out his mother had lied to him his entire life about who his daddy was. That had turned rain to snow. And just three weeks ago, that snow had turned to hail when the woman he'd met online, his "cowgirl," the one he'd been falling for and had allowed himself to trust, turned out to be none other than goddamned Natalie Palmer. Daughter of the man who'd tried to kill Sheridan O'Neil, a bald-faced liar, and a woman who'd had Blue's half sister Cass's diary in her possession for years.

That hail had turned into a solid wall of ice when the River Black sheriff claimed to not have enough evidence to arrest the woman.

Everything Blue had once wanted—and been willing to fight for—happiness, peace, the Triple C, love, family . . . It didn't hold any kind of value for him anymore. He just wanted to keep closed, do his work, forget . . .

"You ain't going to say nothing?" Mac pressed.

Blue turned to stare at the cows. Five of the twelve were staring right back at him. *Your move,* they seemed to be saying. *I ain't got no moves,* Blue answered. *Not anymore.*

"Nothing to worry about here, Foreman," he said on an exhalation.

Mac cursed under her breath. "Bull." She eyeballed him. "I worry, Blue. Christ, I've been worrying since I found out you were a Cavanaugh. You've been tryin' to block shit out ever since. I know how that feels, and how it looks." She rolled her eyes. "I'm married to it, for heaven's sake."

"Yeah, how's Deacon doing?" Blue asked dryly. "Either him or James or Cole find out anything to put that lying bitch behind bars yet?"

Mac recoiled. "When did you start talking like that?"

"Like what? Honest?" He sniffed. "She did it, Mac. Natalie Palmer. Or had something to do with it. I know it. Your husband knows it. You know it."

"No, I don't," she assured him.

"She had Cass's diary."

"Doesn't mean she killed her."

He blew out a breath. "Did you even read it?"

"Of course I read it."

"She was following them, Mac. Cass and the kid. Sweet."

"She had a crush."

Blue shook his head. Pointless. The whole thing. Why was he trying?

"What?" Mac pressed.

"Just strange seeing how gullible and naive looks from the outside."

"I'm not either of those things," she returned hotly. "What I am is cautious. Deacon's private investigator is on this—on her. We're doing everything we can to find out the truth. If she's involved we'll need more proof than a diary. Trust me when I say the whole family is working together on this."

"How nice," he drawled.

She instantly realized her blunder. "Blue . . . I didn't mean—"

"Got work to do, Foreman." The ice was back, colder and thicker than ever. The word *family* couldn't even touch him now. He kicked Rella hard, sending her forward toward those cows. Leaving Mac behind, licking up his dust.

Three

Hunger assaulted Emily as she plopped another scoop of her mother's mashed potatoes on her plate. Tuesday night was Emily's night in their house. Each kid, grown though they were, got to pick his or her favorite meal. Nothing Susie Shiver loved more than taking care of her family. And her fried chicken, mashed potatoes, and corn dressing were the very best in the world.

Emily reached for a third drumstick, and a duo of male snickers came floating her way across the table. She glanced up. Her younger brothers, Steven and Jeremy, were sitting side by side, wide, wicked grins on their faces. Like they were ten and twelve and not twenty-two and twenty-four with facial hair and broad chests covered by work uniforms. Back when she'd been an only child and had all her parents' attention, Emily had made such a fuss when her mother had told her she was bringing home a baby brother from the hospital, and then another two years later. But Lord have mercy, she'd come to adore them. Even with all of their annoying, smelly, loud ways.

"Mama," she drawled. "Tell your sons here to stop passing wind at the table, please. My floral arrangement can only handle so much."

"Emily!" their mother cried from the head of the table. Susie Shiver was always head of the table, boss, baker, and bearer of children that she was. She turned to her grown boys and gave them a reproachful look. "You didn't."

"'Course we didn't," Steven said for them both, his green eyes flashing.

"Then what are you laughing about?" she demanded.

"Emily," he answered.

"And why would that be?" Emily asked before taking a bite of her chicken. When Steven didn't answer right away, she looked to her youngest brother and gave him a smile. "Jeremy, you want to tell me?"

The blond, blue-eyed, baby-faced male snorted. "Not saying a thing," he muttered. "Not one thing."

"Chicken," she accused.

"No," Jeremy said, trying not to laugh. "But interesting choice of words."

Realization dawned and Emily's eyes narrowed on her kin. "You two have a problem with what's on my plate?"

"Not the what, sis," Steven said nonchalantly. "Just the how much."

"Jerks! Both of you." Emily very nearly lobbed

spoonfuls of mashed potatoes at them. Would've if her mother hadn't called out, "That's enough, boys. Leave her be."

"Yeah," Emily said. "Leave me be." Then she slid the spoonful of mashed potatoes into her mouth with a grin.

"After all, she's a growing girl," her mother continued.

All of a sudden that grin died. Heat rushed into Emily's cheeks like she'd just opened the oven. And hell, maybe she had.

"A growing girl?" Steven said with a snort, wiping a bit of chicken grease from the sleeve of his sheriff's deputy uniform. "She's twenty-six. How much more can she grow?"

Granted, the question was innocent enough, but only because they didn't know. Her eyes dropped to her plate. Oh God, she was going to grow. Big. Really big over the next nine months. Soon she wouldn't be able to hide it.

Anxiety pulsed within her blood. Her appetite gone, she put down her fork and released a weighty sigh.

"Look what you did, Steven Shiver," their mother scolded. "Just wait till your father gets home."

This was pretty much an empty threat, as Ben Shiver was moving cattle for the next couple of days. Emily's father was a small-time rancher in River Black. Not nearly doing the business that some places like the Triple C were. But it provided a comfortable life for them all. An honest life. It was too bad that not one of his sons or his daughter were interested in taking over the family business someday. It was her father's greatest sadness.

"Come on, Ems," Steven said, not even a hint of amusement in his tone now. "You know we're just kidding around."

Of course she knew that, and normally it wouldn't have bothered her a bit. Normally, she'd have given it back good—after knocking them each in the face with Mama's mashed potatoes. But what Steven had said . . . about her growing . . . it'd just sent her there . . . to reality, to the end point. No going around it or pretending it didn't exist. She was going to have a baby. Blue Cavanaugh's baby. And she had no idea how she was going to manage it.

"You don't ever mention a woman's appetite, boys," Mama was continuing with her scolding. "Not if you ever want one to stick around."

"You must be mentioning appetites on every first date you go on, Steven," Jeremy put in wryly. "Explains why there's never a second."

"Very funny," he grumbled.

"That's not nice, Jeremy," their mother said.

"Or maybe it's not the appetite comments, but the fact that you don't shower regularly."

Steven's lip curled. "You really want to talk about who smells in this house? Shoot, boy, I share a bathroom with you."

"How was work?" Susie asked quickly. "Jeremy? The construction going as planned?"

Easily distracted, Jeremy thought for a second, then said, "We put the roof on Depro's barn today.

I think we'll be done with all the upgrades by next week."

"And you, Steven?" she asked. "Any arrests?"

"One DUI and a petty theft charge." Steven shrugged. "Nothing exciting."

"It's River Black," Jeremy said with a snort. "Cow tippin' and chicken stealin' are about as exciting as it gets around here. Except for maybe that Natalie Palmer/Blue Perez thing."

Up until now, Emily's head had been elsewhere. Telling her parents, opening her flower shop, moving out . . . all the things a baby needed . . . And then someone had to go and mention Blue.

"Oh, yes," their mother said, nibbling on a biscuit. "Whatever happened with that, Steven? You were at the station that night, weren't you? When the call came in? I remember you telling us something about it."

They were talking about that night. The night she and Blue had officially met. The night he'd come into the Bull's Eye and drank too much. The night she'd taken him home and . . . She swallowed hard and reached for her water glass. He'd been upset. And the next day, Emily had found out why. Steven had told them about Blue and Natalie, how they'd been dating online or some such. How Blue had found Cass Cavanaugh's diary at Natalie's and called the sheriff.

"Nothing too much came from it," Steven said. "All Blue Perez had was that young Cavanaugh girl's diary. Said Natalie had been keeping it all these years. Felt that was suspicious at the very least.

That maybe she had something to do with the girl's disappearance. But Natalie claimed she'd found the diary years ago. Way after the girl's passing."

"Why didn't she turn it in to the sheriff at the time?" Susie asked. "Knowing the case was still unsolved. It is a little strange."

"Maybe so," Steven agreed. "But then, Natalie's strange. Doesn't make her a killer—which was what Perez was insinuating. 'Course, now Deacon Cavanaugh and his brothers are on our ass about it. Want me and the sheriff to investigate the woman. Told 'em if any new information comes to light, I'd let 'em know. Not much more we can do without courting a lawsuit."

Blue had been pretty torn up that night. Emily remembered him saying random things about trust and lies and getting something—someone—out of his head. It was then that she knew she'd made a mistake. That she had to get out of there and forget the whole incredible, amazing, erotic mess ever happened.

Can't do that now, Em.

Beneath the table, her hand came to rest on her belly.

"I remember the day that girl went missing," Susie said thoughtfully. "I held my babies tight." She put down her fork and looked straight at Emily. "Nothing worse for a mother than losing her child. When their mama lost her faculties and had to go to the hospital I understood completely."

Something stirred inside Emily at her mother's

words. Pain for the Cavanaughs and a niggling sense of worry for the life growing inside her.

"I think Everett's stepping out on her didn't help matters," Jeremy put in.

"Don't talk like that, Jere," Susie scolded.

But he was on a roll. "Maybe she even knew about the kid the old man fathered."

"Stop it," Emily ground out.

"Finding out your husband fathered a bastard right after you lose—"

"I said shut the hell up!"

Both her brothers turned to stare at her. Her mother too. They all looked stunned, concerned. She didn't give a damn.

"Don't you dare call him that," she warned Jeremy. "What is wrong with you? Calling an innocent child that!"

"Cripes, Em, I didn't mean anything—" Jeremy tried, but Emily was seeing only red.

"You don't even know him," she continued, her heart slamming hard against her ribs. "His life. What he's had to deal with. Do you think he chose that? A father and mother who had an affair? Can you even imagine what his life is like now? Now that it's out in the open?"

Jeremy was ashen, and Steven cursed.

"I agree with her," Susie put in. "That was incredibly distasteful and ungenerous, Jeremy. Not how I raised you."

Before either of them could respond, Emily was pushing her chair back, standing up. She needed some space, some air. Maybe a hot shower and a good cry. "I'm done."

"Ems," Jeremy said, sounding mournful and embarrassed. "Come on, I'm sorry. I was a jerk. I didn't mean any harm. Perez seems like a decent guy . . ."

She hated hearing the sadness in her brother's voice. Truth was, she believed him. He didn't mean any harm. But hell, he'd used the word *bastard* around her. The father of her baby . . . It was all just too damn close to home.

"I'm going to bed," she muttered as she headed out of the room.

"It's only eight thirty, baby," her mother called after her as Emily left the room.

I'm tired.

And stressed.

And . . . Lord have mercy, she mused as she headed up the stairs . . .

Pregnant.

It was his nightly ritual now. Six o'clock, in the kitchen of the Triple C, at the table, eating the food that his mother had prepared. Did he want to do that? Let her feed him like she had when he was a boy? Shit . . . like he had up until a few months ago? Him and all the other ranch hands?

No.

But the alternatives were few and far between. He couldn't go into the Bull's Eye, and eating at the diner might mean running into her too. Emily Shiver. He felt like a real ass for how that all went down. And he was pretty sure she wouldn't want to see him either.

Without a word, his mother sidled up to the table with her own plate and a glass of water. Instinctively Blue reached out and pulled her chair back for her, then grumbled to himself and went back to his meal.

"Thank you, son."

He didn't answer.

"You know," she said, settling in and picking up her fork. "I'm fine eating in silence as we always do, but if you wanted to—"

"I don't."

"It's just that," she continued, "well, you could eat out. Or make something at the cottage."

What was she driving at? "I know."

She didn't say anything for a few minutes, and Blue was glad as he continued eating. But then: "Maybe you come here because you want to see me? Talk to me? I wish you would talk to me."

Ah, Christ. He looked up, said fiercely, "Mom, I don't forgive you."

A little gasp escaped her, but she continued with a nod. "Oh, I know that. But maybe someday . . ."

His fingers tightened around the fork. For weeks they'd eaten in silence. Sometimes she'd fill her plate and take it elsewhere. For Blue, sitting with his mother at dinner had been a way to be around her without anger filling him up. Without resentment and grief heating up his blood. Why did she have to break that silent agreement?

"Maybe someday you'll let me explain," she added. "Maybe you'll let me tell you that sometimes you get into situations you can't get out of. That you have to make the best of what's in front of you."

His appetite gone, he pushed his chair back.

"Blue, please. The day I found out I was having you was the best day of my life. And I wasn't alone in that feeling. You need to know that Everett was—"

It was all he heard before he walked out of the room and out of the house.

Four

She loved hot showers. Blistering, if she could manage them. Until her skin turned pink and her limbs felt like a rag doll's. But she'd read somewhere that hot showers weren't good for a pregnant woman . . . *Pregnant* . . . Just the word brought on hyperventilation. She was having a baby. There was no question about that. It was just the how . . . and the where . . . and the with whom.

Tilting her face up to the rain shower of warm water, she closed her eyes and allowed the visions of Blue Perez Cavanaugh to take up residence. The problem with that was the last time she'd seen him he wasn't wearing clothes. In fact, he was stretched out on the bed, tanned skin on white sheets—long, lean, heavily muscled body beneath her. Lord, he was the finest specimen of male that existed in the world. A real man. And those hands . . . large and callused, exploring her skin as he kissed her, as he worked inside her, as he lifted her up and down . . .

Her eyes popped open, her mouth too, on a gasp, and she took in a gulp of water. Coughing, spluttering, she forced her thoughts away from images that would only heat her body and screw with her mind.

Turning off the water, she stepped out of the shower and grabbed her robe. After moisturizing her skin with freesia body lotion, she wrapped her hair in a towel, left the bathroom, and padded into her room. She hadn't gotten four steps when she saw Steven sitting at her desk, thumbing through a magazine.

"Damn, Em, leave a little hot water for the rest of us, would you?" He glanced up. "That comment about how I smell is still with me. I think Jeremy gave me a complex."

She rolled her eyes. "Do you ever knock?"

"I knocked."

"And when I didn't answer . . . ?"

"I came in." He shrugged. "The way you were acting downstairs got me worried."

She sighed and sat on the edge of the bed. "Nothing to worry about, little brother. I'm just tired."

"And pissed."

"Well, you guys *were* being jackasses."

"Nothing new there." When she didn't return his smile, he sobered and nodded. "Yeah, we were. And I'm sorry about that."

"Okay. I'll forgive you for insinuating that I'm

the female Paul Bunyan." She flicked her hand in the direction of the door. "Now, off with you."

But he didn't move. Her joke didn't appease him at all. "It wasn't just that. The plate piling. Something's up with you."

As she was taking the towel off her head, her heart stuttered. "You can turn off the inquisition light, Detective."

"I'm not a detective."

"Well, you'd better get on that," she said, drying her hair with the towel.

"Is it a guy thing?" he asked.

God . . . "No."

"A girl thing?"

Her gaze found his and she grinned. "Maybe."

"Come on, Emmie."

"Don't you have to be up early?"

"I'm not on until ten."

"Then why don't you head downstairs and watch *Destroy Build Destroy* with Mom?"

"She gets too competitive," he said, turning to put the magazine he'd been perusing back on her desktop. But in the process, he nearly upended a vase of tea roses, while elbowing her purse and knocking the entire thing to the floor.

There was a thud, and Emily watched the contents scatter. Her eyes caught and held on the pregnancy test. She gasped, looked up. Steven's gaze was on it too. *Shit!* Pushing away from the bed, she dove for it. On her hands and knees, she stuffed things back inside her purse. But he'd seen it. Fucking hell, he'd seen it.

It was quiet. Too quiet. Then . . .

"Emmie?"

Her eyes lifted to meet his. Brows lowered, lips thinned, he looked a hundred different things, from worried to angry to confused.

"Are you?" he uttered.

She could lie. But what was the point? He'd seen the test . . . and in a few months, he was going to see her and her growing stomach. She nodded.

"I'm going to kill whoever it is," he ground out. "Who is it?"

She stood up and went over to her dresser. "Don't be ridiculous."

"I'm not."

"You'll get fired."

"Don't care," he returned easily.

She snorted. "Sure you do. You love that job."

"Are you seeing someone?" he continued pestering. "And if you are, why wouldn't you tell any of us?"

She wasn't going there with him. As she grabbed a set of pajamas, she shook her head. "This is none of your business."

"Are you kidding?" He came over to the dresser. "'Course it is. You're my blood. I care about you."

The truth was, she wanted to hear that, needed to hear it. She was going to need her family in the coming months. But right now . . .

"Does he know?"

And there it was. "Steven . . ."

A growl escaped his lips. "He knows, doesn't he? Oh, hell and Christ."

"Don't start making stuff up in your head," she warned him. "That never turns out well."

He barely heard her. "And he ain't standing by you, right?"

"No."

"That's why you're not talking about it."

"He doesn't know, Steven, okay?" she said, facing him, clutching her pajamas to her chest like they were life preservers. "No one knows except you and me." Just the thought that her brother could actually walk down the stairs and spill the beans to their mother right that moment had her up in his face, index finger pointed. "And you're going to keep it that way."

He looked aghast. "You're not going to tell Mom and Dad?"

She glanced over at the door. "Jeez. Keep it down. I'm not telling anyone right now. Not until I know what I'm going to do."

"What do you mean?" he asked, his tone going rigid.

"Oh, for heaven's sake, I just found out myself." She backed away and headed for the bathroom. "I need some time to process."

He didn't say anything as she changed out of her robe and into her pj's. When she came back out again, he was still by the dresser. He looked young, not like the fierce and formidable deputy she knew he could be.

"Well?" she said.

He unloaded a sigh as his eyes found hers. "Okay . . . I'll keep your secret. But . . ."

Oh, he was so predictable. Her hands went to her hips. "What do you want?"

One dark brow drifted upward. "The guy's name."

Her heart leapt into her throat and she walked past him. "Get serious."

"I'm not going to kill him, Em."

"I don't believe you," she said, picking up her purse and putting it back on the desktop.

"This baby deserves a father."

"Why? So he won't be a bastard?" she tossed back, quoting Jeremy's word at dinner.

"Look, that was stupid and not cool. Jeremy knows it and so do I. He was acting the fool. Neither one of us really thinks that."

She turned and leaned back against the desk. "The baby's father is a good man, Steven."

"A good man would be sitting here with you right now."

"I told you he doesn't know."

"Name, Emmie."

"I swear to God, if you—"

"I won't tell Mom and Dad."

"Swear it."

He put his hand over his heart. "On the grave of Boggs."

Emily stilled, her shoulders falling. It was their thing. Swearing on the grave of their beloved turtle from childhood. Silly, maybe. But she believed him.

She took a deep breath. "It's . . . Blue. Cavanaugh."

Steven's mouth dropped open, and before he could say a word, Emily reminded him, "You promised."

"Wait. I don't get it. How?" He pulled back from the question instantaneously, shaking his head. "Forget I asked that. I know how. I don't even want to think about it."

She made a face. "Stop talking now. Listen, we're not seeing each other. It was one night."

"Oh, Em . . ."

"Don't *Oh, Em* me, Steven Shiver. You're no saint. I want your assurance that you won't go after him. No punching or kicking, et cetera."

"Fine," he ground out, pushing away from the dresser. "I won't kill or hurt him and I won't tell Mom and Dad."

"Or Jeremy," she added.

"Or Jeremy," he uttered.

Emily sighed with relief. Even though it was her little brother, it felt good to tell someone. Get it off her chest. Just while she took some time to figure things out.

They met at the door, and before she could say a word more, Steven gathered her up in his arms and hugged her tight.

"I love you, Emmie," he said. "I'm here for you. We're all here for you, and for this baby. You know that, right? With all the joking around and stupid talk, you know that?"

Tears pricked her eyes. Nothing was more precious to her than family. She sighed and just let him hold her. "I know."

*   *   *

Weather was changing. From those slow, warm days that never seemed to end, to that strange coolness in the air that made a person think about starting school even when those times were long past. Blue had the window down on his truck, arm resting on the frame as he headed up the highway back toward River Black. He loved fall. Or had. Life changing on the ranch. Scenery and maybe new blood. He took a deep breath and blew it out. He'd just come from Hawthorne. Bought fifty head of Red Brangus. Before Natalie's betrayal had completely turned his heart to stone, back when all he'd wanted was to take over the Triple C, it had been part of his plan to expand their brand. His brand, he'd thought. Become a seed-stock producer. Mac had loved the idea, and they'd looked into Brangus being their top choice. He'd forgotten all about it these past weeks, until Mac had asked him just that morning to go on a buying run.

He reached out, grasped at the cool air with his fingers. She was trying to get him fueled again. Get him passionate again. Even if it meant fighting her husband over the rights to his birthplace. Although with Deac, and maybe even with Cole, he'd never thought there would be much of a fight, as the two of them had new lives, new homes. Only one he'd been worried about was James. Granted, the man's fiancée, Sheridan, still worked in the city for Deacon, but James had his horses at the C . . . and he liked hanging around. Whenever he and Sheridan were in town, they stayed in the foreman's quarters.

But Blue's passion, his need to fight, was gone. Most of it was due to all the lies that had surrounded him lately. He had no trust—for others, for his own judgment, for his capabilities. Hell, he couldn't even convince people that Natalie Palmer had been responsible for Cass's death.

Cass.

The one person he actually felt he could trust.

Blue spotted the River Black county line ahead and sped up. She was still there. In everything. As she should be. Blue had never known his half sister, but he missed her anyway. Maybe that was crazy or strange, but it was how it was. When he'd seen that diary, Cass's writing, something had switched on inside him. A protective, brotherly thing he would've never believed he was capable of. It was why he'd jumped, called in the sheriff, pressed them to look into Natalie's past.

His boot pressed low on the gas pedal. He often wondered . . . had Natalie known who he was from the beginning when they'd met online nearly a year ago? Had she sought him out? And if so, why? Had she been trying to get close to the family? He had so many questions, and yet he refused to get them answered. He never wanted to speak to that woman again. And anyway, whatever might come out of her mouth would no doubt be more lies. Sometimes when he was in town, he thought he saw her, thought he felt her—but it turned out to be just his imagination running on.

The sound of a siren behind him jarred him from his thoughts. First thing he did was let up on the gas pedal, then check his speed. Eighty-five in a seventy. *Shit.*

There was one moment, one tiny moment, when Blue thought about running. Slamming his boot into the metal and seeing how far he got. Where he got to. But he wasn't running anymore. Or fighting anymore. He was accepting.

The flashing lights in his rearview mirror sent him to the shoulder and to a dusty stop. The sheriff's vehicle followed, and in seconds the car was near kissing his bumper. *Just write the ticket and let's both be on our way.*

The deputy who stepped out of the patrol car and made his way to Blue's window wasn't exactly a stranger. Steven Shiver hadn't been the one to come out to Natalie's place when Blue had found the diary, but he'd been on duty when Blue and Natalie had been brought into the station. And of course, Blue had met the man's sister later that night.

His gut tightened as Shiver approached.

"Sorry about that, Officer," he said to the dark-haired deputy in the brown hat and aviator sunglasses. "Here's my license and registration."

"Step out of the truck, please."

The deputy's tone put Blue on instant alert. Cold, professional, unyielding. "Why?"

Shiver opened the door. "Out of the truck, sir. Now."

Sir? "I'm due a ticket. I get that. Come on, you know me, Shiver. Here's my license."

"Do I need to pull my weapon, sir?"

"Christ." The guy wasn't kidding. Did he think there was something else going on? Irritation crept into Blue's blood. For one brief second, he contemplated arguing. But a man didn't argue with a cop in Texas. Not if he wanted to keep lead out of his ass.

He climbed out of the truck. But the second his feet hit dirt, Shiver whirled him around and slammed his hands together behind his back.

"You gonna tell me what this is about?" Blue ground out, his instinct to fight humming underneath his skin. "Because it sure doesn't feel like a speeding violation."

The officer answered by slapping cuffs on his wrists.

"Cuffs?" Blue growled. "This is a mistake."

Shiver jerked him back, then led him toward the patrol car. "You better not call it that."

"Call it what?" Blue demanded. "What the hell are you talking about?"

Again, no real answer was given. Instead, Blue was shoved into the backseat, the door slammed shut behind him. He sat there on the cool leather, pissed, confused, wondering if Shiver had gotten him mixed up with someone else. And then it hit him. She'd told her brother. "This is about Emily, isn't it?"

Shiver's face showed up in the rearview mirror.

"So you remember my sister, then. Well, that's something, I suppose."

Blue's face tightened. Along with the rest of him.

"You want to tell me anything, Perez?" Shiver taunted, flipping off the lights on top of the patrol car.

"Like how what you're doing is illegal as hell?" Blue ground out.

"No, that's not it."

A muscle worked in Blue's jaw. He didn't know what Emily had told her brother, but he wasn't going into that night. It was no one's business but his and Emily's. He inhaled sharply and turned to look out the window.

"Fine," Shiver said. "We'll see if you open up down at the station."

Then he threw the car in gear and took off like a bat out of hell.

Five

Emily was going to kill her brother. Or at the very least hog-tie his ass! Was he kidding? A text? On her cell phone? At work? *I have Perez down here at the station. I suggest you come by.* Her heart had flipping jumped right out of her chest. Thank God it was a slow day at the Bull's Eye and Dean had let her go. Or run. Or, as it were, drive straight to River Black's tiny jail.

The parking lot was empty, and good thing too, because the moment she walked in the door, she called out "Steven Paul Shiver?" in a tone that was anything but professional and respectful.

The River Black jail was basically an outpost. The sheriff and sheriff's deputy serviced several small towns in the county, and about ten years back they'd built the three-cell space so people didn't have to make the trek out to Mason whenever there was a drunken situation or a petty theft.

Emily glanced around but saw no one and headed straight for her brother's office. Steven was sitting at his desk, focused on paperwork and drinking a Coke that was beaded with sweat. When he looked up he smiled as if nothing was out of order in the world.

"Afternoon, sis."

"Are you insane?" she accused, walking right up to his desk and planting her hands on the wood top.

He pretended to mull the question over. "I don't think so." He motioned to the chair beside her. "Would you like to have a seat?"

She ignored him. "You arrested Blue?"

"He's not under arrest. Yet."

Clearly, Steven had lost his mind. "You can't do that," she warned him.

"Of course I can," he countered, as arrogant as all get-out. "Your baby daddy was speeding."

"Shut up," she hissed, her stomach lurching. She glanced over her shoulder. The goddamned door to the office was open.

"Don't worry, sis," he said, his tone softening a touch. "Rick ain't here. He's on patrol. Only you and me—and, well . . ." He knocked his chin toward the door.

Emily could practically hear her anger. It was blood, hot and heavy, pounding in her ears. "If he was speeding, then you give him a ticket and send him on his way." She pointed a finger at him. "And don't call him my"—she lowered her voice and whispered through tightly clenched teeth—"baby daddy."

"It's what he is, Em." One brow lifted. "Right?"

"Of course right," she ground out. "But that's not the point."

Steven sat back in his chair and shrugged. "Listen, he was going a good ten/fifteen miles over the speed limit. In this town, I have the right to bring him in."

She crossed her arms over her chest. "Have you ever taken someone in for ten or fifteen miles over, Steven?"

The question was rhetorical. Of course he hadn't. Waste of time and resources. But he was going to keep playing his cards. "Wasn't safe, Em. What if he had you in his truck? Or the baby?"

"Shh! Dammit." Teeth still tightly clenched, she stalked over to the door and slammed it shut.

"He can't hear you," Steven scolded, his eyes filled with humor.

A thought suddenly flickered through Emily's mind, and just like that she felt breathless. Why hadn't she thought of it before? The second her brother's text came in? Steven was being so damn cavalier. Her eyes narrowed on him.

"What?" he said.

"You told him, didn't you?"

"Who? Perez?"

"Yes, of course, Perez. You told him I was pregnant."

"No."

"Steven Paul Shiver," she said in her best big-sister I'm-going-to-pound-you voice.

"I promised you I wouldn't tell anyone, and I haven't."

A thread of relief moved through her, though she wasn't altogether sure she believed him. "Then why is he here?"

"Because, Em"—he leaned forward, his eyes devoid of all humor now—"you're going to tell him."

The blood drained from Emily's face. She could actually feel it. Feel the pale coldness invade her skin. "Damn you, Steven," she nearly growled. "This isn't any of your business."

"Like hell," he shot back. He pointed at her stomach. "That's my niece or nephew you got cooking in there."

"You're such an ass. And don't be gross."

"And don't you be stubborn. You need to tell him the truth, Emmie."

"Not in a jail cell, I don't."

He shrugged. "It's the nice one."

"Not funny."

With a sigh of frustration, he opened the desk drawer to his left and pulled out a set of keys. "No one's around. Not for at least an hour." He held them out to her. "Tell him." His lips turned up at the corners. "And if he tries to bolt, I'll be here to take him down."

"You can't be serious about this."

"I am. That man's not going anywhere until you tell him. Your choice."

Sickened, Emily stared at her brother. He was one hundred percent serious, and she wondered if he'd actually tell Blue in the end, or their mom and dad, if she refused. One thing she did know was that she'd never forgive him if he went there and ratted on her—well, maybe that wasn't exactly true; they were blood . . . but she'd be furious.

Walk into a cell? Face the man she hadn't seen in three weeks—hadn't seen since she was in his bed . . . ? Oh God. She could faint. This was bullshit. What was she going to do?

"God, I hate being related to law enforcement," she growled, snatching up the keys and heading for the door.

"Don't say that," Steven called to her back. "Might come in handy someday."

Her heart slamming fiercely inside her chest, Emily walked out of the office and headed for the small trio of cells in the back of the building. She knew where it was only because Steven had done something similar two years ago when Jeremy had gotten drunk at a party and thought he was capable of driving himself home. One of his friends had called Steven, and Jeremy had spent the night in the jail puking his guts out into a bucket while listening to Emily and Steven go off on him for his stupidity.

Oh God, this was insanity. She couldn't do this. And yet, she kept going, kept walking. Until that night, she'd never been one to run from things. Hard things. Her parents had taught her better. Face your problems. Fix your problems. Move on.

But she hadn't come across a problem like this. And when a man is clearly making love to you because he's pissed off and trying to forget another woman, well . . . you leave.

Dammit, every inch of her was shaking with nerves. And it only worsened when the first cell came into view. She stopped about five feet away and just took a moment to look at the man inside—the man whom she hadn't seen for three weeks—except in her mind, and her dreams . . . memories. Just because his reasons for wanting her hadn't been what she would've liked, it didn't make the experience any less amazing. Or erotic. Or fulfilling.

He was standing in one corner, head down, boots crossed at the ankle. He looked dirty. But the good kind of dirty. Cowboy dirty. Jeans caked in mud, boots worn and caked in mud. Faded red shirt. He looked up then and caught her standing there, staring. For one brief moment, Emily hoped she might see something in his eyes that said he was glad to see her. But instead, his face was dark with anger, like he'd had a lot of time to think.

She swallowed hard and wished she was anywhere else.

He didn't move. Just crossed his arms over his chest and regarded her. "Emily Shiver."

"I'm so sorry about this," she said, coming over to his cell.

"I believe your brother's gone crazy."

"I know." She thrust the key in the lock and

opened the door. Maybe she really wouldn't for-give Steven. Blood or no blood.

"What does he think happened between us?" Blue asked, remaining where he was, despite the open door. "What did you tell him?"

Her gut churned. "What do you mean?"

He gave her a look that said, *Come on, now.* "I should be online paying a speeding ticket, not hanging out in a cage." He stared at her, his gor-geous face all hard angles, his eyes an incredible shock of blue. "This was personal."

"He just thinks we hung out . . . ," she said with forced ease.

"Hung out," he repeated.

"He's protective," she continued. "Overly pro-tective."

Blue was watching her as she spoke, and she could see it in his eyes. He knew she wasn't telling him the truth, and it pissed him off more than his ass being stuck in jail for fifteen miles over.

"It's a brother thing," she finished stupidly.

His eyes flashed and he looked past her, down the hall. "Yeah, well, wouldn't know about that."

Her heart stuttered. God, she was really screw-ing this up. And she didn't want to. It was the first time she was seeing him in weeks, since . . . "I'm so sorry, Blue. It won't happen again. I'll make sure of it."

"Appreciate that." He pushed away from the wall and walked up to her. For just a moment, his gaze rested on hers and a strange softness touched his expression. "It's good to see you."

Her heart pinched inside her ribs. "Yeah. You too."

It was in that moment that Emily remembered how it felt to be close to this man. To be touched by him, regardless of the reason. How his skin smelled and had felt under her hands.

"You all right?" he asked, his gaze concerned.

The question caught her by surprise. Lord, was she all right? Probably not. She was pretty much a confused and scared mess. *Tell him. Tell him, you moron.* "Sure. 'Course."

"And work?"

"Same," she said, her voice near to a whisper. "You should stop in sometime." God, she was an idiot.

His eyes darkened and his lips parted. "I don't know . . ."

"I just mean if you're thirsty," she rambled on stupidly, then instantly wished she could take it back—or crawl into one of the cells and lock herself in.

"I should probably steer clear of bars for a while."

Her gut tightened. Right. Sounded wise. Sounded like a pretty clear message too.

"Then again," he amended, "it was nice having you take me home."

Or a mixed message? "It was nice being there," she offered.

"And yet, you left."

She watched the shadow creep across his face. He didn't trust her. Hell, he didn't know her. Had slept with her, but didn't know her. "I . . . It was a confusing situation. I felt—"

"It's fine," he cut her off, shaking his head. "Don't worry about it. We all make bad decisions, right? Rash decisions—"

His words bit her heart, causing pain to flicker inside her. She didn't think he was meaning to be insulting. Granted, he didn't know what was going on. He was angry about the arrest. But it hurt to know he thought that night was a mistake.

Of course, hadn't she kind of thought the same thing when she was throwing on her clothes and rushing out of his house?

"Well, well. Glad to see you didn't bolt, Perez." Steven's voice echoed down the hall as he came toward them.

Her heart dropped. "Steven, wait—"

"Your sister was kind enough to let me out," Blue replied, his tone cooling further as he turned to regard the man.

"Wouldn't want the daddy of my niece or nephew to have an arrest record, now, would I?" Steven said, then stopped short and asked, "You don't have one already, do you? I didn't even think to look."

"Oh my God," Emily breathed, panic filling her blood. This wasn't it. Wasn't right. How could she turn back time?

"It's all right, Em," Steven said casually.

"I can't believe you," she ground out. She couldn't even look Blue's way.

"Come on, now. The man gets why I had to do what I—"

"Shut up, Steven," Emily growled. "Damn you."

He stalled out, confused. "What?"

She had to. She just had to. Every inch of her skin tight, Emily glanced up at Blue, and when she saw the look on his face she wanted to die. No, she wanted to run. Again. He was staring at her. He looked like someone had punched him in the face. Confused, shocked, pissed . . . but worst of all, betrayed.

Then his gaze shifted to Steven. "You going to book me, Sheriff?"

Realizing what he'd walked in and spat all over without thinking, her brother cursed, then shook his head. "You're free to go. Don't worry about the speeding ticket. I'll take care of it."

"Yeah, you will." And without another word, his body and expression tight with fury, Blue brushed past them and headed down the hall.

Her mind racing, her pulse jumping around inside her blood, Emily stared at his retreating frame.

"Ah, Christ, Emmie," Steven said, shaking his head. "You didn't do it?"

Her eyes cut to him. "You're a jackass," she growled at him.

"And you're a coward," he returned.

"Maybe so. But you had no right to do this. To interfere. No matter what the reason."

"Well, what's done is done. He knows now."

That I'm pregnant. And he'd truly found out in

the worst way imaginable. She had to do something about it. She had to find him and talk to him.

"Don't you follow me," she warned her brother
as she pushed past him.

"Wouldn't dare," he said on a sigh as Emily
took off down the hall.

A few hours ago, he'd been fine. Decent. Doing his
job. Minding his business. Thinking about the fifty
head of cattle he'd just ordered. And then in his
rearview come lights and a siren—then cuffs and
a jail cell—then . . . Christ, the words . . .

He couldn't make sense of it. Was it true? Could
it be true? A sneer came quick to his lips as he
pushed open the front door to the jail and headed
out into the bright fall sunshine. What he knew
was that Blue Perez Cavanaugh couldn't recognize truth if it bit him on the ass. He was damaged
that way.

Maybe the sheriff was just messing with him
for spending the night with his sister.

"Blue!"

Shit. Her voice reached out to him as he headed
toward town. Walking was about all he could do
with his truck being still parked on the side of the
highway. He didn't turn around. He didn't want
to look at her. She was too damn soft. Too eager.
Too beautiful. Just like she'd been that night.

His jaw tightened.

That goddamned night.

But the woman caught up with him anyway.
Keeping pace with him, breathing heavy. It shouldn't

have bothered him. But it did. The idea of her running, being out of breath. He growled to himself.
Hell, wasn't that kind of thing dangerous for a
growing baby . . . ?

"Go back," he ground out. "I got nothing to say
to you."

"Well, I have plenty to say to you," she returned. And with that, she broke ahead and got
directly in his path. Made him stop short. "And
afterward I can take you wherever you need to
go."

"What I need is for you to get out of my way,"
he warned.

"Not gonna happen. You need to listen to me."

"Oh, now I need to listen, huh?" he said. He
glanced around. They were about two hundred
yards from the police station. No businesses in
this part of town except for a small feed store,
which looked pretty quiet this time of day. "How
long, Emily?"

His question surprised her. "What?"

"How long have you known?"

She bit her lip, looked down at the ground.
"Not long. Just found out yesterday."

His guts twisted. So it was true. It was fucking
true. "And you tell your brother first," he forced
out.

"He found out by accident. I wasn't going to
tell anyone—"

"Is that right?" he interrupted caustically.

"Not what I mean, Blue."

His brows lifted sardonically. "So you were going to tell me."

" 'Course I was going to tell you," she said with passion. "After I had a chance to think, you know? Process. Make sure . . ."

She faltered. He didn't like her faltering.

"Make sure of what?" he said tightly.

Looking flustered and uneasy, she turned away and stared at the feed store.

It was like someone was fisting his heart. Shit. He didn't even think he had one anymore. "Make sure you wanted it?" he pressed. He'd meant the words to come out dark, a bleak accusation. Something that mimicked his mood and, fuck him, his fears. But it didn't come out that way. The query was wrapped up in a blanket of unease.

Her eyes came back to him and they were solemn. "No."

A flash of relief went through him. But it didn't last long. "Or maybe make sure you wanted me as the daddy?"

"Blue, please stop . . ."

"Maybe you ain't even sure it's mine." The words had rolled off his tongue with far too much ease. "Is that it, sweetheart?" he growled, leaning in, close to her face. "Not sure who the daddy might be?"

Her chin tilted up and her eyes took on a hardness he'd never seen before. "Wow."

"Because you went home with me pretty easy." He couldn't seem to stop himself. It was like someone else, something else had taken over his brain and his tongue. "Date a lot of customers, do you?"

Her nostrils flared. "Boy, when I'm wrong, I'm wrong. I thought you were a good guy. I thought you were decent and upstanding—"

"Hey," he broke in. "Before we start tossing insults back and forth, let's remember who walked out on who."

"First of all," she began fiercely, "I didn't go home with you. I took you home because you were too goddamned drunk to drive. Real smart and responsible, by the way. The staying part, I'll take full responsibility for that." She took one step closer, shoved her finger in his chest. "And I left because you made it very clear I was only there to take away the memory of your ex-girlfriend."

Blue felt the blood drain from him. What was she talking about? Why would she think that? And ex-girlfriend—

Suddenly, his gaze caught on something over her shoulder. A figure in the doorway of the feed store. He narrowed his eyes. *What is that . . .* Without thinking, he moved, placing himself in front of Emily. The figure disappeared inside the barn, but Blue swore he saw the retreating frame of Natalie Palmer.

"Blue." Emily exhaled heavily. "Look, I don't want to argue. Or toss insults back and forth. We both acted foolishly that night. Let's just agree to that."

He turned back to face her. He didn't want to

agree on anything. Not just yet. Goddammit, it was like one bomb a day was being dropped on him. He couldn't think straight.

"What I want to say is that I'm sorry you heard about it the way you did," she continued. "And I'm not asking for or expecting anything from you."

Blue felt the skin around his muscles tighten. She wasn't expecting anything from him . . .

"I'll see you around," she said finally, then turned and started back toward the police station.

Blue stared after her, utterly stalled. She was pregnant with his baby. She didn't want anything from him. He felt like the world was caving in. Again. He'd been trying not to care—about anything. Not want anything. Just living under the radar. Shutting himself down—off.

And now he had a child . . .

He fought the urge to go running after her. But he had nothing to say or offer. Except maybe an apology of his own? For what he'd said to her now, and Christ, what he had said that night. About Natalie. No wonder she ran. No wonder she'd never crossed his path in the three weeks that followed.

When she disappeared inside the jail, he turned back to the road. He had to get his truck; then he had to screw his head on straight and figure out what he was going to do next.

Six

"You running on batteries tonight or what?" Rae asked as she passed Emily on the way into the kitchen.

Emily gave the woman a tight smile. "It's busy." But what she really wanted to say was *If you stop, you think.* And her thinks would only get her into trouble. Make her feel like crawling under the covers, eating pints of ice cream—and she didn't do pity parties. Sure, she'd cried in the employee bathroom for a solid ten minutes before fixing her face and getting back on the floor, but after that it was all about making money. She had a family to support now. And whatever it took before this baby came, she was going to get that property and open her business.

"Sure is," Rae acknowledged with a glance around the room. "But I'd say you're making double the tips than the rest of us are." She looked Emily up and down and grimaced. "And frankly, honey, I'm not sure how you're doing it. Despite that red rose you got tied into your ponytail, it ain't your best night in the looks department, if you don't mind me saying so."

Oh, why would I mind?

"Not getting much sleep?" Rae lowered her voice, glanced around, then whispered, "Are you seeing someone?"

Emily knew exactly what the woman was insinuating. "No. And no."

Rae shrugged. "Too bad. It's really the only excuse." Then she headed off toward her section.

Grabbing her pad, Emily went to take orders from two new tables. But the first one she came upon had an unwelcome visitor sitting at it.

"You can't be serious."

Steven grinned sheepishly up at her. He was still wearing his uniform. He rarely came into the Bull's Eye, and never in his uniform.

"Can I buy you a drink?" he asked. "Shirley Temple?"

She wasn't in the mood for his cute act. "I'm working."

"I'll wait."

She released a weighty breath. "I'm tired," she said. "And I have a full house here. I don't want to do this right now, Steven, okay?"

"I don't want to do this at all." He gave her that look. That I-screwed-up-and-I-know-it look. He'd worn it, like, every other day when he was a boy. "What can I say except that I'm sorry? It's something that happens to a brother, you know? It comes over us. This wolflike protective thing."

Out of the corner of her eye, Emily could see that her new table of four was starting to get antsy. "Steven—"

"I'm not trying to make excuses . . . well, shit, maybe I am." He quirked his mouth. "Emmie, I just want to make sure you're okay. Both of you."

Tears crawled up into her throat and scratched away. Damn him. She wasn't going to cry on the floor tonight. It was unprofessional and in a bar setting like this one would absolutely kill her tips. She'd seen it happen. "Go home, Steven."

"Emmie . . ."

"Go home."

He paused, then nodded. "Fine. But you forgive me, right?"

Oh, what could she say? Really? This was blood. And like it or not, blood was thicker than stupidity and arrogance and acting without thinking. "Fine," she said on a sigh. "If there's a pizza in the oven and coffee Heath bar crunch ice cream in the freezer when I get home, then, yes, maybe I will forgive you. Crazier things have been known to happen when I'm in a carb-and-sugar comalike state."

He grinned, looked relieved. "I'll see you later."

"Yeah, yeah." She turned away from him and headed for the four-top. Forgiveness, acceptance . . . it all came so easily in the Shiver family. No matter what someone pulled. Because really, what was the alternative? Stay angry and bitter indefinitely?

That was no fun. And pretty much hell on the stomach lining. Her eyes caught and held on the round belly of one of the women at the four-top. And now that she was going to be a strong, capable, single mother, she had to keep her stomach lining—not to mention the rest of her—as calm and relaxed as possible.

Natalie smiled to herself as she slid the lined cookie sheet into the oven and closed the door. It was easy. So easy. All she had to do was watch . . . and wait. Let the chance present itself. And if today was any indication, things would come to her soon.

The smile on her face slipped. Just a fraction. That woman—the waitress—she didn't understand respect. Or men. One night didn't make a relationship. One drunk night where Natalie was sure Blue was thinking only of her. After all, he'd mentioned many a time in his texts that he wanted to be with her, touch her, know her. If she would just reveal herself to him.

Stupid diary. Stupid Cass Cavanaugh. She ruined things even from the grave. But . . . it was a momentary blip. Blue belonged to her. Admittedly, he was angry now. But he would come around.

She would make sure of that.

The scent of perfectly cooked macaroons drifted into her nostrils, and she slipped her oven mitt off the hook near the stove and opened the oven once again.

Seven

The sound that disturbed her sleep was mildly irritating, yet familiar. Emily stirred beneath the warm covers. Sleep wanted so desperately to reclaim her, and she wanted that too. Her body relaxed into the mattress once again. But someone or something was determined she wake.

Bastards.

She came alive with a groan, threw back the covers, and stood up. This time her groan stemmed from half a pepperoni pizza followed by an entire pint of ice cream. But seriously, what was a girl to do if she couldn't have wine?

Throwing on her robe, she padded over to the window. The sound that was forcing her awake was coming from the glass. Or something up against the glass. What was it? Rain? Tree limbs?

"What in the world?" she exclaimed as a sprinkling of tiny rocks struck the window in front of her. She waited for another just to make sure she wasn't having a middle school flashback. Not that any of the boys she might have liked back then took the trouble to come to her house and toss gravel at her window. But that was always the fantasy.

When the rocks came again, splattering against the glass, she flipped the lock and pulled up the window. With the screen, she couldn't really stick her head out very far, but she tracked the front yard with her gaze. Even with the half-moon, it was pretty dark. She couldn't see anything but shadows and trees and—

"Emily." The voice lifted to meet her. The rough, male voice that after today she wasn't quite sure she'd ever hear again.

"Blue?" she called down.

A figure stepped out from the shadow of the grand oak. A tall, imposing, devastatingly handsome figure that she recognized right away.

Reflexively, Emily glanced over her shoulder. Dark bedroom, door closed. Silent house. She had to make sure it remained that way. When she turned back, she called down in a strained whisper, "What are you doing here?"

"I need to talk to you."

"It's . . . God, what time is it?"

"Three," he said without even a hint of an apology in his tone.

She shivered against the cold air rushing in from the open window. "Can it wait until morning?"

"Emily?"

"What?"

"I need to talk to you. Now, are you coming down or am I coming up?"

Jeez, this was nuts. This guy was nuts. And stubborn. Way too stubborn. She sighed. "My father or my brothers will shoot you if they catch us down there."

"So I'm coming up, then?"

Beyond stubborn! And with a possible death wish. "Make no mistake about it. They'll shoot you up here too," she added dryly. "You're not going to climb this tree, Blue Perez. You're over fifteen years old and—" She stopped talking when he completely ignored her and started walking toward the tree, and then she panicked when he hitched himself up to the first branch. Unbelievable. He was going to do it. "Okay. Stop. Wait a second—" She blew a breath. Dammit. "Get away from the house and back into those shadows. I'm coming down."

She didn't even wait for a response. After closing the window, she tightened the sash on her robe, stepped into her UGG boots, and hurried downstairs. She made the journey as quietly as possible and, once outside, ran across the yard to the trees where she knew he was waiting. She was pretty sure she looked like death warmed over. Or at the very least, puffy and bloated. Thank you, pizza and dairy. But that couldn't be helped.

"It's freezing," she said, joining him under the heavy limbs of the oak. "How long have you been out here?"

"Never mind that." He took off his coat and put it around her. Then he reached for her hand and led her toward the driveway.

"I'm not in the position to go anywhere, Blue," she said.

"Don't worry," he said as they reached the truck, which was parked back a ways and in the shadows.

How covert, she thought. No wonder she hadn't seen it from her bedroom window. "I see you got your wheels back."

"You mean I got back to my wheels?" he said dryly.

Damn Steven. Why had she forgiven him so easily? With just the suggestion of carbs and sugar? "Hey, I did offer to drive you," she reminded him.

He opened the passenger door for her. "Come on. It's warm in here."

She climbed in, and when he was sitting beside her, the truck running with enough heat so her teeth stopped chattering, she allowed herself a good look at him. As cold and as curious as she'd been, she hadn't really stopped to see him properly. Her eyes did a quick sweep. He had on jeans as usual, but these ones were faded and molded to his powerful thighs. Up top he wore a thick cream sweater that set off his tan skin real nice. His chiseled features looked even more striking with the fine dusting of dark stubble. She remembered that he'd had that the night she'd left him in bed. Her insides softened. He'd kissed her with that stubble. And it had felt really good, raw. Her nostrils flared.

"What are you doing, Emily?"

"Hmm?" she mumbled.

"Eyes are up here, honey."

As she realized what he was saying, and what she'd been thinking, heat surged into her cheeks. She dragged her gaze upward from his mouth. His very kissable mouth. "I'm still half asleep," she explained. *That's right. Blame the staring on that. Good plan.*

"I know," he acknowledged. "And I'm sorry about it. Three o'clock in the morning is not a friendly hour for anybody. It's crazy and not fair to you, but the thing is, I can't sleep. I can't think." Those eyes were serious now as they delved into hers. "I need you to tell me, Emily. Like this. Face-to-face."

Her brain was still foggy. "I don't understand."

"You were going to tell me. Your brother got the news first." He exhaled, ran a hand through his thick, dark hair. "I just don't want anyone else to hear until I do—until you tell me."

"Oh . . . ," she breathed, understanding now. He wanted to hear her say that she was pregnant. She blinked, feeling as though her lungs weren't producing oxygen properly. "But you already know . . ."

"I was coming out of a jail cell when your brother blurted out the news. And I retaliated by saying some really stupid and shameful and untrue words to you." He shrugged. "Not exactly the way things like this should go."

"Glad you recognize that last bit," she said, lifting her chin.

"So." He leaned in a little. "I'm asking you now . . . will *you* tell me?"

Their proximity, the heat off his skin and coming from the vents—and the need she saw in his eyes—held her there, captive, unblinking. Barely breathing. A blade of fear slashed through her heart. It was odd, but she felt like the words he wanted to hear from her, the words she was about to utter, might connect them. In a way that felt strangely permanent. And though she was clearly attracted to him, she didn't know where his head was at. Where his heart was at. Maybe he was seeing someone. Maybe he had plans with that person, for a future, for . . .

She cut herself off. None of this was her business. It was one night. She didn't have a claim on him. Hell, where was *her* head at? *Her* heart?

Her eyes locked with his. "Blue. I'm pregnant."

For a moment he just stared at her, his thoughts unreadable. But then his expression relaxed and he nodded. "Thank you."

Thank you? She wasn't exactly sure how she felt about that response. Not that she had expected him to jump up and down and say it was all he'd ever wished for. But maybe something besides . . . *Thank you.* "And again, I'm sorry about my brother, the jail."

"It's okay."

"Really?"

He shrugged. "You know, if I had a sister . . ." He paused a second. "One that I knew and had grown up with anyway . . ."

He was talking about Cass. She couldn't imagine what was running through him about all that. The lost time. The wondering. The pain.

"Well," he continued, "I'd probably jail the guy who got her pregnant too."

"Well, that's generous of you," Emily told him. "But Steven will be leaving you alone from here on out. No threats, no pressure. Me either. Like I said earlier, you don't have to do anything. You aren't responsible for anything."

His expression darkened suddenly. "Why do you keep saying that to me? About my not doing anything?"

"I don't know," she began, confused by his quick change of mood. Why was he so mad? She was trying to take the pressure off him. After all he was going through, might be a relief. "It was one night, Blue. We don't have a relationship. We weren't in a relationship. I don't know your circumstances now, if you're seeing someone . . . I don't want to screw something up—"

"I'm not seeing anyone," he said definitively. "And that night, I wasn't seeing anyone." He looked away a second. "Not really." When he turned back to her, his eyes were cobalt. "Whatever I said to you, it wasn't because I had some great, unrequited feeling for someone else. It was because I was angry at myself."

Her heart kicked her chest. "Why?" she asked. "Because of Natalie? What you found in her apartment?"

The news had spread far and wide about Blue

and Natalie's online romance and the fact that he'd found Cass's diary in the woman's house. But he didn't look keen on discussing the subject. "What I'll say is that Natalie Palmer is a liar. She's dangerous." His jaw tightened. "And I didn't see it. Should've seen it."

Emily stared at him as the car's heater kept pumping out warm air over her skin. The questions that hummed on her tongue . . . For goodness' sake. And yet, she knew pushing him for answers was a bad idea. If Blue Perez wanted to tell her more, maybe he would . . . in his time.

"I want to talk about you now," he said, his eyes serious and concerned as they probed hers. "How have you been feeling?"

Strange. Tired. Slightly annoyed. And slightly turned on. "All good. Fine."

He nodded. "Have you been to see a doctor yet?"

"I have an appointment tomorrow."

One brow lifted. "I'd like to know what he says, if you don't mind."

Without her consent, a wave of disappointment moved over her. Realistically, she knew Blue wasn't about to ask or demand to come to her appointment, but the feeling was there all the same. "'Course not."

"And how . . . everything is progressing," he continued.

"Sure. No problem." Her smile was tight, forced. And the heater wasn't working because she felt suddenly chilled down to her bones. "I should get back."

He looked momentarily dazed, but then his gaze cleared. " 'Course. Listen, I'm sorry about the rocks on your window. Waking you up. I just couldn't . . . I needed . . ."

"It's fine," she assured him, reaching for the door handle. "I understand. I do."

Blue was out of the car in an instant and came around to her side. "Let's get you back in bed, darlin'."

The words were meant exactly as they'd been spoken, but instead of taking them that way, she found they hummed diabolically inside her. She couldn't help her physical reaction to this man. Call it the hots or call it appreciation, it had been there before and it was back with a vengeance.

He took her hand then and started for the house. The cold night whipped around her, but all she could think about was how those warm, strong, callused hands had felt on other parts of her body.

Idiot.

You need sleep. And maybe therapy.

When they reached the front door, Emily started to pull away. But Blue held her a moment before leaning down and giving her a quick peck on the cheek.

It was simple. A little nothing. And yet the gesture spread through her body like wildfire. Blood pumped hot and heavy, and sleep was the very last thing on her mind. Lord have mercy, she needed to get inside before she did or acted without thinking.

"Sleep well, Emily," he whispered as she opened the door and slipped inside.

"You too," she returned.

Her skin both chilled and overheated, she closed the door and ran across the foyer to the stairs, careful to be quiet. It wasn't until she entered her bedroom and slid under the covers that she realized she was still wearing his coat.

As much as he'd tried not to, Blue had slept in the next day. Only for an hour, but still . . . Problem was, after he'd gotten home, sleep had still managed to elude him. Emily was running through his mind. Her eyes, her voice, how she looked in that robe, her curls all mussed, her cheeks pink from sleep and the cold. She was pregnant with his child, and he couldn't make out how he felt about it. Was he scared? Curious? Happy? Worried? Angry? Was he excited?

Should he have been excited?

What was there in him that said *Dad*? He didn't know a thing about that. Was never shown that.

Goddamn you, Everett. Maybe if you hadn't been so ashamed of me, of claiming me, I'd know what to do now . . .

Heading up to the main house, the sun high in the sky, Blue forced those thoughts out of his head. He needed to get to all the work that was surely waiting for him. He just had to fill his belly first, maybe gulp down a cup of coffee before getting saddled up. He hoped the cowboys were down in the south pasture starting on those fences. It'd be a good day if they could finish before the sun went down.

He took the porch steps two at a time. He hadn't talked to his mother since he'd walked out on her the other night. He'd tried like hell to keep himself even, unaffected, but things like that, holding on to anger, were getting harder and harder for him. Not only was he growing curious about the past—wanting to hear those stories about her and Everett. How they'd met. Why they'd fallen for each other. How Everett had reacted when he'd heard Blue was coming along. And with that last bit, even more so now. But with Emily pregnant, baby on the way, the actions of his mother scarred him deeper still. How could she have let him grow up without a daddy?

He sure as hell wasn't going to let that baby grow up with a question like that.

He entered the house and walked down the hall to the kitchen. Normally, he got a whiff of what was for breakfast and heard a few sounds of pots banging or dishes being washed. But today, the good smells were accompanied by a ton of chatter. Blue's guts twisted, and for a second he contemplated turning around and heading to the diner for eggs and bacon. They weren't usually here. The Cavanaughs. And by the sounds of it, all three brothers, and two of their women, were tucking in to Elena's vittles.

He stopped at the open door, his back to the wall, and listened. They were talking about Cass and Natalie—and the diary. The cold anger he'd tried to shrug off a moment ago was back. With a damn vengeance. Natalie. Such an accomplished liar. Stood there in her house not three weeks ago, looking confused as he'd demanded to know what Cass Cavanaugh's diary was doing inside one of her cookbooks. She'd found it, she'd said. A long time ago, she'd said. And why was Blue looking at her like that? All accusatory?

A growl exited his lips. How had it been so easy to fool him?

"To me it just sounds like a girl with a crush." It was Mac talking, still refusing to see what was right in front of her nose.

Blue shook his head. His once closest friend was deluding herself.

"You do remember who her father was, right?" James's fiancée, Sheridan, stated in a tight tone. "How he nearly took my life. And all that he said to James, all that he implied about Cass's disappearance. Maybe he knew Natalie had something to do with it. Makes sense that he would try to protect her . . ."

"Your woman's pretty smart there, J," Cole put in.

"It's one of the many reasons I'm marrying her," James answered.

"And that makes you smart," Sheridan answered, a smile in her voice.

"Okay, maybe Natalie is a little unstable," Mac acquiesced, forcing the conversation back. "But do you guys really think she did this?"

"I do," James said.

"And I believe people are capable of anything," Deacon added like he was in a board meeting or something.

"Listen to this," Cole said. " 'Diary of Cassandra Cavanaugh. May 10, 2002. Dear Diary, my new friend is the best. She doesn't think anything's wrong with Sweet being older than me. In fact, she says she likes an older boy too. It's so great to have someone to talk to about this stuff.' "

Cole stopped reading. "Do you think that's true?" he asked. "That Natalie was seeing someone? Or was she talking about Sweet? Aka Billy Felthouse? Because if she was, we need to put your man on that too, Deac."

"Let's give Billy a call," James suggested. "See if he knows any more than what he told us at the barbecue."

"I hate that she had to search out someone else, especially Natalie Palmer, to talk to," Mac said softly. "I wasn't doing my job as best friend."

"Not even close to being true, honey," Deacon said. And Blue imagined the man stealing an arm around his wife. "Billy did say he remembered her being around. With these diary entries it's getting clearer and clearer to me that Natalie was stalking them. I can't believe it wasn't clear to the sheriff."

"They're not seeing it from a family's point of view," James said. "It's a girl having a crush on a boy. They've seen that a hundred times without an outcome like Cass's."

"Well, that may be so," Deacon countered. "But they need to see it from all points of view to get at the truth."

Blue was glad the Cavanaughs were taking this seriously. He'd been concerned that they weren't. That, like Mac, they believed it was just a crush and that Natalie had found the diary and was guilty only of keeping it from them all.

He pushed away from the wall and headed into the kitchen. Surprisingly, Elena wasn't there. But the Cavanaughs were just where he'd pictured them: huddled around the table, the plates in front of them licked nearly clean. He went straight for the coffeepot near the sink and poured himself a cup.

"Hey there, Blue," James called out.

"How's it going, Blue?" Cole this time.

"Morning." He turned to see the lot of them. All three brothers, Sheridan, and Mac. The latter gave him a kind, hopeful smile.

"There're pancakes and bacon," she said.

"Not sure I'm all that hungry," he said. *Or that I want to stick around long enough to eat it.* "Might take something small to go."

Mac's smile faltered. She always seemed to be looking for a different expression on his face, a different way of talking to her. Anything that signaled things were back to the way they used to be.

He wished she'd just understand that wasn't about to happen. Too much muddy water under the bridge. Not enough time for him to slug his way out of it yet.

"Have a seat, man," Cole said, cocking his head toward an empty chair next to Mac.

"Yeah, Blue," James agreed. "Maybe you can help us figure this out." He grabbed the diary and held it up. "After all, you were in close contact with Natalie for a while."

He couldn't help it. His jaw went tight as a trap. Even though he was glad the brothers were taking this shit seriously, he hated that his online relationship with Natalie had become so public. Hated that people knew how stupid and vulnerable and gullible he'd been. But that's what happened when you called the sheriff. *Why had he been at Natalie's? How did he know her? How had he found the diary?* At the time, Natalie herself had been pretty forthcoming on the subject. Real proud of their connection. Blue, not so much.

"I don't really know anything," he said, then took a healthy gulp of his coffee.

"She ever mention life outside of River Black?" Deacon asked, cutting up a stack of pancakes. "Like vacations she took or a cooking school she went to?"

Cooking school? What the hell was that about . . . ?

"No."

Deacon's brows lifted. "I find that hard to believe. Especially the school. My PI's on it, and he says it was a huge part of her past."

"We didn't talk about the past," Blue said between tightly clenched teeth. "Didn't get personal."

Cole snorted. "That's online dating for you. Sure glad I don't have to suffer that hell anymore."

"Cole," Mac scolded. "Insensitive much? Jeez."

He looked confused. "All I'm sayin' is I'm grateful to have my baby, Grace."

"I got work to get to," Blue said, setting his cup in the sink. He stuffed a pancake and some bacon into a napkin and headed for the door. "See you all later."

"Hey, Blue," Cole called out. "I didn't mean anything by that, you know."

"Sure, I know," he called back.

"Seriously. We're nothing but thankful. You got Cass's diary for us. We owe you."

Those last words followed him out the door and onto the porch. *We owe you.* Ever since that night three weeks ago, he'd just sort of given up— the fight for understanding his past, the fight for Cass, the fight for the Triple. He was out of gas. Not worth the battle. But this morning things were different. Felt different. Having a home, a secure home, and a livelihood long-term was about more than himself now. After all, he thought as he headed down the porch steps and out into the sunlight, munching on his pancake, a new life was coming into this world. A Perez.

No, he supposed, a Cavanaugh.

Eight

Emily flipped through the magazine and pretended to be interested in Diaper Genies and baby slings. But really her mind was on the exam she was about to have. Nerves skittered through her. Mostly because she didn't really know what to expect. Blood tests? Ultrasound? And it wasn't a doctor she knew. She'd picked someone three towns over so there wouldn't be any talking in River Black. After all, she had yet to tell her parents. She'd wanted to wait until after the doctor's appointment, until she knew that everything was as it should be, before she dropped the bomb.

"Emily Shiver?"

Emily glanced up to see a nurse standing in the doorway leading to the examining rooms. "Yes." She rose quickly and followed. The exam room was very neat and clean and homey, with pale green paint on the walls and black-and-white photographs of the Texas countryside. After asking a ton of questions, making her pee into a cup, and then taking her vitals, the nurse left Emily alone to change.

Nothing like a paper gown that leaves your ass uncovered to make a girl feel comfortable and at ease. She grimaced. Good thing she'd told Steven her appointment wasn't till next week. Having him tag along, asking dumb questions and making fun of her paper dress, would've only made things more uncomfortable.

After she was done and sitting on the exam table, she played on her phone for a few minutes before there was a knock on the door. "Miss Shiver?"

"Yes," she called. "I'm all ready."

The nurse stuck her head in. "The doctor's actually going to be another five minutes."

"Oh, that's fine. I can wait."

"There's a Blue Perez out here," the nurse continued. "Says he's the baby's father."

Emily's heart stalled inside her chest. Blue? Outside? Telling people he was her child's father. What the hell? She wasn't sure she'd heard the woman correctly. But then again, yes, she had.

The nurse looked expectantly at her. "Should I let him in?"

"Umm," she answered dumbly. "Okay. Yes."

After the nurse left, Emily stared at the door. How in the world had he found her? Yes, she'd told him she had an appointment today, but not where it was. And she hadn't told anyone else either. She was miles away from River Black, for heaven's sake.

Just as she was attempting to Sherlock Holmes the answer out of herself, the door opened.

"I'm sorry I'm late, darlin'." Blue walked in, confident, charming, looking all tall and bronzed, blue eyes blazing. A Texas girl's dream. "Ten head broke through the newly fixed fence and ended up getting stuck in a three-foot bog."

Well that explained things.

Not.

She suddenly became aware of how she looked. Not confident or charming. And definitely not ranch-sexy like this one. No. She was sitting on the table in a paper gown, bare legs hanging between those cold metal stirrups, toes not at all polished, hair piled on top of her head—absolutely no makeup.

God, it wasn't fair.

Why was he here? Really? Yesterday, he'd said he'd wanted to know *what* the doc said, not that he was coming to the appointment.

The nurse left then, closing the door all gentle. And Emily turned on her surprise visitor. "Late?" she repeated.

"What?"

"You're not late, Perez. You're not even supposed to be here."

Shadows moved across his eyes. "I think this is exactly where I'm supposed to be."

"That's not what I mean, and you know it," she said, trying to appear casual and together in her paper robe.

"Do I?" he asked tightly.

"Yes." She huffed out a breath. Damn this man. "Look, I didn't mean to make it sound like you weren't welcome. It's just that you said you weren't coming, so this is all a big shock."

"That's not exactly what I said," he amended. "I said I wanted to hear what the doc had to say." He came over to her then, stood near the examination table she was sitting on, and looked down into her face. "Do you want me to go, Emily?"

Breathless, she stared up at him. Did she? Want him to go? Her heart squeezed and she released a breath. "No." She gave him a half smile. "No. I'm glad you came."

Before she could ask him just how he'd managed to find her, there was a knock at the door and both the doctor and the nurse came in.

"Morning," the doctor called brightly as he stepped into the room. He was around Emily's height, her father's age, very trim, and had the kindest eyes she'd ever seen. He stuck a hand out to Emily first. "It's good to meet you."

"You too," she told him.

Then he reached for Blue's hand, shook it heartily. "I'm Dr. Page."

"Blue Perez," Blue told him.

The doctor turned to Emily with just a quick lift of the eyebrow.

"This is the baby's father," she said, her chest feeling a little tight as the words were released. What would Dr. Page think if he knew she and Blue were practically strangers? Not that she planned on telling him or anything.

"Well," the doctor began, "we can go in any order you'd like, Emily. This is your show. You run it how you see fit."

Ease moved through her at the man's words. It had been a real crapshoot going outside River Black for care, but the Yelpers had been right on the money. She was thinking she might've hit the lottery with this one. "What do you normally do?" she asked him. "I think I'd be fine with that."

"Usually, I like to do the ultrasound first," he said, pulling up his gray leather wheely chair and sitting down. "Then a chat in my office where you can ask me a ton of questions and I do my best to answer them. Then we'll take some blood, and I know Mary Louise here likes to follow that up with a doughnut."

Emily glanced over at the nurse, who grinned at her. "I take care of mine, honey. Got some glazed chocolate back there with your name on it."

Oh yes, this could in fact be my favorite place on earth.

"So we'll start with the ultrasound, then," the doctor said, starting to set up, pulling out a pair of gloves.

"Is it possible to see the heartbeat?" Emily asked.

"We're a little early yet, but we can give it a try." The doctor motioned to Mary Louise, and the nurse took over setting up the metal tray and ultrasound machine. "Let's have you lie back, Emily. Mr. Perez, over here," he said, guiding Blue to stand near Emily's shoulder so he could see the monitor while giving her a little privacy.

The doctor took the long wandlike instrument the nurse handed to him. "Now, this might feel a little cold."

As Emily stared at the screen, she felt the wand slip gently into her body. She'd heard about ultrasounds, seen pictures of little bean-shaped babies, but it was something altogether different to know that what she was seeing on the monitor was hers. At first, as a few shapes came up, she didn't know at all what she was seeing. Then Dr. Page started pointing things out.

"This here is your uterus," he said, indicating something that looked like a dark, kidney-shaped swimming pool.

"Does everything look okay?" Blue asked from beside her. He sounded a little anxious.

"Everything looks wonderful," the doctor assured him. "Just as it should be."

"Okay." Blue leaned closer, squinting at the screen. "Well, I don't see anything. Are you sure it's all right? The baby—"

"It's fine, Blue," Emily said, glancing up. He looked pensive as he stared at the monitor, his jaw tight. She couldn't believe how nervous he was. And yet it filled her with just the slightest breath of hope.

"Mary Louise will show you, Mr. Perez." Dr. Page moved the wand a little. "Right . . . there."

The nurse came around and pointed to a small crescent just resting against the bottom of the kidney-shaped pool. For several moments, no one said a thing. Just stared. Recognized. Comprehended. Realized. For Emily, though, it was as if the world shifted. The world she'd known before. Free, single, independent. It no longer existed. She was a mother now. That little crescent relied on her, needed her. Her heart kicked inside her chest. The future no longer belonged to just her.

"Is it okay?" Blue asked the doctor, pulling Emily from her thoughts. "It's so small."

"The fetus looks healthy," Dr. Page assured him. "Measures well. We should see a heartbeat the next time you're in." He gently removed the wand and covered her. "Mary Louise got a picture for you. Your first baby picture."

Again, Emily's heart kicked. This was real. More than real—it was happening and she needed to be prepared. Needed to get her life in order. Needed to tell her family.

The nurse handed her a black-and-white copy of what she'd seen on the screen. Her little crescent. "Here you go, honey."

"Thank you, Mary Louise," she said. "And you too, Dr. Page."

The man gave her a brilliant smile and rose from his chair. "Why don't you get dressed and meet me and Mr. Perez next door in my office."

She nodded and watched as they all filed out the door. The gravity of what she was facing was now pulsing through her. Oh, Lord, yes. She would do right by this child. No matter what it took.

After dressing, she headed for the door, but stopped a moment and took out the picture from her purse. The little crescent stared back at her. Her little crescent.

Hers and Blue's.

He hadn't told her he wanted to come. Hadn't even asked. A woman's time with her doctor was private, wasn't it? And yet . . . today, out there, under that great dome of sky and sun, where he'd always felt like he belonged—the only place it seemed like anymore—he felt angsty. Maybe because it wasn't where he belonged in that moment. It had taken him an hour calling around, telling every receptionist who answered that he'd forgotten the time of his girlfriend's appointment, didn't want her to go through their first doc visit alone. A little subterfuge had procured him a time, a place, and an "Aww, you're so sweet."

"First time, Mr. Perez?"

Blue glanced up, addressed the man sitting across from him behind the enormous desk. "First time for what, Doc?"

The man's brown eyes warmed. "Being a daddy?"

The question was simple, and so was the answer. And yet, Blue couldn't get anything to come out of his mouth. Emily was pregnant. That was right. She was going to have a baby, be a mother. He had helped create that baby. But the word . . . *Daddy* . . . it was just like a knife, cutting a hole inside his chest. Over and over. How could he be one when he'd never had one?

The door opened then and Emily walked in, looking soft and beautiful in a pale pink T-shirt and blue jeans. Her hair was down, curls touching her shoulders. Would their baby have those curls?

The question had come hard and fast and without his permission. His gut tightened and he turned back to face the doc. Emily came to sit beside him, and as the doctor talked to her, Blue listened with half an ear. Rest and good diet, blood test important, and she needed to take vitamins.

"I'm writing down a prescription for a good prenatal vitamin," Dr. Page said, scribbling away on the pad in front of him. "With your mother's history of preeclampsia, I want to make sure I'm seeing you every two weeks."

The fog in Blue's brain suddenly evaporated and he jerked to attention. "What was that you're saying? Pre-what?"

"It's called preeclampsia," the doctor told him.

"And it's nothing to worry about," Emily assured him.

Blue stared at Dr. Page. "Is it nothing? Doesn't sound like nothing."

"It can be serious if not treated," the man said. "But we'll be on top of it. Checking and monitoring Emily's blood pressure as well as—"

"Well, damn," Blue interrupted. "What can happen to her?"

Dr. Page looked incredibly calm as he sat behind his big desk. "It's rare, Mr. Perez, but she could develop a blood clot. Seizure or a stroke is also a risk. As well as liver and kidney function issues. But again, we will be monitoring her."

Fear was suddenly rushing through Blue like cold water from a hose. He sat forward in his chair. "Are there symptoms? How would she know if something's wrong if she's not here?"

"Blue," Emily said, cutting in. "I know all about this, what to look for. It's fine."

He wasn't listening. Not to anything but his fear. "Can it hurt the baby?" Blue pressed Dr. Page. Christ, his entire body was rigid.

"With the reduction of blood flow to the uterus, there can be some complications, but again—"

"Like what?" Blue interrupted. "What complications?"

"Blue," Emily said, her voice a forced calm. "My mother had preeclampsia and three healthy babies."

"Like what, Doc?" he said through gritted teeth, glaring at the man. He knew he was getting worked up, but he just couldn't stop himself.

Dr. Page released a breath. "Premature birth, stunted growth—"

Blue turned to Emily. "You need to stop working at the Bull's Eye."

"What?" she exclaimed, staring at him like he was crazy.

And he probably was. "Now."

"Okay, that's enough." She tossed him a warning look. "You're not going to start acting like a caveman with me, Blue."

"And you're not going to risk your health or the baby's—"

"I would never . . ." She stopped, took a breath. Then she turned away from him and stood. "Thank you, Dr. Page. That's all the questions I have for now." She reached for his hand, shook it. "I'll see you in two weeks."

"It was a pleasure to meet you both," Dr. Page said, an understanding smile on his lips.

"You'll see me too," Blue added forcefully before following her out of the office.

Emily didn't say a word until she was at her car; then she whirled to face him with eyes that were trying like hell to be calm and understanding.

"Okay, I know I got a bit nuts in there," he started with a heavy exhalation.

"A bit?" she asked.

"That pre-thing sounded scary as shit."

"That's because you know nothing about it. It's pretty common. And if I do get preeclampsia, it's not until later in the pregnancy." She sighed, her irritation stripping away. "You don't have to worry, okay? About any of it. It's all covered. This baby will be fine. I have my whole family looking out for me. My mom knows all about this. I don't need you—"

He felt himself go rigid. He looked away. Her words had cut him.

"Come on, Blue," she said, recognizing her blunder pretty quickly. "I didn't mean it like that. All I'm trying to say is please chill out a little. Everything is going to be fine."

Fine. *Fine.* He sniffed. Was it? Christ, nothing had been fine in the past several months. Why should he believe that this would be any different?

"Look, I need to go," she said, turning around

and opening her car door. "I have work." Before she slipped inside, she gave him a tight smile. "I'm glad you came. Really. But next time, maybe it's better if I go on my own."

He stared at her, flinched as the door slammed shut. And as the weight of her words sank in, and she drove off into the late-morning sunshine, his guts twisted with pain. It wasn't the kind of pain that stemmed from a fist to the jaw, but the emotional kind—the kind that came from fear and loss.

And a moment of hope, shattered.

Nine

Emily was in Willy Wonka's candy factory, running beside the chocolate river. Her stomach growled with hunger and she bent down, scooped up a handful of the cold chocolate, and brought it to her lips. Rich, creamy goodness met her tongue and she groaned.

More.

Spotting a mushroom to her right, she leapt at it, digging her fingers into the cream and custard. Nothing tasted so good.

"Do you like it here, Emily?" Mr. Wonka asked.

He had appeared at her side. Resplendent in purple and gold. His smile wicked, his eyes gleaming. She nodded enthusiastically. "I wish I could stay forever."

"I know, but you can't," he told her. "You have a job."

She blinked at him, and his face—the one she

knew from television—morphed into one she knew from home. From the Bull's Eye. Rae?

"If you don't go back to work," the older woman said, adjusting the sleeves of her purple suit, "you'll lose that business space. No flower shop. No future for your baby. Is that what you want?"

Confused, Emily glanced down. She couldn't see her feet. Her belly was huge. What in the world . . . ? Suddenly, a pain gripped her side, and she cried out and doubled over. She couldn't breathe. It hurt too much to breathe. Oh God, the baby was coming . . .

She woke on a gasp. Sitting up, she gripped the comforter and looked around her room. The moonlight was streaming in, and it was raining. Wait. How was it raining with the moon . . . ? She stared at the window. *No . . . not rain . . .*

Oh God.

Not again.

Wiping the sweat from her brow, she rolled out of bed. Still caught between her dream and this strange reality, she stumbled over to the window. Flipping the lock, she yanked it up and looked out. It was freezing. She stared down at the dark yard below. Where was he? Somewhere in the shadows with his hands full of rocks.

"Emily?" came a whisper.

Startled, she jerked her head up so fast she nearly rapped it on the top of the window. No shadows. He wasn't on the ground or behind the tree deep in the yard. He was right there, in front of her, not five feet away, in the tree.

"Are you insane?" she hissed, fully and completely awake now. "You're going to get your neck broken."

He stood up—actually stood up—and held on to one thick branch. He stared at her with the cocky confidence of a boy half his age. "I've been climbing trees since I was five. Besides, it's not that high."

"I wasn't just talking about the fall," she whispered harshly. "My mom, dad, and brothers are just down the hall."

His lips twitched. "We'll need to be quiet, then." Lips that were, she couldn't help but notice in the moonlight, bracketed by a couple of days' worth of beard. Something close to amusement lit his eyes. Unbelievable. "You going to invite me in?"

"Can I possibly say no?" she asked.

Those bluest of blue eyes turned serious. "You can always say no, Emily."

"Oh my God, this is madness," she grumbled, but did indeed unhook the screen and step back.

He moved to the edge of the thick branch that touched the side of the house, then easily swung himself inside, like a flippin' Tarzan in spurs, into her room. He barely made a sound as he landed.

"Something tells me you've done this before," she whispered dryly.

"A lot of trees on the Triple C property. And a lot of time on my hands when I was kid." He glanced around her room. "I feel a little like Peter Pan."

"Well, I was thinking Tarzan—"

"Oh, I like that better."

"This is getting ridiculous, Blue," she said as she reached for her robe, which was hanging off the side of the bed.

"I agree."

"Then maybe this is your last attempt at entering my house through the upstairs window?"

"I just want to talk, work out things." He exhaled. "It'd be much easier if we lived under the same roof."

She laughed softly. "True. But I don't think you'd be welcome here. 'Course, Steven might share his room with you. Seeing as how he owes you."

"There's plenty of room at the Triple C," he said, not exactly meeting her gaze. "You've been there. It's pretty nice."

The smile on her face started to fade. What was he doing? Saying? Something told her he wasn't kidding around with that suggestion. She stared at him for a moment, taking in his contemplative expression. "You're not serious."

His eyes flickered to the window, then back to her. He shrugged. "Maybe it's something to consider."

Her mouth fell open. "Something to . . . ? What the hell is going on with you? Freaking out at the doctor, coming to my house two nights in a row, waking me up."

"Ah, shit, I don't know," he said, raking both hands through his hair. "I get that I'm acting nuts, but I can't seem to stop myself."

"I think you need to."

His eyes flipped up, scored her. "You're having my baby, Emily."

"No," she countered, though her insides were revving up. "I'm having *my* baby."

She didn't want there to be a question about that. It was harsh, but true. But even so, the words had a deep effect on the two of them. Emily retreated, grew quiet and pensive, and Blue left his spot by the window and stalked cagily toward her. She stared . . . at all that six-foot-two, denim really working below the waist, his white T-shirt straining over hard, tanned muscle above. When he came to stand before her, her eyes moved over his tense, yet strikingly handsome face. His eyes were dark blue like the sky just before dusk, and his hair had grown a bit since that night they were together. There was some curl in it. She wondered what it would feel like between her fingers.

"Make no mistake, darlin'," he said with a possessive edge to his voice. "I will be a part of this child's life. It will know who its daddy is. You know what I'm saying?"

Staring up into such a brutally gorgeous face, those resolute eyes, Emily lost her breath for a moment. He was talking about his own life, and the father he never knew existed until the man's death. Yes, this child was hers, would come from her body. But truly, would she ever deny Blue Perez knowing his son or daughter? No. Of course not. For the child's sake as much as his.

Then again, she mused, lifting her chin, she wouldn't be bullied or told what she could and couldn't do either.

"I know what you're saying, Blue," she told him. "But you better know what I'm saying too. I'm not quitting my job, doctor's visits won't be stressful and an opportunity to freak out over your fears, and you can't keep coming here in the middle of the night."

His eyes flashed. "Some women might find that last part romantic."

Her belly clenched and she said in an almost breathy tone, "Others would find it exhausting. But you know, you could always go find one of those women."

For a couple of seconds, he just stared down at her. Then, his lips curved up at the corners. "I don't think so." He brought his hand up and let his fingers brush over her cheek. The pads were rough and calloused and the feel of it on her skin made a sound escape her throat. A cross between a moan and a whimper.

"I thought I'd imagined it," he said with a soft laugh.

"What?" she asked, her breath now caught in her lungs.

"How soft your skin was. How it felt against mine." He glanced at his hand, fingers. "Rough and worn . . ."

"I remember," she said without thinking.

His eyebrow quirked up and amusement lit his eyes. "Really?"

"I wasn't the drunk one, remember?"

"I wasn't all that drunk," he protested, then brushed his thumb over her cheekbone. "Or hell, maybe I was. For a few days, I actually thought it was a dream."

"A good dream?" she asked, foolishly. Because, really, how horrible would she feel if he said—

"The best."

Her breath caught. Her eyes held. Lord Almighty, how was it possible that they were standing in the middle of her bedroom, lights off, moon spotlighting them, just a few hours before dawn? It was crazy. And yet, she felt utterly, wistfully happy for the first time in weeks. Well . . . happy and sexually charged. Her heart jumped into her throat. If he kissed her, and things progressed . . . as they did . . . would they end up on her bed? Her childhood bed?

"I know the moving-in thing was stupid," he said, his gaze so charged, so intense. "I'm just trying to figure things out, Em, you know? I want to be around. You. I need to."

For a split second, her mind conjured an idea, a very depressing idea. *He wants to be around you because of the baby. Only because of the baby.* Then her ears pricked up as she heard movement down the hall. Someone was going to the bathroom.

Panic seized her and she broke from his grasp, the moment lost. "You have to go," she whispered.

He didn't move, didn't even look worried. "Why?"

"I hear someone." She pointed at her door. "In the bathroom."

"I'm not afraid of your brothers or your parents, Emily. They're going to need to get used to seeing me around." He shrugged. "Especially if we're not moving in together."

Oh, she was so not in the mood for his jokes. "Go," she whispered, grabbing his arm and pulling him toward the window. "Please."

"Fine," he said, ducking down and climbing out the window. "But think about what I said. I want to see you. Be there."

She heard the water running in the bathroom. "Go, Blue."

For a second, she thought he was going to protest, maybe even climb back inside. But then he slid onto the branch, and, like a monkey, easily climbed down. Her heart in her throat and her insides still warm with awareness and longing, Emily watched him cross the lawn, then get into his car and drive away.

The cold night felt good on her skin. It attacked the fire that raged inside her. The woman—that waitress—she just couldn't do it, could she? Keep away from Blue. Didn't she have enough? A nice home, two parents who loved and cared about her?

Natalie sneered as she watched the window she'd just seen Blue escape from. And she believed it was an escape. *Why would he be there when he loved* me? *Wasn't right.* Clearly, it was time to act. Make a new friend. It would be nice to have a friend. It had been a long time. Of course, they never stuck around very long. Maybe that was her fault. She had a lot of faults. Blue had seen her faults.

A light clicked on in the woman's bedroom. It was the only light on in the house. Maybe she was thinking. Feeling guilty about taking what didn't belong to her. Maybe she couldn't sleep. Natalie knew how that was. There was forgiveness and understanding—and help—within her heart.

She could help Emily Shiver sleep.

Pulling her coat closer around her, she continued to watch the light. It was an hour before she left the shelter of the old playhouse and made her way home.

Ten

Sweat poured off Blue's face, and he grabbed a bandanna from his pocket and mopped things up. He'd just come from feeding, and another try at the fence, and was now cleaning out one of the Triple C's guest room closets. He'd picked the nicest room—lots of light, an apple tree outside the window, nice pale yellow paint on the walls. And it was the closest room to the one he'd lived in his whole life. Well, up until recently anyway. It wasn't for Emily. He shook his head, recalling that crazy, desperate moment he'd had last night. Moving in with him . . . Christ, the woman barely knew him. No, the room was for his child. Granted, it might be a while before anyone stayed in it. But he needed the distraction—the action. To do something. Offer something.

Show Emily he was going to be there no matter what.

Maybe show himself that too.

"What are you doing?"

He poked his head out of the closet. His mother was standing just inside the door, looking around, curious. "Just cleaning up."

"Why?" she asked, confused. Then without waiting for an answer, her hands flew to her cheeks, and she gasped. "Oh, Blue, are you moving back into the house?"

The pure, undisguised joy on her face made his gut wrench. It was hard sometimes to face the truth that this woman wasn't just the person who'd lied to him his entire life. She'd also been his caretaker, his nurse, his friend, his supporter. Goddamn, he missed it. Missed her.

But anger and resentment was a stronger force than sentimentality.

"I may be moving back in," he said. "But I won't be alone if I do."

Again, Elena looked confused. "Are you talking about your brothers?"

He sniffed with derision. "Don't have brothers."

She gave him a look. Pursed her lips. No doubt she was getting tired of hearing his passive-aggressive bullshit. Didn't stop her from trying to reason with him though. "Blue, 'course you do. And they want to build this bridge you keep tearing down."

He turned away. He wasn't up for talking about the past or the present. He was doing something for the future. That's all he wanted to think about.

"If it's not for a Cavanaugh," she pressed him, "who's it for?"

Six months ago, Blue would've told her everything. No doubt with a huge smile on his face. She would've loved it. She was going to be a grandma. Every mama's dream. But it was a gift. That knowledge. And right now, today, it was a gift he wasn't ready to give.

"I'm going to keep working on this," he said.

She didn't say anything for a moment. Then, "I can help you. I'd be happy to."

"No." He looked back at her once again. Was resolute. "Thank you. I've got it."

He felt the weight of her disappointment. It saturated the air between them. There was a part of him that despised himself for treating Elena like this. No matter what had happened, what she'd done, she was still his mother, and she deserved his respect. But the rest of him, the raw nerve he was now, just couldn't allow it. When you are vulnerable with someone, *to* someone, and they betray you, that bond, that respect, is severed. Who knew how it could be fused again. Or if . . .

For a moment, as Elena stood there in the doorway, Blue thought she was going to keep pressing him, ask him to reconsider. But she didn't. Without another word, she turned and left the room. And his gut wrenched once again.

Emily didn't make it a habit of showing up at people's homes or work, but this morning she'd woken up with an urgency that couldn't be ignored. She imagined she'd be feeling a lot of that over the next nine months.

"I want to talk to the owner."

Aubrey was seated behind her metal desk in her small office at River Black Properties. Her makeup was expertly applied, but when she smiled up at Emily, there was a bit of pink lipstick on her teeth. "Oh, honey, is that why you're here? I thought you did the smart thing and asked your parents for the money."

No, she hadn't asked them. Hell, she hadn't even told them about her little crescent yet. She wanted things in place before she did. "I think if I could just explain things, we could work something out."

"Emily," Aubrey began with that look that begged someone to just stop right there, since whatever they were about to say was futile.

But Emily was immune to nonverbal negativity. Especially when it stood in the way of her future. "The thing is, people who grew up here in River Black . . . You know, there's an understanding, a respect for hard work and . . . special circumstances."

"What special circumstances?"

She shook her head. Aubrey wasn't getting that news yet. Not before her family did. "All I'm saying is, they want to help each other out."

"Of course, but—"

"And I have a sizable down payment," Emily added quickly.

"There's an offer on the table, hon." Aubrey looked sheepish, like it was really the last thing she wanted to tell her eager client. "All cash."

Emily stopped, stared. "No."

"I'm sorry, hon."

This couldn't be happening. Really. Her head started to spin. The property she'd been coveting and working toward owning for two years suddenly had an offer on it. Granted, people came around to look at the space from time to time, but no one committed. It was so small . . . "Is it a client of yours?"

"No," Aubrey told her gently. "It's an out-of-towner actually. Well, sort of. He used to live here when he was a boy. James Cavanaugh."

Her guts flipped over. Cavanaugh? "The horse-whisperer guy?"

Aubrey nodded.

And Blue's half brother. "Why in the world would he want business property in town? He's a celebrity who travels. This doesn't make sense."

Aubrey shook her head. "No idea. Except maybe he's moving back? Got that fiancée now, horses on the Triple C property. All the Cavanaugh brothers seem to be showing their faces 'round here lately. And no one's decided on who's going to take over that ranch of theirs."

A sullen quiet came over Emily, and her shoulders fell. It was the last thing she'd expected in coming here. She gave Aubrey a forced smile. "Okay then."

"I am real sorry, Emily. But when you're ready, we'll find you another place. Just as good. Better!"

"Sure" was all she could say. As she left the office, her stomach felt like a lead balloon. When she was ready? She was ready now. Like, big-time ready. And she didn't want another property. Hell, there weren't many to be had around River Black. And the few she'd seen were too big, too expensive, and didn't have the office and living space she wanted.

She walked down the sunlit street toward the property she felt was meant for her. Her flower shop. Her future. This baby was coming—and its mother just had to be settled into a solid career and a business of her own before it did.

As she passed the diner, she spotted the eldest Cavanaugh brother, Deacon. Tall and broad like his half brother, the man was seated at the counter having breakfast. Emily knew Deacon had purchased land just outside town, had built a massive ranch property, and had married the Triple C's foreman, Mackenzie Byrd. Were those boys back home to stay? Was Aubrey right? And if so, what did that mean for Blue? His life, his work—where he belonged?

You need to worry about yourself and this baby right now. Blue can take care of himself.

She inhaled sharply. Maybe there was something she could do . . . maybe the person she needed to talk to wasn't the current owner of the property—but the potential new one.

James Cavanaugh.

Eleven

Mucking stalls was pretty much the worst job on the ranch. But hell, he'd lost a bet with Frank, so there it was. Kicking some shit off his boot, Blue headed into the next stall. He had six more to go before he could stop for lunch, and boy was he hungry. Breakfast had pretty much been a bust, and that cooler over by the door was calling his name.

That is, until someone else did.

"Hey there," came an old, grizzled-sounding voice Blue knew as well as he knew his own. "Found this little lady wandering around. You ever seen her before?"

"Sam," the woman chided. "For cripes' sake, you know me. And I know you. Burger, rare with sharp cheddar, bacon, and plenty of hot sauce."

Blue turned, his gut tightening at the sound of Emily Shiver's voice. It had this sweet, smartass quality to it. *Out of bed anyway*, he thought as he stood up and looked over the stall door. Christ Almighty, he shouldn't be thinking stuff like that. And yet, as she walked toward him, the Triple C's barn manager beside her, all Blue could do was think about it. Her hair was in a sort of side braid with a few small white flowers tucked in. She was wearing a pale pink sundress that was tight up top and at the waist. And if that wasn't bad enough, the pretty thing was cut to midthigh, and Emily Shiver had the longest, sexiest legs he'd ever seen.

Wrapped around me and holding on tight, even better.

His nostrils flared. Shouldn't be thinking things like that. Emily Shiver was not his woman. She was the mother of his child—and he needed to keep that straight. Especially as the months rolled on, and they became closer . . . friends.

"Hey, Blue," she said as she approached, her expression a little wary. Or was it shy? He didn't know. Hell, he didn't know all that much about her, and yet he wanted to. Really wanted to.

"Howdy." He touched the brim of his hat. He might be an irritated jerk most of the time lately, but his mama had raised him to be a gentleman. And that didn't leave a body once it was ingrained. He gave Sam a wry look. "The lady is here to see me. So feel free to get back to whatever you were doin'."

"Why'd she be here for you?" Sam challenged with a snort. "That's like a rainbow seeking out a bucket of horseshit."

"A little too on the nose there, cowboy," Blue said dryly, knocking his chin in the direction of his pitchfork.

"Actually," Emily said with a little shrug, "I came to see James."

"Ha!" Sam said with a chuckle, pointing at Blue with glee. "What'd I tell ya?"

Blue's upper lip curled, heat snaking through him. A wicked heat. One he hadn't felt in a long time. Strange . . . What was that? A jealous heat? Cripes, no. Couldn't be that. With grit, he pushed the feeling down below the surface of his skin, but that kind of heat refused to be repressed.

"Haven't seen him around," he told her with just a hint of irritation. "Why you lookin'?"

With the toe of her boot she kicked a single horse plop he'd yet to pick up. "Just need to discuss something with him; that's all."

Discuss something? With James? Did they even know each other? And how well? Blue's gut twisted. He didn't like this at all. He put the pitchfork against the wall and came out of the stall, nearly colliding with that scuffed up wheelbarrow full of manure, the one that had no doubt been used for the same job for the past fifty years.

"Hey, Sam," he said. "My mom made fried chicken for lunch. I know she has extra if you're interested."

The old man's eyes narrowed. He looked from Blue to Emily, scrunching up his lips. Hell, he could contemplate all he wanted to, but no one could resist Elena's fried chicken. Not even for some potentially juicy barn drama. In seconds, the man was shrugging, giving up, wishing Emily well, and heading out of the barn.

"So is James staying here?" she asked. "Or is he in town? At the hotel?"

Blue took off his gloves and tossed them on a nearby bench. "What do you want with him?" he asked a little too brusquely. "You know he's engaged, don't ya?"

Her chin lifted and her eyes locked with his. "Of course I know that." Those eyes narrowed and her lips thinned. "What are you implying?"

He blew out a breath. What was he implying? More like imagining. Not wanting to imagine. "Look, I'm sorry," he said at a near growl. "Didn't mean anything. He's coming by later. I can tell him you want to talk to him."

She held on to her ire for a couple more moments, then seemed to shake it off. "Okay. Thanks."

He nodded.

"See you."

"Yeah, see you." He waited for her to turn around and leave. After all, she hadn't come by for him . . . But she didn't move. Just stood there surrounded by all the ancient tack and hay bales. "Are you all right?" he asked her with a gentleness he hadn't believed still existed inside him. "You feeling okay?"

"I'm fine."

She didn't sound all that convincing, and it made his instincts flare. Dammit. What'd she want with James? How were they connected? Was his half brother going to make her feel better? Put that pretty smile of hers back on her face? Christ . . . he didn't like that. Really didn't like that. Not that he was going to show it. Vulnerability was an unforgiving asshole. You opened yourself up to it and ran the risk of being destroyed.

And yet, the pull of something beyond logic and reason and lessons learned was in play . . . "I want you to know," he began. "I'm here for you and this baby."

Her eyes widened, but she didn't say anything.

"Things started how they did," he continued, "and that can't be changed. Hell, wouldn't want it changed. But like I said last night, I want to be around."

"I know, Blue."

What was that, he wondered, in her eyes? Sadness? Worry? He was trying like hell to alleviate some of that. "Not just a few hours here and there either." His gaze dropped, momentarily settling on her flat stomach. "I want to see it grow. I want to feel it move."

She released a breath. Weighty. And a sudden softness touched her expression. "I would like that, Blue."

A bit of her hair had escaped her braid and was sort of covering one eye. She looked so damn beautiful. Without thinking, he reached up and tucked the strand behind her ear, then let his fingers drift down her cheekbone. She had the softest skin.

Her breath caught and she leaned into his touch.

His eyes searched hers. "What? What's wrong?"

"How do we do this? You? Me? The baby?"

His nostrils flared and his chest expanded. "We'll figure it out."

She didn't say anything.

"Yeah?" he prodded. He needed to know she believed him.

She nodded, her cheeks going pink again. He couldn't help himself. He ran his thumb over that cheek once again. Oh yeah. Softest goddamned skin on the planet. Christ, he wanted to kiss her. *Just a taste. The bottom lip . . . that full one . . . just one taste; then you let her go.* Without thinking too hard on it, he leaned in. Right away, she closed her eyes. Parted her lips. Pink and full, and so ready. Blue stared at her mouth. Seconds ticked by. What was wrong with him? The breeze off the meadow came rushing into the barn. The Triple C's barn. Shit, what was happening to him? His entire body humming with a need he hadn't felt since that night . . . that night they'd created the life inside Emily.

Overtaken with far too many emotions he refused to deal with—not now anyway—Blue eased back, releasing her.

Instantly, Emily opened her eyes. And when she realized what had happened—and what hadn't—she turned bright red.

Blue's chest tightened. He was such an ass. He wanted to kiss her. Like a drowning man wanted air. And she'd wanted him too. So what was he doing pulling back?

She moved away from him. "I should go." Her voice was slightly breathless.

No. Fuck no, she shouldn't go. She should stay here until he figured out what screw was loose in his brain, what piece of his wrecked heart was missing.

"Let you get back to mucking stalls." She forced a smile. Didn't get anywhere near her eyes. She was upset, confused, embarrassed.

And he was the ass who had made her feel like that.

"I appreciate that," he said dryly, then gave her a sort of half smile that was supposed to carry an apology along with it. "Nothing I'd rather be doing."

She returned the tight smile. "I'm sure. How'd you get stuck with that job anyway?"

"Lost a bet."

She laughed softly, shook her head. "You boys and your bets."

"Yeah," he said. Goddammit, he was always so afraid of getting close whenever he was around this woman. He wanted her. Just wanted to taste her, feel her lips on his. Again. Sober this time. *Then grab her, idiot. Fuck the fear and take her in your arms and kiss her like you want to—like she wants you to.*

But he didn't. Pussy. He stayed where he was and cracked a joke. Best medicine there was for keeping distance between people. Lose the emotion and go hard on the humor. "That's why you're really taking off, isn't it?" he said. "Between the sweat and the manure, you can barely stand to be around me, right?"

"Clearly I can stand it just fine," she said dryly. *Oh yeah. He was an ass. A stupid, scared ass.*

"Besides," she continued, "I come from ranching people. Sweat and manure is a special brand of cologne 'round these parts." Her eyes filled with a sad warmth. "You wear it well, Blue."

He stared at her then. The humor he'd been clinging to falling away. This woman. Not only did she cast fear into his cold heart, but she made him question things. Like what he was doing. Why he was doing it. If maybe something good and real could actually be possible in his life. And then the weight of all that had gone down over the past month snaked through him again, biting at every hopeful thought.

"Better get to these stalls," he said, turning away. "But I'll make sure to tell James you stopped by. If I see him."

"Okay," she said.

Blue heard her walking away, then stop.

"I'm telling my parents tonight," she called out to him.

His head came up and his eyes connected with hers. "That won't be easy."

"Maybe not. But I suppose it's got to go better than how you found out." She gave him a half smile and shrug.

He laughed softly. "Hopefully it won't end in anyone's arrest."

"Right," she agreed. "Okay. Well. See you later?"

"You will," he said.

She nodded, then turned to go.

Blue watched her walk away, his gaze running down from her pretty neck to that pink dress, long legs, and—melt his frozen heart—those cowboy boots. Whereas ten minutes ago, he'd been starving and ready for lunch, now all he wanted was Emily Shiver. Legs wrapped around his waist, arms around his neck, and that smile inching closer until their lips locked.

He'd thought he'd felt lost before, but this was something else entirely. He grabbed his pitchfork and got back to work. For a man who'd sworn to keep himself closed off and protected, there was no one more dangerous to want than the woman who was carrying his baby.

"Everyone here, Mr. Cavanaugh?" Franklin inquired, taking his seat and placing three files on the conference table.

Deacon nodded to the private investigator and sat back in his leather chair. The massive conference room on the twenty-sixth floor of Cavanaugh Enterprises was sparsely populated. Just Eric Franklin, James, and Cole. Deacon had decided to meet with the PI in Dallas, as he was already in town for work. Same with Cole, who was ordering equipment for the new training gym he was opening in River Black. James had been flown in on the *Blue Bull* not thirty minutes ago, without Mac, who'd decided at the last minute that there was too much happening at the ranch for her to get away.

Franklin was seated to Deacon's right. He eyed all three men before diving in.

"Five and a half years ago, Natalie Palmer attended cooking school at the Debenroux School in New Orleans."

"Never heard of it," James said, reaching for the glass carafe in front of him and pouring himself some water.

"I'm not surprised," Franklin said. "The cooking school she attended wasn't a prestigious institution. And I only say that because when one of its students went missing, it was hardly talked about or investigated."

"Someone went missing?" Cole said tightly.

"A young woman," the PI told him. "Her name was Erica Keller."

"Is she still missing?" James asked, a note of concern in his voice.

Franklin nodded. "Yes, sir."

Deacon felt his insides tighten. "Did she know Natalie Palmer? Were they friends?"

"No, sir," Franklin answered.

"Well, shit," Cole ground out, taking off his Stetson and dropping it on the black marble table. "Then what does all this even matter?"

"Cole," James said, shooting his tatted-up brother a look. "Let the man finish."

Lips twisting, Cole turned to Franklin. "Sorry."

The man nodded. "Natalie knew Erica's roommate at the time. A Gary Schnull."

"A man?" Deacon asked. "Were you able to locate him?"

Franklin nodded. "Yes, sir. We spoke in detail for several hours."

"And?" Cole pressed. He was leaning on the table, hungry for answers. Hell, they all were.

"During their time at school," Franklin continued, "Miss Palmer took an interest in him. At first it was just your usual flirtation. But then it grew into love letters and phone calls. She showed up at his apartment several times. Wasn't pleased with the female roommate and was even less pleased when Mr. Schnull told her that he wasn't interested. That he wanted to date Miss Keller. Though Miss Palmer didn't act angry or spiteful, Mr. Schnull believes she may have sabotaged a few of Miss Keller's dishes. He couldn't prove it, of course."

"Did they question Schnull and Natalie when Miss Keller went missing?" James asked, the water in front of him completely forgotten.

"Yes." Franklin took out some paperwork from a gray folder. "Natalie was never looked at closely, but Schnull was a suspect for quite a while. In fact, he was questioned just last year when Miss Keller's family put pressure on the local district attorney. But without a body . . ." He didn't finish. He didn't need to.

"Don't suppose he kept any of those letters?" James said with a snort.

"He did."

They all turned to stare at Franklin.

"One. The same one he showed the police back when Miss Keller went missing. They believed it was irrelevant, as Miss Palmer was only interested in Mr. Schnull and had little contact with Miss

Keller. He kept the letter, found it several months ago when he was moving into a new house with his wife." He slid a black file toward Deacon. "I made a copy, sir."

Jaw tight, Deacon picked up the folder and slid the letter out. His eyes moved over the copy. And with every sentence, every word, his chest filled with both pain and hope. With this new information, he could go to the sheriff and demand they open an investigation into Natalie Palmer's involvement in Cass's death.

"Is it something we can use, Deac?" James asked.

"Yeah," Cole added, his almost vulnerable expression a true contrast to his heavily tattooed neck and arms. "Out with it."

Deacon looked at each one in turn, then said, "We might just catch Cass's killer after all."

Twelve

Ben and Susie Shiver were arguably the best parents in the world. They loved their children like each was a gift to treasure. They supported them, pushed them, made them laugh, and when it was time to cry, held them tight and reminded them that tomorrow was a fresh day full of possibilities. But . . . they were also fiercely protective and opinionated. Hell, Emily and her brothers hadn't gotten those two attributes from nowhere.

"I know you love your flowers, but baking could be your true calling," her mother cooed as she sliced into the chocolate cake Emily had frosted near an hour ago. After all, dropping a bomb required large quantities of sugar and carbohydrates. "This is gorgeous, Em."

"It is," Steven agreed. He glanced her way, one eyebrow raised. *What's the occasion?* he seemed to be asking. In the past couple of days, he hadn't pushed her to tell their parents about the baby. In fact, since the incident at the jail, he'd been kind of quiet. It was weird. Like either he felt guilty, or a storm was brewing inside of him. Emily wasn't giving him the chance to explode with the news he'd been holding on to. Tonight was the night.

"Just thought we all deserved a little something sweet," Emily said, her stomach clenching with each word.

Her father grabbed her mother's hand. "I got my something sweet. Right here."

"Oh, Ben," her mother said, blushing.

"No PDA at the table, okay?" Jeremy said wryly.

"Hey now," their father said with false sternness as he leaned in and kissed his wife on the cheek. "That PDA brought you into this world, young man."

Jeremy grimaced. "One thing I'm not going to miss."

"Miss?" their mother repeated, returning to the cake and her slicing duties.

"Just saying I won't miss you and Dad pawing on each other when I move out."

Emily's brother said the words all casual-like, but she saw his eyes dart around the table. A table that was now uncomfortably silent. Everyone was staring at the youngest Shiver. Emily couldn't believe her brother. Bringing up something so pivotal. Right now. Where the hell was his soften-the-blow cake?

"You leaving the nest already, son?" their father said, his tone curious as he passed the boy a slice of cake.

Jeremy took it with a quick thanks. "Just moving to town. I think it's time. Don't you?" He glanced at Steven questioningly. But the sheriff's deputy had his gaze pinned to his coffee cup.

Emily sat there, feeling unsure. Her little brother was moving out of the house. Her *little* brother. And he was saying it was time. It was strange, him saying that—especially tonight.

So what now? she thought, looking at each Shiver in turn. Did she just come out with it? Drop the second bomb of the night? Or did she wait? Lord, did they have enough cake?

As always, their mother was thinking practically. "Who's going to feed you, Jeremy?" she asked him. Feeding her boys, and her girl, was of top importance, and a huge part of her mama's DNA.

Jeremy smiled and said a very simple, "I will."

Susie blinked at him, as though she couldn't imagine this. And frankly, Emily wasn't sure she could imagine it either. Jeremy didn't even know how to work the burners on the stove—didn't know where the washing machine was "hidden."

"What he means is, he'll go to the diner," Steven said dryly. "And if that ain't open, over to the Bull's Eye."

Jeremy elbowed him in the ribs.

"What?" Steven asked. "Bugging our sister while having some wings and a beer? I think I'll move out too."

Both men chuckled, but Susie looked crushed. Ben patted his wife's hand. "Babies need to leave the nest, darlin'. Hell, soon as they decided not to go into the ranching business, they had one foot out already."

Jeremy frowned. "Oh, come on, Dad."

"No offense or judgment," Ben said. "Just truth."

"What do you think, Em?" Steven asked, his eyes on her now. "About all this? About babies? And nests?" He raised his brow again. Was this the coming storm? Had Jeremy's news pushed him over the edge?

Emily gave him a look of promised death.

He just shrugged. "Curious is all."

"Emily isn't going anywhere," her mother said with a confident smile. "Are you, honey? Baby girls don't move out of their mamas' houses until they're married. Or that's the way it was in my day."

Oh God. This was awful. She couldn't take it anymore. The knowing looks from her brother, the never-ending stress of keeping a secret from her parents. She just needed to—"Speaking of babies," she began slowly.

"What about them, sweetheart?" Susie asked, handing Emily a plate of cake. "Someone we know having one?"

Her stomach was churning. She stared at the cake, her appetite completely gone. "Yes, actually."

"Oh. Who?"

God, God, God. Just do it. Rip the damn Band-Aid off. Her mouth was extraordinarily dry. Maybe she should have some water first. She reached for her glass just as the doorbell rang.

Perfect. Another interruption.

"I'll get it," Steven said, then gave her an encouraging yet annoying nod. "You keep talking, Em. Keep on with what you were saying."

She gulped down the water, eyes narrowed at his retreating frame.

"How exciting," Susie was saying, pouring Ben a cup of coffee. "A new baby in River Black. Do we know if it's a girl or a boy?"

"No," Emily said, putting her glass down and clearing her throat. "We . . . I mean I . . ." *Oh God.* "I don't know. Yet."

Band-Aid off.

Cue reaction.

Churning stomach and dry mouth, she held her breath as neither one of her parents picked up on what she'd said. Well, not right away anyway. They were far too busy with creamer and sugar cubes. They still used sugar cubes! But, Lord, Jeremy had understood. He was sitting there, fork poised at his open mouth.

Then he dropped the thing on his plate. "*You don't know?*" he said. "Wait . . . Em? You're not saying that you're the one . . . ?" He leaned in. "Are you *pregnant*?"

Oh . . . okay, this was it. Emily felt like a vacuum was sucking the air out of the room. She didn't want to, but she did. Her eyes shifted. Susie and Ben Shiver were staring at her now, eyes wide and confused.

As pale as the cream she held in her hand, her mother uttered her name like it was a question.

"Emily?" A strange combination of horror and happiness glittered in her pale brown eyes. "That's not what you meant, is it?"

"Sorry I'm late."

The male voice, the deep, almost chiseled male voice Emily recognized—would always recognize—boomed into the room. Dressed in blue jeans and a dark gray chambray shirt, Blue Cavanaugh entered, followed by a tight-faced Steven. He carried a small collection of wild flowers, and when he came around the table, he handed them to Emily, then leaned down and gave her cheek a quick kiss. Confused, touched, horrified, Emily turned back to her parents. They still looked confused.

"Blue Perez Cavanaugh," he said to them, sticking out his hand. "I think we've met before, Mr. Shiver. Cattle sale or over at the feed store."

"I know who you are," her father said tightly. "Work at the Triple C, right? You're Everett's . . ." He stumbled. "You worked for Everett."

Seemingly unaffected by the awkwardness of her father's blunder, Blue turned to her mother. "Mrs. Shiver, it's a pleasure."

She shook his hand, her expression stunned.

"Well, this is going to be fun," Steven muttered, sitting back down.

"Did you know Emily's pregnant?" Jeremy asked him, his tone accusatory.

Blue heard and looked relieved. "So Emily told you our good news—is that right?" he asked her parents.

Susie's eyes widened even further. "Oh my goodness. Well, she said there was a baby . . ." Her face grew paler. Skim milk with those large, bewildered brown eyes that were now settling on Emily.

"Mom," she began.

"I know it's a bit of a shock," Blue said, taking the empty seat beside Emily. "But we're happy about it. Right, Emily?" He took her hand.

"What are you doing?" Emily hissed at him.

"Ben . . . ?" her mother was saying in that breathless voice she reserved for mice in her kitchen.

"Emily?" her father said. "You're pregnant?" He glanced at Blue.

"Yes," she said, wanting to melt into the floor.

"How long have you two been . . ." Her mother looked from Blue to Emily, then back again. "Seeing each other?"

"Not long," Blue confirmed. He sounded completely at ease. Confident. Lucky bastard. She couldn't believe he'd come. Why had he come? Her brain was spinning. He should've asked her. Discussed it with her. She didn't like being blindsided.

"How did this happen?" Ben Shiver said in a cool tone.

"Oh, Ben," her mother said, shaking her head.

The man reddened. "What I mean is . . . what are your intentions, son?"

No, no, no. "Dad—"

"To be there for your daughter," Blue cut in, then gave her hand a squeeze.

Oh my God. Emily glanced over at her brothers. They were listening, enraptured.

"And the child?" her father pressed.

Before Blue could answer, Emily jumped in. "You don't need to answer that."

"Of course he does, honey," her mother said, almost as though she was insulted.

"I don't understand any of this, Em," her father continued. "Why didn't we know about this? Why wouldn't you tell us?"

"That's right," Susie added. "About him or the baby?"

"Something tells me there's no relationship here at all, Sue," her father continued.

Her stomach clenched. "I . . ." They wouldn't stop. Her parents. The questions. All they needed was an interrogation light. Emily felt as if her mind had dissolved inside her skull. The room was feeling small, and the walls were breathing. She wasn't going to faint, was she? "I . . . we . . . Blue and I . . . you see . . ." Oh God. What the hell did she say? It was one night of drunken sex. Well, he was drunk, she was . . . No, that wouldn't work. "The truth is—"

"We're planning on getting married," Blue said.

Emily gasped as all eyes once again shifted to Blue Perez Cavanaugh.

Jesus.

He didn't. He hadn't. Emily stared at him, her eyes wide and questioning. How could he say that . . . blurt something like that out at her family's dinner table? Something that was never going to come to pass.

She felt a wave of nausea—a wave that had nothing to do with her pregnancy—overtake her. She wanted to get out, away, think . . . And then the room exploded into a cacophony of opinions and agreements.

"I don't like it," her father said. "The secrets. But marriage is the sensible option. Better than living together."

"We hardly know this young man, Ben," her mother said. "Emily should just stay here, and they can keep seeing each other. I'll help with the baby."

Keep seeing each other? Right. Sure. She wanted to bust out laughing, but she was worried it might come out sounding kind of insane.

"So I guess my news was small potatoes compared to what you got up your sleeve, big sister," Jeremy said, grinning. "Or in your belly, as the case may be."

"Shut up," Steven warned him. "You sound like an ass."

"And you don't sound very surprised," he retorted.

"You're not at all concerned about how this town will react, given she's not married?" Ben asked his wife.

"Oh, what do I care? This is 2015, for goodness' sake. And maybe in time, they will get married."

"Mr. Perez," Ben started. "What are your plans? For work, I mean. I know you're a cowboy—"

"I'll be moving up to foreman when Mac Byrd leaves, Mr. Shiver," Blue returned in a deadly serious tone, though his gaze did dart to Emily and back a few times. "As you may know, the Triple C is one-quarter mine."

"One-quarter—" Ben started. "Hmmm . . ."

"But I intend to own the entire property," he finished, his voice resolute.

"Is that so?" Ben snorted, impressed in spite of his objections to their news. "Now . . . my daughter and grandchild living at a competing ranch. I don't know. 'Course we sell different stock . . ."

As they continued to discuss her, her future, her reputation, and her baby, Emily set her flowers on the table, pushed back her chair, and stood. Without a word, she left the room. This was madness. Never in her life had she felt so out of control, so exposed, or so furious at anyone.

Or, Lord, so painfully alone.

Ben Shiver was talking to him about Angus and an idea he was having to bring on some dairy cows in the coming year. But Blue was only watching Emily. Her back, more like, as she left the room. He knew she was pissed at him, and he didn't blame her. Married? Christ. Married? Where the hell had that come from? He hadn't intended it. First the moving in, now the married . . . his subconscious was clearly trying to prove something. That he was no heel, maybe. That he didn't get a woman pregnant and walk away. That he didn't refuse his last name to both the child he'd helped create, and its mother.

That he wasn't Everett Cavanaugh?

He cursed softly and pushed his chair back.

"Where're you going?" Jeremy asked him.

"After her," he answered simply.

"Don't think she wants you to, and I believe maybe I need to punch your lights out."

Steven shook his head. "No, you don't."

"You did know about this, didn't you?" Jeremy accused.

The deputy just shrugged.

As Ben and Susie Shiver turned on Steven and started questioning him about what he knew and when he'd known it, Blue left the room. He went back the way he'd come in. He'd heard the front door close, so he knew she was outside. It was a chilly night, autumn coming on fast now. When he spotted her walking down the driveway at a brisk pace without a coat on, he felt his gut constrict. His fault. He jogged toward her, easing up only when he caught up to her.

"Hey, there," he said, falling into pace beside her. "Slow down?"

"You." She whirled on him and stuck her finger in his face. "You don't get to tell me what to do. You don't get to tell me anything!"

"All right. Fair enough." He took off his coat and put it around her. She, in turn, ripped it right off and shoved it at him. "I already have one of these, remember?"

Did he remember? Shit, he remembered everything. "You're pissed. I see that."

She sneered at him. "You don't see anything.
You're blind."

"Maybe," he acquiesced.

"And heavy-handed."

"Oh, probably."

She glared at him. "What the hell were you
thinking? Coming here, uninvited, and telling my
parents we're getting married? Have you lost your
fucking mind?"

He stilled, frowned. Lost his mind? Yes, he had.
A few months ago.

"No, really, Blue," she continued when he didn't
answer. "I want to know your thought process on
this."

He exhaled, scrubbed a hand over his jaw and
just let it rip. "You said you were telling your parents tonight, and I . . . shit, I wanted to come and
support you."

"Then why didn't you?" she demanded. "Why
didn't you just have my back instead of blindsid-
ing me?" She stared at him, all strawberry blond
curls and fierce eyes, pink cheeked and wind-
swept, and so goddamned beautiful it nearly took
his breath away.

Oh Christ, what the hell was happening to him?

"Your parents were doing all the talking," he
explained. "Demanding answers. I said what I
thought would defuse the situation."

She looked away for a moment. "Jesus in
heaven."

"It wasn't planned, Emily—"

"'Course not."

"But I stand by it."

She turned back and gave him an indignant snort. "Oh, how valiant of you, Blue."

Her sarcasm was like a blade running up his spine. "Come on, Em. I was just trying to help."

Her finger came up again. "Don't you call me that. You aren't my family, my boyfriend, or my husband. Hell, I don't know what you are." She shook her head. "You need to go."

His jaw tightened. "Fine. And what are you going to be doing?"

"After I take a second to calm down I'll have to go back inside. Tell them the truth."

That was going to go over well. "I should go back in there with you. This is all my fault—"

"No. I can handle it. All of it. In fact, I'm beginning to think that's how this needs to go down."

The icy wind that had blown around him only seconds ago was inside of him now. "What does that mean?"

She looked away, at the house, for a moment, then shook her head. "Everyone is trying to decide what's best for me. Except me." She turned back and raised a brow at him. "That changes. Now. I'm going back in," she stated flatly. "And you're going home."

Goddammit, he'd really fucked up. This wasn't what he'd come here for, to drive a wedge between them. If anything, he wanted to know her better, get closer to her. "Emily, wait, please—"

But she was already gone, walking away, back up to the house.

He blew out a breath. "Come on. We need to talk about this," he called after her.

"Go home, Blue," she called back.

Home. The word felt foreign to his ears. Where was that exactly? Home? Used to be the Triple C. But he wasn't exactly sure now. He pulled on his jacket, fisted his keys, and started for his truck. A home was where you felt like you belonged. There was family there. Love. And trust.

He wasn't sure he had any of that anymore, but, Christ Almighty, there was something inside him tonight that'd hoped he might just find it here.

Thirteen

"Be right back with that salad, Miss O'Shay," Emily told the River Black middle school teacher, who was wearing her usual steely gray pantsuit and slicked-back bun. She looked like a drill sergeant.

"Extra ranch, okay, honey?" the woman called, reminding.

As if Emily needed a reminder. Miss O'Shay was a regular. And so was her order of extra ranch. But she just smiled and tossed a friendly "You got it" over her shoulder as she headed for the kitchen.

It was barely eleven a.m., but in River Black, Texas, that was lunchtime. Folks were up by four and on their horses come five.

In the kitchen, she ripped off her ticket and handed it to Dutch.

"This for Mandy O'Shay?" the cute twenty-five-year-old tattooed cook asked her.

"What gave it away?" she asked with a grin. "The extra ranch?"

He snorted. "Thinly sliced eggs. I swear she measures."

Emily laughed and filled a glass with iced tea.

"You just get here?" Rae asked, strolling into the kitchen and ripping off a ticket. "Here you go, Dutch. Extra crispy on those fries." She turned and inspected Emily. "You all right, baby girl?"

"Perfect," she lied easily. "Why?"

"You look tired."

Now why would that be? Not much sleep perhaps? "Rae, I swear, you're this close to giving me a complex."

The woman laughed. "Not to worry, hon. You're gorgeous. Nothing can take that away from ya. Just worried you're not sleeping." Her lips formed a wicked grin. "Unless it's that man you're not telling me about."

"No man," she lied again. *Except maybe the one who'd blurted out at my dinner table last night that we were getting married.* Or the older man—her father—who'd tried to get her to talk to him. Or the two younger men—her annoying little brothers—who had insisted on taking her to work today.

"If I didn't expect a rush in about an hour, I'd tell you to go home and take a nap." The woman shrugged. "But it's going to be a busy day. I can feel it."

Rae could always feel it. It was weird. "I'm really okay," Emily insisted. "And I need the money." To her right, a salad with extra ranch and thinly sliced eggs was placed on the pass. "Thanks, Dutch."

"Tell her I measured them myself," he called to her back as she headed out the double doors and out onto the floor.

Laughing to herself, she made her way to Miss O'Shay's table. Once there, she gently placed the salad in front of the woman and stepped back. "Dutch sends this along with his compliments."

Miss O'Shay's sharp eyes lifted to meet Emily's. "The eggs?" she inquired slowly.

"He measured them."

Those eyes narrowed. "We'll see about that."

Same old, same old. *Gotta love the River Black folks.* "Okeydoke." Emily grinned. "You enjoy, Miss O." She turned around to the two-top behind her and greeted the waiting customer. "Afternoon. What can I . . . ?"

"Emily Shiver?" came the man's husky baritone.

Whoa. Could've knocked her over with a feather. She'd seen him, both back in the day and on the covers of magazines now. But she didn't know him. James Cavanaugh was one striking guy. Lots of light brown hair, prominent cheekbones, and eyes the color of the ocean. Eyes that sort of sparkled with curiosity as they looked at her.

"I was told you wanted to talk to me," he said.

"Oh. Right. I did. I do," she stumbled. "But I thought it could be a phone call . . . You didn't have to—"

"Blue made it sound like it was pretty urgent."

He smiled. The man was totally movie-star hand-some. "Actually, he made it sound both urgent and like he didn't want me anywhere near you."

Her insides warmed traitorously. She was still angry with Blue. Had spent an hour explaining the marriage mistake to her parents, while her brothers listened, enraptured, grins blazing. "I'm sorry about that."

"Don't be," he said good-naturedly. "It's nice to see him interested in . . . you."

She gave him a tight smile. Right. Interested in the baby, more like. "Can I get you something to eat? Drink?"

"Coke and fries?"

"Coming right up."

"Hey." He stopped her before she could pass the table. "But first can you tell me what you need from me?"

Emily did a quick sweep of the Bull's Eye—well, her section anyway. She had three tables going, one of them being James Cavanaugh's two-top. Every-one was occupied, either talking or eating. Even Miss O'Shay was digging into her salad, clearly content with the width of her egg slices.

Now was as good a time as any, she supposed. She chewed the inside of her cheek a second be-fore speaking. "See the thing is . . . well, I'd heard that you might be interested in the small property on Main."

He looked surprised that real estate was what was on her mind. "Sixteen and a half?"

Her heart thrummed in her chest. "That's the one."

"I am interested," he admitted. "How'd you know about that?"

"My agent, Aubrey Perdue, told me," she explained, feeling super-awkward. "I'm moving out of my parents' house. Looking for a new place to live. I like that space." She sounded like a moron.

"Oh. I see. Well, it's actually an office space for me. I'm spending more and more time in River Black, and I thought I needed to have somewhere to do business out of. That property had been vacant for a while, and, well, it suits my purpose."

"Oh," she exclaimed softly. "So you're not in love with it or anything?"

"In love?" His brows knit together.

"As in, the space isn't your heart's desire. You're not emotionally connected to it." She shook her head. "I'm sure I sound insane."

"Not insane, just confusing."

She heaved a sigh and did something she'd never done before. She pulled back the chair opposite James and sat down at a customer's table. "Look, here's the thing. I've been in love with that property for a long time, Mr. Cavanaugh—"

"James," he corrected.

"James . . . and when I heard you were interested in it too, I wanted to speak to you . . . see if maybe I could talk you out of it. You know, if you weren't head over heels for the space or anything." She shrugged. "Maybe I could even help you find something else."

His eyes clouded over. "I'm real sorry, Miss Shiver—"

"Emily," she corrected.

"Emily. I signed the paperwork yesterday. And so did the owner. Money's already been transferred."

Her stomach dropped. "Oh."

Sensing her heavy disappointment, he asked, "Did you make an offer . . . or . . . ? I mean, I wouldn't have—"

"No. No." She stood up, feeling embarrassed. She didn't want to tell him about her lack of funds. "It's fine. Really. Congratulations." She forced a smile. "Thanks for coming here. You didn't have to, and I appreciate it. I'm going to get you that Coke and fries now—on the house. And again, congratulations." She turned to go.

"Hey, Emily?" he called out.

She stopped, turned back. "Yeah?"

"I might be able to offer you a compromise of sorts. If you're interested." He gave her a small smile. He had very gentle eyes. They were the eyes of someone who was naturally kind. She could see the horse whisperer in him. "If you're looking for a place to live, I do plan on renting out the apartment above the office space. It's not big, as you probably know. But it's . . . cozy. Even has a separate entrance."

"Really?" she asked, surprised.

He nodded.

A low hum started working within her. It wasn't exactly how she'd planned it, but maybe it was exactly what she needed—right now, at any rate. . . "When would it be available?" she asked him.

That movie-star smile widened. "You can move in anytime you're ready."

Blue thundered across the Triple C land. Some days it felt like the earth went on forever. Just long stretches of green and tan and blue sky. Blue might get lost in it if he had a mind. He and Barbarella. And many times over the past few months, he'd either done that or wanted to do that. But things were changing—and changing fast—in his life. Things he had no control over. Things that made him think and act differently. A baby was coming into the world. And its mama was occupying much of Blue's brain space. How she felt. Whether she was safe. Happy? Christ, he felt on edge, straddling two different worlds—caught between what had happened these past months and what was possible in the months to come.

He slowed Rella, halted her in the middle of the vast south pasture.

Mac followed suit, pulling up alongside him, laughing into the wind. "It's like old times," she called out. "Racing across Triple C soil. 'Course, we never stopped until I won."

He turned to look at her. Oh, Mac. She was always doing that. Always trying. Bringing up the past. Mostly the good stuff in hopes that they could find their way back to the close friendship both of them had enjoyed—even counted on. For the past couple of months, Blue had ignored her attempts to connect. He just couldn't manage it. Didn't want it. He knew she hadn't been a part of the lies and betrayal, but she was married to a Cavanaugh brother, and it made him feel like he couldn't be vulnerable with her.

But today, instead of turning away, he did something crazy. Something reckless. He turned *to* her. Maybe it was a bad idea. Maybe he'd end up regretting it. Maybe she'd tell her husband all about it and they'd have a good laugh. But damn, he needed her. He needed his friend. Now more than he ever had.

"Can I ask you something?" he said as Rella snorted and tried to walk on. But he held her firm.

Beside him, Mac instantly sobered, a little flash of hope crossing her features as she too held her horse in check. " 'Course."

"You think someone who didn't have a father, didn't know his father, could be a decent one himself?" Hell, his entire body felt tighter than a newly twisted wire.

She stared at him, her expression curious and intense. "I think anyone who's willing to put the work into parenting will succeed at it."

He nodded, then turned and looked out over the land.

"Want to tell me why you're asking?" she probed, as gently as she'd ever said anything to him.

"Not just now."

"Okay." She was quiet for a moment. Then she blew out a breath. "You know, I think Deacon would probably wonder the same thing."

That brought Blue's eyes back to her. "But he had a father."

"Yeah, early on. But after Cass . . . not so much. The relationship was strained at best. You could say he was more damaged by the parenting he got than supported by it."

As the sun clipped his gaze, Blue squinted at her. He'd never thought about Deacon or James or Cole missing out on a daddy. Because, hell, even if yours was a loser, at least you had one. But maybe Mac was right. To be a good parent, successful, really do right by your little one, you just had to want it, work at it—never give up on it.

"Don't know why you're asking," Mac continued. "But if you ever choose to become a father, you'll be amazing at it." Her eyes connected with his. They were warm and sentimental, and they cut him deep. "We all have our crap that we take into any relationship, Blue. Husband, wife, brother, sister, mother, child. We can't escape it. No matter how hard we try. We all have a couple strikes against us. But I gotta believe, if there's love, and a willing heart—"

"If there's love," he interrupted, the bitter edge in his tone barely audible in the cool breeze. "That's a problem. I wouldn't know love if it bit me in the ass. Probably because it has, a couple of times lately."

He expected her to answer right away, give him

a gentle but uplifting speech about how it was people who had the sharp teeth, not love. But she didn't. Maybe she didn't want to press things after he'd opened up to her. Or maybe she just thought he was a fool and a jackass, and she didn't want to waste her breath.

"Another fence is calling," he said.

She nodded slowly, smiled gently, her eyes so soft on his. "There's always another fence."

A smile touched his lips. "Something to count on."

"Yup."

"Well, then. Should we get 'er done? Mac?"

Her eyes widened, then suddenly pricked with tears. He knew it was because he'd only called her *foreman* these past two months, since he'd found out that Everett was his father and fell into a dark place where no one could be trusted. He'd put the wedge, the protective barrier, there between them, in the form of a word. *Foreman.* Now it didn't feel right. She was Mac. And they were out riding the land once again.

A slow smile spread across her features, and she gave her horse a kick. She circled around him once, then pulled her Stetson low. "You ready?"

"Born ready," he answered.

"All right then." And in the space of a breath, she kicked her mare into a gallop and took off across the plain.

His heart just a shade lighter than it had been a few minutes ago, Blue followed.

Fourteen

She'd done it.

She'd actually done it.

Granted, the move had been quick and head-strong and maybe not all finely planned—zero furniture until tomorrow—but it felt good. She felt good.

Leaning against the massive broom she'd found in the office closet, Emily stared around the room of her new apartment. One bedroom, one bath, a cute but small kitchen, huge windows, flowers everywhere she could manage, and loads of charm. It didn't have the space and comforts of home, but it had something else. Something she thought might end up being more important in the end. The ability to teach her autonomy.

She headed downstairs and put the broom away. She'd spent the past hour working on the floors and cleaning the bathroom and kitchen. Now it was time to get her bags. She hadn't brought much.

A week's worth of clothes and toiletries, some books and music, a few candles. Her brothers were coming tomorrow with all the rest. She smiled as she thought of them, how they'd insisted. That smile waned slightly when she opened the door to her car and saw the two food warmers, each with a Post-it note on top. Her mom. Susie Shiver hadn't given her any grief when she'd told her the plan. But her eyes had filled with tears, and her arms had stayed around Emily for a good five minutes before allowing her to leave.

Just call me, Em. Let me know you're okay. I love you, Baby Girl.

Emily swung a bag over one shoulder and scooped up the two food warmers in her hands. She was on her way inside when someone stepped directly into her path. "Shit!" she said on a gasp.

"I'm so sorry," came a woman's voice.

Righting herself, Emily glanced up. When she saw who it was, her heart stuttered inside her chest. "Oh . . ." Had the woman slipped inside the house when Emily had been digging out her luggage from the car? "You scared me."

"Didn't mean to." The woman smiled. "I'm Natalie, by the way."

"I know who you are." Realizing she sounded a bit abrasive, Emily pulled back a little. "I remember you from school and from the bakery."

"And maybe from Blue?" she said hopefully.

Bags in hand, Emily stood in the doorway, unsure

of how to proceed. What exactly to say. What she knew about Natalie Palmer was sketchy at best. But she'd definitely heard about the woman's father and what he'd allegedly done and how he'd passed away before he'd even gone to trial. She knew a little about Blue's online relationship with her. And she knew that Blue had found Cass Cavanaugh's diary at Natalie's place and believed her to be involved in the girl's disappearance. She hadn't known until that very moment, however, how hung up on Blue Perez Cavanaugh Natalie Palmer was.

"Has he talked about me?" Natalie pressed.

Emily glanced past her to the street. This was incredibly strange and awkward. And yet, she felt compelled to answer. "A little, I guess," she said warily.

Like a little girl hearing she's pretty for the first time, Natalie beamed at the news. "He's a good guy."

"Yeah, he is," Emily agreed.

"Are you two seeing each other?"

"Um," Emily stumbled, "I don't . . . you know, I really have to get going."

But instead of nodding, saying good-bye, and heading down the street, Natalie turned and ventured back into the building. Emily followed. This chick was weird. Social-cue simple. What was she going to have to do to get rid of her?

"I love this space," Natalie was saying, looking around the room. "When I saw that it was for sale, I was thinking about it for my bakery. But it's just too small."

"You're opening a bakery?" So maybe that was it? Why she was here. Same as Emily. She'd just really liked the—

"It's always been my dream," Natalie cut into her thoughts. "And us girls need to follow our dreams, right?" She smiled broadly, but the gesture didn't reach her eyes.

A shiver moved through Emily. "Sure."

"Even if the road is paved with obstacles," Natalie went on. "We can't give up. So many people try to bring you down . . . have you noticed that?" She raised a brow at Emily.

It was rare that Emily felt at a loss for words, but as she stared at this woman, dressed in a lovely green-and-yellow sundress, she couldn't muster a response. Was Natalie just trying to connect with her? Had she been passing by a space she'd also been interested in, and thought, *Hey, I'll take a look inside and say hi to the new tenant . . . ?* Or did she have other motives? Like sending a passive warning regarding Blue? She was obviously still interested in him.

"You know," Emily began, "I really need to get going—" She lifted her bags and knocked her chin in the direction of the stairs.

"Oh, of course," Natalie said, looking suddenly normal and friendly and upbeat. "I'm so sorry to keep you. I was on my way home, saw the light on." She gave Emily a wave before turning and heading for the door. "Have a great night."

Yeah. "You too."

Emily followed her out the door, then watched

as she walked down the street. It was only when the woman was three blocks away and had turned onto Metcaffe that she went back inside and up to her new apartment.

The River Black jail was pretty much the last place Blue ever wanted to return to. Being inside felt constricting as hell, and it smelled worse, like a combination of cleaning products, old coffee, and suspicious brother.

Just like the one who was sitting across from him right now, staring and waiting.

Cursing, Blue glanced at his phone, checked the time.

"So?" Steven Shiver pressed. "Where are they?"

He gave the deputy sheriff a shrug. "Hell if I know. They told me to meet them here at five."

Shiver pointed to the clock on the wall. "It's five now."

"Hey, you can tell time." Blue's brows lifted. "Does River Black Elementary know about you?"

"Funny. I can see why my sister ran away from you."

A muscle in Blue's jaw pulsed.

Steven grinned, glanced down at some paperwork on his desk, then back up again. "So what? You want to sit in silence? Or keep jabbing at each other? I have a brother, so I'm real good at that. I got a million of 'em."

Blue dropped back in his chair. "What're my other options?"

"Oh, I don't know. Talk about you and—"

"No."

"You *and* Em, was what I was going to say," he continued, "and what's going on with the two of you. What you're thinking. What your plans are."

If he had the answers to all that, he'd be sitting pretty right now, instead of checking his phone to see if she'd called or e-mailed or texted. Thinking and plans? Not even close. "And if I don't, am I going to end up in handcuffs and behind bars?"

Steven snorted. "Come on now, Perez. When are you going to let that go?"

"It's Cavanaugh. And never."

Shiver just moved right on by that. "I mean, you should be thanking me."

Blue stared at the man. Christ on a cracker, Shiver had balls the size of Texas. "You want me to thank you for locking me up and leaving my truck on the highway?"

A shrug and another grin. "Hey. I got Emmie to tell you about the baby, didn't I?"

The word rolled through him like a soft, gentle wave. It was crazy the effect it had on him. Just the word, the idea. What was happening to him? No—what was threatening to change him? "I'm sure she would've told me," Blue said. "In her time. That whole pull-over-and-arrest spectacle wasn't needed."

"First of all, you were speeding," he pointed out. "Second, and more importantly, you clearly don't know my sister."

Blue didn't answer. Just scrubbed a hand over his face. Where the hell were the Cavanaughs?

"Mom and Dad are beside themselves, by the way," Steven told him. "Emmie's done a complete one-eighty on them. She's always been their little homebody. Grown up, but content to live at home. And yet, she came home from work today, packed up a few things, and said she'd see us on Sunday. For dinner." He tossed his hands in the air. "Like it was nothing at all."

"What?" Blue sat forward. He didn't give a rat's ass about dinners and Emily's parents' reaction. "She moved out? Already?"

Steven's brows drifted upward. "You didn't know?"

"'Course I didn't know. I would've been there. Helping her. Why aren't you there helping her? She's pregnant, for Christ's sake!"

"I'm here waiting on your goddamned brothers!" Steven nearly shouted. "And for the record, she didn't want any help. She only brought clothes and some personal stuff. She had this idea of going it alone—especially for her first night. I didn't like it. None of us liked it. But you've seen her in action. She's stubborn as shit. And an adult. So she can pretty much do as she likes." He inhaled and dropped back in his chair. "Anyway, me and Jeremy will bring all the rest tomorrow. Check in on her."

Frustration hummed inside of Blue. He hated this. Not knowing where the mother of his child was. Hated that she hadn't told him, hadn't asked him for help. "Where did she go?" As in, how had she found a place in such a short time? It didn't make sense.

And yet, something in his gut told him that his pushing her on moving in and getting married was part of the answer.

"An apartment above the new shop your brother owns," Steven informed him, giving him a pointed look. "On Main. She's been coveting that place for a long time now. Had wanted to buy it and turn it into a flower shop. It's her dream, you know?"

No, he didn't know. He should know. Hell, he should know everything about her. Not just how her skin felt, or the bright sweetness of her smile when she was happy, or how pissed she got when you surprised her. He should know what was in her heart. What was worrying her, paining her . . . what she wanted most out of her life.

Voices rang out in the hall then, followed by heavy footfalls. And in seconds, the Cavanaughs strolled into the room. Deacon regarded both Blue and Shiver and said a quick "Evenin'" before taking a seat. But Blue was single-focused now. He had his eyes on James. The offender. He pushed out of his seat and approached the man. "You let her move into your apartment?" he accused.

Confused, James put his hands up. "Whoa. I clearly walked in on something."

"Damn right you did," Blue shot back. "A pregnant woman living alone. No family. No . . ." He stopped right there before he said something to the effect of *man in her life*.

Cole and Deacon exchanged looks.

"Emily's pregnant?" James asked, stunned.

"Yup," Steven said, still seated behind his desk. "And your brother here did it."

"You asshole," Blue ground out, shooting the man a dirty glare.

Cole busted out laughing. "Holy shit."

Deacon, however, remained quiet, contemplative.

"Wow," Cole said. "Congrats, man."

"Forget that for a moment." James eyed his eldest brother. "You get what this means, don't you?"

"Perhaps," Deacon said.

"Well, I do," Cole said with a grin. "That baby's going to be related to us. Our niece or nephew. I hope it's a niece. Be nice to have some female Cavanaugh energy—"

"Who says this baby is going to be a Cavanaugh?" Blue said with a bite to his tone. "Or if any of you will be a part of its life."

All three of them turned to look at him. But it was Cole who spoke, his expression offended. "Why do you have such a goddamned problem with us? It wasn't me or Deac or James who did the steppin' out all those years ago—"

"Cole," James began, his tone laced in warning.

But Cole wasn't listening. Probably had that shit bottled up inside of him for quite some time. "Wasn't us who lied to you. If anyone should be pissed around here, it should be James, Deac, and me."

"Oh?" Blue ground out. "How do you figure?"

"All you've wanted since you found out we're

related was the Triple C. No relationship. No family."

"As if that's what you all want," Blue shot back.

"You never even gave us a try," Cole said. "As hard as it was for us hearing about our father's many sins—and it was hard—we've opened up to you. But you're a fucking locked door." Then for good measure he uttered, "Little brother."

"That's enough." It was Deacon who spoke now. Low, commanding, all business. "We didn't come here to argue family issues or discuss Blue's relationship with your sister, Deputy."

"Then why did you come, Mr. Cavanaugh?" Steven asked.

Deacon leaned forward and placed an envelope on Steven's desk.

"What's this?" the man asked even as he opened it and took out the single piece of paper inside.

"That, Deputy Shiver, is what you're going to use to open an investigation of Natalie Palmer for the abduction and murder of our sister."

Fifteen

Emily had spent the past two hours cleaning the small apartment. The kitchen shined and the bathroom sparkled. Now she was going to grab a shower, then hunker down with her mother's very welcome dinner and the second season of *Downton Abbey* on her laptop. But the water had just barely turned to hot when there was a knock at the door.

Nerves skittered through her. After the strange encounter with Natalie Palmer, she was kind of hoping for nothing else to go down tonight. She slipped her robe back on, grabbed her cell phone, and went to the door. Another knock echoed through the room.

Could it be James? she wondered, tightening her grip on her cell. To see if she's settling in. Or maybe it was her brothers . . . "Who is it?" she called brusquely.

"Blue."

A tsunami-sized wave of relief crashed over and through her. She tightened the tie on her robe and opened the door.

Standing there, filling up the doorway, was one extraordinarily handsome man. Like, toe-curling, gut-tightening handsome. But it wasn't just his blessed facial features or long, hard body that made him so. It was this air he walked around with: confident, ready, hungry, strong.

"Hey," she said, her gaze running over his faded jeans and black T-shirt. "What's going on?"

Blue's eyes were pretty much doing the same thing. Taking in what she was wearing. Or not wearing. "Your brother said you left the house."

"I did," she confirmed.

"Without anything but your clothes?" He nodded at her robe. "And it looks like maybe you didn't even bring that."

She smiled. "All the rest of my stuff is coming tomorrow. I just wanted to go . . . you know? Just needed to jump into the deep end."

"Without a bathing suit?"

"I'm just crazy like that."

"Is this because of me, Emily?" he asked, his incredible blue eyes wary. "Did I drive you out of your home with all my talk of moving in and getting hitched?"

"No." She leaned against the doorframe. "Well, maybe."

"Ah, dammit." He shook his head and sighed.

"But not in the way you're thinking. This was coming on for a while, Blue. I loved living with my family. They're the best. And I was comfortable. Maybe too comfortable," she admitted with a slight cringe. "But I'm having a family of my own now. Changes things. Changes perspective. And the drive within a person. Not to mention how one sees the future."

His jaw went tight. "Speaking of the future, where do you plan on sleeping tonight?"

She looked at him strangely. "In my bedroom."

He raised a brow. "I mean on what? If you only brought some clothes—"

"Oh. I have blankets, and a pillow."

He looked horror-struck. "That's what I thought. Not going to happen, Em."

She laughed. "Come on. It's fine. It's one night . . . Blue, where you going?"

But he'd disappeared. Emily stuck her head out the door, only to be met with the end of what looked like a brand-new rolled-up mattress. No . . . futon. What was this? What had he done? She had no choice but to back up into the apartment as he carried it inside.

"Where's your bedroom?" he demanded.

"To the left, past the bathroom," she said. "But—"

He was already moving in that direction. Emily followed him, confused, stunned. The sales tags were still on the thing. As she came to stand beside him, he had the rolled-up futon on the freshly mopped floor beneath the window and was taking out his Swiss Army knife.

"Stop right now," she said. "This is crazy."

"You're not sleeping on the floor." He clipped

whatever was holding the thing together, and it uncurled and spread out beneath her window. "Triple C bunkhouse can always roll out another. I'll take it back tomorrow when Steven and Jeremy bring over your bed. Hell, I'll be helping them, so it's easily done."

"What?" she exclaimed. "No. You don't need to do that."

He turned to look at her. " 'Course I do. Look, I know you're angry with me for meddling, and that's understandable and all. But it's only because I want to do right by you, Emily. I want to help, be here." He shook his head. "I should've known. About you moving. Where you were going."

Something pinged inside her, near her heart, as she looked up at him. The sincerity she saw there, the want and need and worry . . . He cared.

"You're carrying my baby, Em," he said plainly.

Yes, he cared. About the baby. Her gut tightened. That's what mattered to him. All that mattered to him. Granted, she was glad for it. She wanted her child to have a father who loved and cherished it. Knowing that made her feel safe and protected. But she also was hoping . . . ever since that night they'd spent together . . . that maybe he might come to want her too.

"Thank you for the mattress," she said, going over to the bedroom door, making it plain it was time for him to leave. "It was very thoughtful of you. And don't worry. I'll keep you informed in the future. Of all the baby's comings and goings."

He picked up on her tone and her meaning immediately. His eyes softened and he shook his head. "Come on, now, darlin'. You know it's not just about that."

The ping came back, but she shoved it away. "Isn't it?"

He inhaled deeply, blew it out. "No. Wish it was, though."

"Damn you, Blue."

"What?"

"You start off all nice, then toss that in at the end. You wish you didn't care about me? 'Preciate that."

"You don't understand," he began, scrubbing a hand over his jaw. "Seems like lately, caring about someone, whether it's family or a person you met online and believed was honest and real, turns out real badly. I feel like I'm a wrecked man, Em. Can't trust. Closed off. Nothing much here to offer, if you get my meaning. And you . . ." His gaze moved over her, slow and almost hungry. "Shit, honey, you deserve something far better than damaged goods." He turned around then, and started making her goddamned bed—with the blankets she'd brought and the pillow.

"Please don't tell me what I deserve," Emily said softly. "And don't do that."

He was quiet for a second, his eyes on the small vase near the window. It held the flowers he'd given her last night at her parents' house.

Yes, I've been thinking about you, Emily said silently. *Wrecked man though you claim to be.*

"You hungry?" he asked, dropping her pillow into place.

The question was so out of the blue, she didn't answer right away.

He turned to look at her, those eyes sweeping over her face. Why did he have to be so beautiful?

"We can go to the diner," he suggested.

"My mom actually sent something with me."

He seemed disappointed, pensive. It was a very sexy look on him. But then again, what wasn't? "They're going to miss you, you know?"

"My parents? Yeah, they will. And I'm going to miss them. But it really is time." She glanced around the room. "Experience life on my own. Figure things out before I'm not so on my own anymore."

His pensive look intensified. "I suppose your mama didn't pack enough for two."

Interesting. He didn't want to leave. And in truth, she didn't want him to go. But there was this fear that clung to her insides, played with her mind. *He's here because of the baby. He never sought you out after that night, Emily. Get a clue.*

"Right," he said, taking her silence as rejection and heading her way. "I know I'm being a pushy bastard. I'll see you tomorrow."

She stopped him just as he passed, going out the door. Her hand on his biceps. It was like wrapping her fingers around granite. But such smooth, warm granite. Her belly clenched with awareness.

"Stay," she said.

His eyes caught hers, held. "Yeah?"

She nodded, feeling breathless. "If you want to."

His mouth curved into a smile. A slightly wicked smile. "Oh, Emily Shiver. You know I want to."

Oh Lord. Was that heat surging into her blood? She released his arm and stepped back. "I need to take a quick shower first. That's where I was when you knocked. About to turn on the water." She needed to stop talking.

His expression changed in an instant. From soft, simmering interest to an almost untamed need. She'd never seen anyone look like that. And certainly not aimed at her. *Shower. Go take a shower. And maybe make it a cold one.* "I'll be out in ten minutes," she uttered, her insides so hot and liquid now, she had to quell the urge to moan as she moved past him and headed for the bathroom.

"I'll be here," he returned, his voice near to a growl.

"You know that eating-for-two thing is a myth," Emily said when Blue handed her another piece of bread.

They were sitting on the blanket-clad futon, enjoying a picnic of lasagna, bread, fruit, and rice pudding. Mama Shiver sure could cook, Blue thought. Even rivaled Elena, and that was saying something.

He grinned. "Can't help it. I just want to feed you. I feel like my mother when I was in high school. Always pushing plates on me."

"Well, you needed it," she said. "You were a beanpole back then."

He didn't deny it. Beanpole was actually stretching things. More like a pushpin. "I swear I could eat a side of beef followed by a vat of pasta and nothing stuck."

"Lucky bastard," she said with a grin.

He laughed. "Yeah, but it killed my social life. Girls barely gave me the time of day. Bones weren't nearly as attractive as muscle."

"Well, you certainly overcame that obstacle," she said, her cheeks going pink. "If only those girls could've had the foresight to know what was going to happen in a few years." Her gaze flickered over him, then returned to his face. "Probably kicking themselves now."

Heat was pulsing through him. Shit. It had been since she'd opened the door, in her robe. "You're making me blush, Em Shiver."

"No, I'm not."

"Okay, you're not. But other things are happening to me, I guarantee you."

Her eyes widened and she gasped, nearly choking on her piece of lasagna.

He laughed. "Careful, now."

She swallowed thickly, then cleared her throat. "Okay, back to the high school discussion. There must've been someone, right? Someone who saw through the bones?"

He thought for a second, popping a few grapes into his mouth. "I dated Sheila Erickson in ninth grade."

"Oh yeah. I remember her." She gestured to her

mouth. "She had those blue braces. I was so jealous. I had the ugly metal kind."

"Sheila," he reminisced with a sigh. "Wasn't the nicest person in the world, but damn could she kiss."

Without thought, Emily tossed her bread at him.

He laughed. "I'm just giving respect where it's due, ma'am. Despite the metal, Sheila knew what she was doing."

Emily pressed her lips together. "Where is Sheila now?"

"She's an orthodontist in Austin," he said with a straight face.

"No!"

He laughed again. "I don't know. Lost track of a lot of people when my mom and I moved into the Triple C. Was a strange time." He picked at his lasagna, not sure he wanted to continue, and yet there was something about the moment, with Emily, that pushed him. He'd wanted to get closer, get to know her. Maybe that included her getting to know him too. "My mom was keeping Everett together. The brothers were gone. The house just always felt in mourning, you know? I didn't do much on the social front during that time."

Emily was watching him closely. Looked like she was trying to decide what to say. Push him on the past or keep things light. She opted for the latter.

"Poor Sheila," she said on a sigh. "I bet she regrets not keeping in touch with you."

He shrugged. "She didn't call. She didn't write." He smiled halfheartedly.

They ate in silence for a bit. Then Emily asked, "Did you ever wish you hadn't gone to live there?"

"The Triple C?" he said.

She nodded.

Her question slowed him a bit, forced him to think, reflect. It wasn't his favorite thing to do these days. He put down his fork. "I don't know. There have been times in the past few months where I would say absolutely, yes. But . . . not sure that's the truth. The Triple C is my life. Always has been. For better or for worse. Everything I am is wrapped up in that ranch. I'm in the soil, you understand?"

Her eyes were pinned to his as she nodded.

"Things were pretty good until Everett passed," he said. "More than good. Had my mom and Mac. Had Everett. He treated me like a fourth son. His were gone, Cass was gone, and Deacon came back and tried to destroy the C . . . I thought, what a terrible thing to have sons like those." Blue laughed, but it was a bitter sound. "I had no idea what was really behind their anger. I never questioned Everett's kindness and affection for me. I just basked in it."

" 'Course you did," she blurted out, impassioned.

He looked at her.

"Well, why wouldn't you?" she continued. She started cleaning up, stacking their plates and putting everything back in the basket her mother had sent. "Why do you think he didn't tell you, Blue? About being his son? Or why didn't your mother?" She put the basket on the floor behind her. "I mean, after Mrs. Cavanaugh died, why would they still hold on to the secret?"

He inhaled deeply. "I'm sure there's an answer to that question."

"You've never asked?"

He shook his head. "My mom wants to tell me. Talk to me. Lay the whole mess out in front of me to dissect. But I don't know. I don't know if I want to hear the reasons. I don't think I want to forgive her or him."

"Yeah," she whispered.

His eyes lifted to meet hers. No judgment there, only curiosity and interest. "Sometimes I feel like my anger is the only thing holding me together. Keeping me sane. Keeping me from making the same mistake over and over."

"What mistake is that?" she asked.

"Trusting."

She made a soft, sad sound. "Oh, Blue . . ."

He shook his head. "I don't know why I'm telling you this," he said on a frustrated growl. "I shouldn't be."

She scooted closer to him, then reached out and put her hands on either side of his face. "Look at me," she demanded. When he did, when his eyes connected, locked with hers, she said, "Just because you were vulnerable with a few people and they screwed with that, doesn't mean everyone will. I . . ." She stopped, bit her lip.

"What? What, Em?" he pushed.

For a moment, she didn't answer. She looked like she was trying to find the right words, or decide if she should continue—and what it would mean if she did. Then she released a breath. "I wouldn't. Just so you know." She shrugged lightly. "I wouldn't screw with that."

Her words touched him. Deep. Hit a place inside of him that had been dead for the past several weeks. And then when she leaned in and kissed him—one soft kiss that made his insides erupt, made his hands clench into fists, made his head fuzzy—well, he just plain broke. Inside out. Cage around the heart.

"I don't have the blue braces," she said against his lips. "But I'm a pretty good kisser."

"Yeah you are," he whispered huskily.

"Maybe better than Sheila Erickson?"

"Who?"

She eased back, locked eyes with him and shook her head. "Oh, boy, I like you something awful."

Her tone was a mixture of hunger and melancholy. Blue knew exactly what she meant. This was probably not the best of ideas. It was complicated. And yet neither one of them could help it.

"I like you too, Em."

She leaned in and lapped at his bottom lip with her tongue. "Prove it."

Oh, that did it. Her hot, pink tongue. Her challenge. Made his rational, reasonable mind exit through his ears. With a growl of possession, he picked her up and placed her on his lap, forcing her to straddle him. And she did—instantly—wrapping her legs around his waist and her arms around his neck. Hungry and impatient, Blue captured her mouth with his own. A groan escaped him as he tasted her, sucked at her bottom lip. Sure, he'd kissed her that night—that fateful night—and it had been ravenous and hot. But this . . . this time he was completely and totally sober. He was all here, all in. And it felt so real, so perfect—like every breath she took, every moan she made, belonged to him.

Her fingers moved through his hair, gripping his scalp as their kiss intensified. Blue pulled her closer, wanting to feel her, the softness of her, the strength in her, and he groaned with pleasure as she pressed her breasts against his chest.

How could something as simple as a kiss turn rabid? Within him? And going by what he felt from her, how she moved and reacted every time he bit at her lip or suckled it into his mouth—she was right there with him. In his foggy mind he warred with the idea that this woman, this beautiful, incredible, intelligent woman, if she really knew him—his ravaged heart that seemed to crave vengeance against anyone who had done him wrong—she'd pull away and demand he get the hell out of her apartment and her life. But then again, maybe she did know . . .

Didn't care.

Wanted him anyway.

His hand slipped between their bodies and cupped her sex. Through the thin layer of cotton pajama bottoms, he felt wet heat against his palm. In that moment, whatever was left of that rational, reasonable—sensible—mind departed for parts unknown. And all that remained was a man who had been in a state of unfulfilled desire for weeks—ever since the night three weeks ago when he'd sat at a bar with a flower-haired angel.

He slipped his hand inside the loose waistband of those thin pajama bottoms and followed the hot trail down her lower abdomen until his fingers brushed her soft pussy. Instantly, Emily bucked and pressed herself against him, releasing a sigh of need. As his mouth gently played with hers, as his eyes opened from time to time to catch her looking at him, he started making small circles over her clit. The tight bud pulsed beneath the pads of his fingers, matching his rapid heartbeat.

"Why does this feel so good?" she uttered against his mouth, her tone breathy and strained. "With you . . . you . . ."

That's right, only me, he wanted to say as he pinched her ever so slightly.

"Oh God," she cried out and started grinding against him hard.

"You want to come, Em?" he whispered, circling her, then giving her a couple of gentle flicks.

"Yes," she breathed. "And no." She laughed softly, pained. "I want it to go on forever. Never stop touching me, Blue."

"Christ, darlin'," he said, his entire body rigid with need. His cock so hard it was leaking at the tip. It wanted her. Wanted to be the one she craved.

Wanted to be the one who touched her. So deep she couldn't talk, couldn't do anything but cry out, moan, scream his name.

And then he felt it. The initial shock waves of her coming orgasm, and the lights of thought went out. His mouth took hers, hungry and fearsome, and as she canted her hips and thrust against him, he circled and pulled gently at her clit. He kept his motion steady, instinctive, until she froze.

"Oh God!" she cried out. "Oh, Blue. Please."

It was like a possession had taken her. She thrust her hips and gripped his scalp and drove her tongue into his mouth as she came. And Blue loved every goddamned moment of it. He relished it. His angel. His Em. Her pleasure belonged to him.

There was nothing he wanted more than to be inside her at that moment. His cock. As deep as she could take him. But he knew that if he did that right now, he was going to lose himself, and his mind, and his will. Emily Shiver was too sweet. Addictive. And if he made love to her—again— what little there remained of the protection around his busted heart would be gone. He'd be open to her, falling for her. She'd have the power to utterly and ultimately bring him down.

Before she could touch him, he wrapped her in his arms and dropped back against the futon.

She felt the disconnect immediately and asked, "Blue . . . ?"

"Yeah."

"You don't want me to touch you, do you?"

Shit! Of course he did. He wanted her soft

hands all over his body, her fingers wrapped around his cock, stroking him as he kissed her so hard and so thoroughly, she came again.

"Not tonight," he pushed out, his voice a raw nerve.

"Why?" she asked sadly. "Is it me?"

Yes.

Fuck, yes.

"I just want to touch you tonight, Em," he said through gritted teeth. "Want to make you feel good. Isn't that okay?"

He prayed she wouldn't fight him on that. Want to talk it out, probe. He couldn't take it if she did. Couldn't resist if she was determined to make him feel good too.

Just the idea made him groan.

But instead of pressing him, she snuggled into him. Which, frankly, was almost as bad. She wanted to be close, to connect. The Blue of three months ago still lurked somewhere inside him. That man wanted a goddamned connection so bad he'd missed any and all signs of a relationship built on-line and on lies.

"You staying?" she asked, her voice threaded with hope and the fading huskiness of climax.

His body flared once again with heat. He should go. Get up and get out. If it was logic and reason and rational thought he craved in this moment, then heading for the cold air and his truck was the right thing to do.

And yet, how did he leave this woman? Warm.

Wanting him. His child resting easy inside her belly.

"I'd like to," he managed. "For a while at least."

She didn't say anything at first, but he felt disappointment. At the last bit he'd uttered. Felt it in the way she nuzzled against his chest. "Just don't go before I wake up, okay?" she whispered.

His gut tightened at the irony of that request, and he pulled her closer. "Okay."

Sixteen

The sun was barely up when Emily woke. Well, not exactly woke, but opened her eyes and rolled over to . . . good God, what a view. He'd slept over. He'd actually stayed. In her bed, wearing his jeans and T-shirt. Next time? No jeans *or* T-shirt. She smiled to herself. She could have all the slumber parties she wanted now that she was on her own.

Huge perk.

Through her still sleepy haze, she studied him. He was truly the most beautiful man she'd ever seen. She wanted to touch him everywhere, memorize how his skin felt against her fingers. Without thought, she reached up and brushed her thumb over his lower lip. Then over his jaw. It was dusted with stubble, and the feel of his sharp yet soft hair on the pads of her fingers made the muscles inside her sex tingle.

Again.

Memories of the night before barreled through her. Hands, lips, fingertips . . . She shivered.

A low, masculine growl rumbled between them, but Blue's eyes remained closed. "Keep touching me like that, darlin', and we won't get out of this bed today."

"Futon," she corrected, playing with a shock of hair near his ear. "We won't get out of this futon."

Before she had a chance to take her next breath, he was up and rolling her to her back. He gazed down at her, all dark and foreboding. "Smartass."

Her lips twitched. "You're finally getting me, aren't you?" she chided, feeling his cock through his jeans, hard and thick, pressed against her thigh.

One dark eyebrow jerked up. "I thought I got you last night. And good."

Her grin broadened. "Some of me," she clarified.

"Well, that's not right," he drawled, then started moving down her body until he was lips to her navel.

She gasped at the feel of his warm breath on her skin, then giggled. "That's not what I mean, Blue."

"That's what I mean." His fingers were already in the waistband of her pj's and he was pulling them down. "That's what I want." He accentuated that last word by tossing her pj's over his shoulder.

Emily laughed, but only for a few seconds. The man was shouldering himself between her legs, his eyes pinned to her sex.

"Just a quick taste," he uttered, dropping his head. "Before I dig in. Before I eat you up."

Oh God, his words . . . they made her crazy. As his tongue swiped at the seam of her pussy, Emily pulled in air and fisted the blanket beneath her. She'd never been this close to a guy. Never been touched this way—or tasted. The one man she'd been with besides Blue had only wanted straight-up, girl-on-the-bottom, boy-on-the-top sex. This . . . what was happening now, Blue's head between her legs, and his tongue dancing . . . it was something she'd only fantasized about.

He had spread her wide then, and was gently flicking her clit with his tongue. So light it made her insane, made her need, pissed her off.

What was happening between them? Picnics on her futon, deep conversation, opening up to each other—sleeping together? Were they . . . dating? Were they messing around? Did she care?

His tongue was pressed against her clit now and he was moving back and forth. Tugging. She moaned. No. She didn't care. She was lost at sea. The perfect eighty-degree sea.

"Christ, you're sweet, Em," he said on a groan, then pulled her tender bud into his mouth.

Crying out, she abandoned the blanket and grasped his head, her fingers in his hair. So thick. She wanted him. Him inside her. *I want you deep!*

"I want that too, sweetheart," he growled. "You have no idea how much."

She was talking, in her head, and outside too. The ache was terrible.

The need to come.

And the need to be filled.

She jerked her hips up, circling them. Blue followed, his mouth ravaging her now. He was making those hungry sounds that drove her mad, wild—over the edge.

And then he slid one long finger inside her.

A gasp escaped her throat. It sounded so raw to her ears.

Then a second finger. And a third.

Oh fuck!

Was this how it was supposed to feel? Like divine madness? Like purity just out of reach—and yet you don't want to get there . . . don't want it to ever be over? Don't want to come down from such an incredible high?

His thrusts were quickening now, and his lips were drawing on her clit. She wasn't going to be able to hold herself in. Not another moment. She had to release. Had to fly.

The waves of climax erupted inside her, and she pumped against his fingers, hearing the sounds of her wet heat, hearing Blue's groans as he ate her out. And then she was wriggling down. She had to get to him too. Taste him. Feel him. Own him like he owned her now.

In her blind haze, she found the waistband of his jeans. Gritting her teeth, she snapped open the button, ripped down the zipper. Almost. She almost had him— Before he stopped her. Again.

"No," he growled. "No, Em."

Her eyes opened. Panting, she blinked at him.

What . . . Goddammit. He was standing up. He was off the bed. No, the futon.

"I just wanted you," he said, his eyes darker than she'd ever seen them. "You gave me all I could ever want. On my lips, my tongue."

This was insane. He was shaking. His jaw was clenched so tight he could barely get the words out. What was going on? His lips were still shiny from her sex. He looked like he wanted to fuck her so badly it was paining him. And yet, he was resisting. Why?

"Blue?" She stared at him, trying to gauge what was going on. "Talk to me."

His cobalt eyes, lit with a fierce fire, nearly assaulted her in their brilliance, their hunger.

"Blue," she said again when he didn't answer her. "I know you want this, me—my hands on you."

"No," he ground out. "No, I don't."

Emily's heart faltered. She hadn't heard him right. Couldn't have. Because if she had, this man would be saying he didn't want her to touch him. Had to be something more, something else. He was feeling something for her, something he didn't want to feel, so he was backing the hell off—saying shit he didn't mean.

She knew how badly he wanted her. It was obvious as hell.

"Shit," he cursed, running a hand through his hair. "I have to go."

Was he serious? For a second, she thought about confronting him, pleading with him . . . But screw that. He might have had a shitty past to deal with, but that was over now—that wasn't about her. And hey, a girl has her pride.

She just nodded at him. "Okay."

His eyes found hers and they were stormy, like a battle was being fought behind them. No, no, no, she warned herself. She wanted to reach out to him, tell him she could help him fight that battle—after all, that was her nature, how she'd been brought up. But she knew in her guts that only Blue himself could decide whether that war he was waging was worth winning or not.

And shit, again—pride.

She pulled back the covers and got up. Didn't say another word as she walked straight past him and into the bathroom.

Blue had meant to go. He'd opened the front door intending to leave, intending to get in his truck and head back to the C—back to the ranch, his work, his life as an angry, distrusting cowboy. Only to feel every inch of him pulled back inside. He paced Emily's bedroom floor, trying to get his mind together, his anger tamped down—and worst of all his desire under control. But the sound of the shower was wreaking havoc on him. And the picture he had in his head . . . Emily, naked, water falling over her body . . . Emily was no doubt pissed off at him. And for good reason. He'd wanted her to be pissed. Wanted her to stop asking questions. Wanted her to stop looking at him that way, hungry, needing, open, reminding him of the emotional shit he'd said to her last night. She wanted him. Wanted him to go deeper, inside her body and no doubt inside her heart as well. And mother-fucker, he'd wanted that too!

Christ, hadn't he learned?

His gaze swung to the bathroom door. Did he believe that Emily Shiver was like Natalie? A liar and a manipulator? Or like Everett and Elena? Keeping him from his true self, his true family? No. But the fear that she might be kept the walls, the armor, unbreakable, and the shitty, hurtful words coming.

His gut clenched. That woman in there was trying like hell to get through to him. She was kind, funny, stunning—and she had his baby growing inside her. At the very least, she deserved an apology.

But instead of sitting down on the bed and waiting for her, he went to the bathroom door and turned the knob. Wasn't locked. His skin pulled around his muscles as he went inside. Steam enveloped him, causing him momentary blindness. But the closer he got to the shower, the more he could see. Her silhouette was art through the glass. Tall, long, with curves that made his insides liquid. Heat and anticipation pulsed through him as he started to strip.

What are you doing, asshole?
She's pissed at you.

His cock, as hard as granite, rested against his belly. Maybe she'd tell him to get lost, get out . . . he wouldn't blame her. But he had to try. He had to see her, look her in the eyes and know she didn't hate him, even though he was deserving of it.

He eased back the shower door and stepped inside. She was facing the spray, her eyes closed, letting the water just cascade over her. She had an amazing body. Long legs, tight, toned ass, curved waist, and breasts that begged for a man's hands— his hands.

He could barely contain the growl rumbling in his chest. Or the arms that wrapped around her waist as he sidled up close to her.

She gasped, then instantly relaxed, even pushing back into him. "Hey."

"Hey," he said, pressing a kiss to her shoulder. "Christ, Em . . . I'm sorry."

"Oh, Blue," she breathed. "Just talk to me. Please. Tell me why you don't want me to touch you."

"Darlin', I want it. You can feel how much I want it." He rolled his hips and groaned. "I want you. Right now. I want your hands on the shower walls, your ass in the air, and my cock buried deep inside your pussy."

She turned in his arms, stepped out of the spray. Her lips parted and she stared up into his eyes. "Then, why . . ."

Blue struggled with the answer. With saying it out loud. It was dark and ugly, and it was about him—not her. And yet he had to give her something. "I want this, Em. I want you. And it scares the shit out of me."

Her eyes pinned him. "I wouldn't hurt you. I wouldn't lie to you."

He let his hand drift from her belly upward. "I want so much to believe that."

When he cupped her breast, rolled her nipple between his thumb and forefinger, she moaned, "Then do."

His nostrils flared as she fisted his cock. "Not that easy."

A slow, sensual smile touched her lips. "But you'll try."

He returned that smile. "Fuck. Yes, I'll try." Then he groaned when she started stroking him. Her eyes were pinned to his as her hand moved up and down his shaft. Blue had felt ready to explode since last night, so it took every ounce of restraint he had in him to calm down and not come right then and there.

She forced him back against the tiles, dropped a hand on the side of his head, and just worked him over. She had magic hands, soft and wet, and Blue could only imagine her guiding his dick to the entrance of her pussy, slipping it inside.

He growled and let his head fall back against the tiles. He was so screwed up. *Just take what you want. Take what she wants to give you. What is your goddamn problem?*

Her eyes left his and she bent her head, ran her tongue over his right nipple.

"Fuck, yeah," he groaned.

Her grin was nearly audible. Blue put one hand on the glass door to steady himself. She'd latched on now, biting and sucking his nipple while she stroked him, using his pre-cum as a lubricant, running her thumb over the seam in the head of his cock.

Grinding himself into her hand, his ass clenching, he remembered that night. On his back, Emily above him, riding him, her hair around her shoulders, and the scent of flowers commingled with the scents of their arousal.

With a hard thrust and a guttural groan, he came. The lights shut off in his mind and he just allowed himself to feel. Her hand, hard strokes, then gentle, then release . . .

After a moment, she wrapped her arms around his waist and let her head fall to his chest. He pulled her closer. He was still partly erect, and he wanted to lift her up and place her down on him. Let her ride him, then press her back against the tiles and take her all the way to climax again. But the water suddenly turned cold and made the nearly impossible decision for him.

"Guess I'll be speaking to my landlord about this," she said dryly as he turned off the water and stepped out of the shower. "I want hours of hot water."

He had a towel waiting for her the second she emerged.

"James," he ground out. "Leave it to the Cavanaughs to ruin a perfectly good morning."

As he wrapped her in the fluffy white towel, Emily grinned up at him. "Nothing ruined here.

But I would say he just might've saved your virtue."

Ruined long ago, darlin', he wanted to say. But frankly, he'd said too much already. All he wanted was to just hold her.

Seventeen

"Come with me," Blue urged, leaning against the kitchen counter. "You've got to be hungry."

Emily let her gaze roam over his naked torso. "I am." Couldn't he just put on a shirt? He was killing her here.

His nostrils flared as he stared at her. "Swear to all that is holy, I'm not going to be able to get my ass out of here. Forget my 'virtue' as you call it; I'm in danger of losing my job. I have cattle coming this morning. Bought and paid for by me. I have to be there."

Clad in only a towel, Emily shrugged. "Okay." Then she gave him a bright smile. She was pretty sure she was trying to kill his virtue. Or his chivalry. Or whatever it was that was really keeping him from taking her against the counter right that very minute. Because truly she didn't understand why he was holding back. They'd been together before.

He crossed his arms over his perfect chest. "Can I come back?"

"Maybe," she said coyly. "When?"

"Well, I'm helping Steven and Jeremy with your stuff around four. Then I could just stay."

"I'll be at work until six."

"I could have dinner waitin' on ya," he suggested.

A smile broke on her face. She was pretty sure it rivaled the sun in its intensity. "Really?"

He nodded, grinned, seemingly pleased with her reaction. "Any requests?" he asked, his eyes heavy-lidded and sexy. He needed to stay over again. Morning Blue Cavanaugh was her favorite.

"I have a few," she answered, then slowly readjusted her towel, not being very careful of what parts were exposed to his gaze.

His eyes darkened. "Cattle, Emily."

She laughed and covered herself properly. "Fine."

"Dinner?" he growled. "Tell me."

"I'm not picky. I'm sure whatever you get will be great. Here." She reached over and grabbed the extra key off the counter and gave it to him. "Take this. So you can come and go, let my brothers in. It's for the private entrance. And whatever you do, don't lose it. We don't want your ex-girlfriend finding it and showing up here again, uninvited."

It was like all of the air was suddenly sucked out of the room. Blue's brow furrowed; then he stalked toward her. "What do you mean, again?"

"She came by when I was moving in yesterday," Emily explained, a little stunned by his ferocity. "She kind of hung around a little too long and said a few things . . ."

His face drained of color. "What did she say?"

"It was no big deal," she assured him. "I'm making it into something, obviously—"

He didn't buy it. "Emily."

She sighed. "She was talking about you, how great you are. I think she was fishing to see if we're dating or hanging out. I think she's still pretty hung up on you."

His face was a mask of apprehension. "Listen to me," he said, taking her hands, pinning her with his electric-blue gaze. "Deacon's PI might've found something that links her with the disappearance of a girl at a cooking school she attended in New Orleans."

A thread of unease moved through her. "What?"

"Natalie liked the girl's male roommate."

"Was the girl found?"

"No."

Now it was her turn for the facial blood drain. "Could be nothing. Could be a coincidence."

"Could be," he agreed. "But just as a precaution, I don't want you anywhere near her."

She broke away from him and headed back into the bedroom. "Not sure how that's possible unless I remain in this apartment twenty-four/seven."

He followed her. "I guess that would be pretty extreme."

"You think?" She laughed tightly, nervously. She didn't like this Natalie Palmer thing. She'd sensed something was off with the woman last night. "I'll just be really careful," she said, unzipping her duffel bag and taking out her uniform.

"Or maybe . . ." he started.

She glanced over her shoulder at him. "Maybe what?"

He shrugged, grabbed his shirt from the bed. "I dunno. Maybe you could rethink moving out."

Okay. "No way," she said with heat in her tone.

"I know we weren't really considering this seriously before, but you could always come home to the Triple with me," he added, tossing on his T-shirt.

"Don't start this again, Blue," she warned, giving him the serious-girl eyes. "You know what this means to me. Living here. On my own. How important I feel it is for me."

Fully dressed now, he went over to her. His eyes moved over her face. "Is it wrong for me to want to keep you safe?"

Her heart melted. Just like that. Ice cube in the blazing sun. "Of course not. I know you want to protect the baby—"

He didn't let her finish. "Now it's you who needs to stop. This isn't just about the baby and you damn well know it."

Did she? She wanted to believe that.

He took her by the shoulders. "You know how I feel about you."

"I know you care about me," she began.

"Shit, woman. It's more than that. Has turned into more than that. And I would never forgive myself if something happened to you."

"I get that, and I get the risk. But I'm not going to panic because of something the Cavanaugh brothers *think* they might know. Granted, that doesn't mean I'm going to be stupid either. I'll be safe and steer clear of her. Okay?"

The moment of silence that stretched out before them then felt like hours. Blue looked as though he was attempting to invade her thoughts while trying to keep his own hidden. She didn't like it when he did that. Filled her belly with unease.

"It'll be okay," she assured him. "Yeah?"

After a moment, he finally released a breath and nodded. "Okay."

She smiled softly. "I'll see you later."

"Yeah, you will."

"With dinner?" she added, widening that smile as she gathered up her purse and a jacket.

A sliver of warmth touched his eyes once again and he smiled back. "Can't wait, darlin'." Then he leaned in and gave her a kiss before leaving the apartment.

He's fucking her. Blue is fucking that stupid worthless waitress.

Inside Gaby's Books and Stuff, through the picture window at the front of the store, Natalie watched her man get into his truck and drive away.

That bitch had to be manipulating him in some way. It was the only reason Blue would do something like this. Natalie had to find out. Then she could help Blue. He was so vulnerable right now. With all he was going through. He'd shared everything with her. Told her she was the only one he trusted. The only one who understood him.

I'm sure he's told that bitch nothing.

Emily Shiver didn't truly care about him. And Blue needed to know that.

Eighteen

"Morning," Elena called as she entered the kitchen.

It was past breakfast time, and the kitchen was cleaned up already and shining in the sun. But Blue needed something to tide him over until lunch. Instead of grabbing a meal at Mirabelle's, he'd headed straight back to the ranch. His cows were coming in, and there wasn't time to order and go. "Just grabbing a few biscuits if that's all right."

"'Course it is." She gave him that strained, hopeful look he was used to. "How 'bout a little coffee to go with them?" She opened a cupboard and took out a large mug.

"I can get it."

"It's no trouble." She poured him a cup, placed it in front of him at the counter.

"Thanks," he said tightly.

"I didn't hear you come in last night."

He didn't answer. Just took a bite of the still-warm biscuit.

"Did you stay down by the river?" she fished.

"Nope."

"Oh."

A tense silence followed. Within Blue, that same conflict he'd been wrestling with for the past few days emerged once again. A need to connect, to share with his mom what was happening in his life. About Emily. About their news. About his feelings for this woman. He wanted to ask her advice, tell her how scared he was to give himself to somebody again. But the other part of him, the one that continually refused the call, started going back over all the instances of betrayal. His whole life was a lie. How did he forgive that?

"I've got cattle coming in," he said in a voice far gentler than Elena was used to.

"You could always bring her here," Elena said.

He gulped down the coffee, then said, "Not sure what you're talking about."

"I'd love to meet her," she added hopefully. "Is it someone I know?"

The expression on her face cut into him deep. She looked so excited, full of curiosity and life and caring. She looked truly happy for him. And she had no idea . . .

"Thanks for the coffee," he said tightly, rinsing the cup and putting it in the dish drainer. "And the biscuit."

He wasn't talking, wasn't sharing, and she understood that immediately. Her face fell; the glow of excitement gone in a heartbeat. " 'Course," she managed, opening a drawer and taking out a few place mats. "That's my job. Feed the cowboys."

For a second or two, he just stood there, disgusted with himself, watching as she set up for lunch. It was starting to get to her. Break her down. He could see it in her eyes. His apathy, his coldness. Everything in him, forged from a wonderful childhood with this person, told him to just let it fucking go, forgive her, move on. Maybe if he did, he could be with Emily. Really be with her. Not just as a father to her child.

And yet, his guard remained in place as he left the kitchen and headed for the front door.

Emily viewed the large table she'd just been given with interest and slight trepidation. They'd been in the Bull's Eye before. Many times, in fact. Separately, all together, and just the girls. In her gut she knew they'd asked for her section. What she didn't know was why.

She approached the table with an apprehensive smile. "Afternoon, folks. Can I start you off with something to drink?"

Mr. Ocean Eyes was the first to look up, first to smile with familiarity. "Hi, Emily."

She nodded. "Hello, James."

"Everything okay with the apartment?"

Well, the hot water . . . "All good." *And strangely, it came with your handsome half brother.* She left off both of those thoughts, the memory of last night and this morning still very much with her, making her belly clench. "Thanks again."

"My pleasure." He gestured to the woman beside him, the woman he was holding hands with. "This is my fiancée, Sheridan."

"Hi," Emily said. Sheridan was very pretty with her hair tucked in a bun, and far fancier than most of the women in River Black. She suspected Sheridan came from the city.

"It's so nice to meet you," she returned warmly.

"And you know my brother Cole," James said, pointing to the fierce but definitely good-looking tattooed man across from him. The man nodded. "And his fiancée, Grace."

Emily knew Grace. Probably best of the bunch. The town's veterinarian came into the Bull's Eye pretty frequently.

"Hi, Emily," Grace said. "It's good to see you again. Would you like to sit down?" The woman instantly realized what she'd said and grimaced. "I'm sorry. I know you're working." She glanced at Cole and shrugged her shoulders.

Emily eyed the Cavanaugh clan, and, not being someone who shied away from uncomfortable situations, she said on a sigh, "You all know, don't you?"

The women looked instantly sheepish, while Cole just stared at her hard like he was trying to read her mind.

"I don't think Blue meant to tell us," James admitted. "Came out when he was hollerin' at me about renting you the apartment."

Of course it did. Emily shook her head and blew out a breath. "I'm sorry for that."

"Don't be. That's not why he's mad at us."

"It's because he wants the Triple," Cole put in, his black eyes flashing.

"Chill out, Cole," Grace said, giving him a pointed look.

"I'm just laying all the cards on the table. Me and Deac are fixed with housing, of course, but James is still up in the air. Everett was a damn jackass for splittin' it four ways. He had to know what a problem he was causing. Probably why he did it."

"Or maybe he just wanted the four of you to talk," Grace tossed back.

"Not here, you guys," James told them. "Emily has nothing to do with any of that."

"Her baby does," Cole said, keeping his voice low, so only Emily and the people at the table could hear. "Or will. First Cavanaugh baby." He gave Grace a wink and a look that belonged behind closed doors. "First of many, I hope."

"I really need to get back to work," Emily interrupted, feeling as though she'd walked in on a family discussion that wasn't meant for her ears.

"Of course," James said. "Sorry."

"Really sorry," Grace put in, looking at Emily and trying to convey a girl-to-girl understanding. "I'll have a beer. Whatever's on tap."

"Same," Cole said.

When Emily had taken all the drink orders, she left the table and headed to the bar. *Well, that was uncomfortable*, she mused. *And enlightening.* So the Cavanaughs knew she and Blue were having a baby—well, most of them of anyway. She didn't know about Deacon and Mackenzie Byrd, although she could assume they probably knew too. And they were feeling what? Sentimental about it? Guarded? Worried? Suspicious? Blue did seem to be bent on owning the Triple C. She wondered what that dynamic was. Did James want it too?

Dean strolled back behind the bar, a bottle of red in his hand. "What do you need, Em?"

"Three tap, and a white wine," she told him.

"You got it."

As she stood there waiting, a thread of unease moved through her. This was a small town, and the news of her pregnancy was going to get out. Would she lose her job? Her gaze swung to Dean. He was filling glasses with cold beer. Her manager might not want some pregnant woman waiting tables in his bar. Kinda killed the mood . . .

She had a few months before she started showing, if she could keep her news quiet. A few months to find a new space and a loan. A few months to get the flower shop off and running.

"Here you go," Dean said, drawing her out of her thoughts.

"Thanks." Tray in hand, she headed back to the Cavanaughs' table. She was going to ask them, each of them, including the dark-eyed fierce one, to keep her pregnancy to themselves. For now. But she hadn't taken more than a few steps when she felt something. Something strange. Her heart skittered in her chest and she stopped between two four-tops and glanced around. She didn't know what she was looking for. Or who.

Her gaze traveled the entire bar, but there was nothing of note. Nothing strange. No creepy guy. No Natalie Palmer. Damn Blue. He was filling her head with fear, and now she was thinking she was seeing things—or feeling things.

Rolling her eyes, she headed for the Cavanaughs' table.

"You okay?" James asked her when she arrived, his concern real. "Saw you stopping short over there."

"Fine." There was no way she was bringing up Natalie now, to this crowd. But she did have something she needed to get off her chest. And this was as good a time as any. "Before I get your food order, can I ask a favor?"

The entire clan looked up and gave her their full attention.

"About this little bun I have in the oven . . ."

Nineteen

Well, hell, he was no gourmet or anything, but he'd sure picked up a few things from Elena over the years. One of them was how to make soup. His mother liked to say it was easy and filling and could be pretty comforting on a cold night. He'd paired it with some biscuits, which he'd bought from the diner, and he felt pretty good about what was waiting at home.

Not home, Blue corrected himself as he leaned back against a tree outside the Bull's Eye. That tiny apartment was Emily's place. Which was all hers, and decently furnished now, thanks to him and her brothers.

He checked his watch. Six o'clock. He hadn't wanted to go inside. Give her a chance to say no, tell him she was fine getting home on her own. Granted, she probably was. But he wasn't dealing in *probably*s anymore—not since he'd met her, and not since Natalie Palmer was skulking around.

"It's only a couple of blocks, you know?" she called out to him as she exited the bar in jeans and a brown leather jacket.

She looked hot. Pushing away from the tree, he grinned. He was starting to know this woman. "I'm trying to be a gentleman here. Walking a girl home."

When she reached him, she gave him a suspicious look. She knew his motives for waiting on her weren't purely chivalrous. But she didn't say anything about it.

"How was work?" He reached out and took her hand as they started back toward the apartment.

"Fine."

He didn't like that word. It meant too many things. "What happened?"

She shot him a look. "You need to relax, Blue."

Yeah, maybe he did. But his unease wasn't about this—about her. "Tell me."

Realizing he wasn't about to give up, she blew out a breath. "Some of your family was in today."

His gut turned. *Damn Cavanaughs.* "I don't have family," he said as they crossed the street. "Except for my mother, and she's never set foot in the Bull's Eye. That I know."

"I'm talking about the Cavanaughs," she said, interlacing her fingers with his. It was just a small thing, but it spoke to her comfort, her ease, with him. "And they don't see it that way. You're their brother whether you want to acknowledge it or not."

He snorted, unconvinced.

She glanced over at him and raised one eyebrow. "And thanks for spilling our beans, by the way. Our one little few-weeks-old bean."

He frowned. *Damn Cavanaughs.* "Didn't mean for it to come out. I'm sorry."

"It's okay. I've asked them to keep it to themselves. For a few months at least. I can't afford to lose my job right now."

"That's not going to happen," he said confidently, squeezing her hand. "But if it did, you know you're taken care of."

They reached the side door of her apartment. Emily stopped and looked at him. "Blue, listen to me. I'm not asking to be taken care of. By you, my parents, anyone. I don't want that. I'm finally in charge of myself, finally pushed myself out of the nest, and I'm not looking to fly back in. You understand?"

Conflicting emotions coiled within Blue. The part of him that wanted this woman, cared for her, and for the life growing inside her, felt like growling with irritation. Refusing her words. It was his job, his pleasure, to take care of her. But then there was the part of him that found her claim on independence admirable and damn sexy.

"Come on now, darlin'," he said. "Let's go upstairs."

Her brow lifted. "That's not a proper response."

He opened the door with his key. "I'm just saying we can argue this point inside as well as outside. Nice and warm in there, and far more comfortable."

Her eyes probed his, trying to find the root of

his humor and deflection—but she didn't push him to answer her previous question. In fact, she forgot it altogether when she stepped inside her apartment moments later.

The rich scent of chicken and vegetables wafted into her nostrils and made her smile. "Did you cook?" she exclaimed.

She looked so shocked by the possibility, he laughed. "I'm not completely useless around the house."

Her eyes flashed with a sudden heat. "Oh, I know."

That heat went straight into his gut and dropped. His nostrils flared. This desire he had for the woman before him seemed to keep growing. Keep intensifying. Right that very moment, the urge to take her into his arms and claim her mouth was hard-core.

Reservations be damned.

But he never got the chance. She eased her hand from his and started for the bathroom.

"I'm going to take a quick shower. Scrub the Bull's Eye off my skin."

Shower?

Oh, baby. Me want.

That primal part of him was screaming. Go after her—follow her, be her washcloth, that bar of soap. . . guiding it from her toes upward . . .

But once again, he refused himself the pleasure. With tight jeans and a tight jaw, he watched her go, then headed into the kitchen to grab a beer out of the refrigerator and check on the soup.

*   *   *

Emily's stomach was in love. Warm and happy and in love. "This is so good."

"You sound surprised," Blue said, glancing up from his steaming bowl of chicken soup.

"Maybe a little." She laughed. She was sitting across from her chef du jour at the extra dining set her parents had kept in the basement. It was small, perfect for an apartment, and Susie and Ben had insisted that Steven put it in the back of the truck. "The dinner," she continued. "The apartment. These flowers." She nodded in the direction of the glass vase with pink roses inside. "You and my brothers did a fine job today. Thank you."

"You're welcome. You know, I'm pretty decent at the caretaking." He shrugged. "I think I'll make a pretty good dad."

Her insides softened. If this man would just let the past go, let his anger and resentment go, and just trust—in both himself and her—they could really make a go of it. "I bet you had a good teacher," she said.

He was silent, and a muscle in his jaw twitched.

"Sorry," she said. "I know this is a sore subject right now."

"It's fine."

Her gaze traveled over him. Rigid, a heart full of pain. "Doesn't seem like it. You're not eating your soup anymore. And this is some killer soup."

His eyes connected with hers. They were a deep, thoughtful blue. "I don't know. With all I'm mad about, the grudge I'm holding on to for dear life, I can't deny her skills as a mother." That gaze turned a little sad. "She was the very best. She gave out the perfect amount of toughness and love. Taught me that being a man was about many kinds of strength."

"Not just muscles?" she teased ever so gently. She didn't want to lose the mood. Didn't want him to stop being vulnerable with her.

"Nope." His eyes softened to affection. "Character and drive, honor and kindness."

"I like the sound of that." She ate a little more of her soup. "Have you told her, Blue?"

His brows came together. "About?"

"The baby?"

"No." He picked up his spoon and started eating again.

"You plan to?"

"I don't know."

She watched him. Granted, it had been hard telling her parents. They weren't rigid in their beliefs or anything, but explaining a baby born out of what she'd told them was a very short-term relationship was rough in any family. But to actually contemplate not telling them at all . . . about their grandchild . . .

"Right or wrong," Blue began, his expression darkening. "Well, it's a sort of gift to know about the baby." His eyes lifted and connected with hers. They were resolute. "I'm not giving her any gifts right now. She doesn't deserve them."

A tingle of tension settled over Emily's heart. "This part of you scares me, Blue."

"Which part is that?" he asked tightly.

"The cold, unfeeling, unforgiving part."

"Well, I'm sorry, but I have reasons for the way I am, the way I react."

"I believe it. Anger and bitterness are real and reasonable feelings—reactions to the tough shit that happens in life."

"But . . . ," he prodded, ripping apart his biscuit with no intention of eating it.

"But they're not building blocks to anything good, anything solid and lasting. If they're held on to, they only destroy and keep on destroying."

His expression hardened. "You don't understand."

"Maybe not," she agreed. "I've never gone through what you're going through." She wiped her mouth with her napkin. "But I don't think what you're doing is going to give you the results you want."

"And what do you think I want?" he asked coolly.

That chill didn't push her off or scare her. She told him. "Protection . . ."

He snorted, grinned.

"From getting your heart broken. Again. And again."

The grin faded. He stared at her, his biscuit and soup completely forgotten now.

"Like I said last night, I'm not looking to do that," Emily said, her own food a distant memory as well. "Not sure you believe me—or can allow yourself to believe me—but there it is."

His eyes were so fierce as he stared at her. Like

he was trying to see straight through her, or into her—into her mind and soul. See what she was truly thinking—if what she'd just said could possibly be sincere.

And then he pushed back his chair and stood.

Emily looked up at him. "You want to leave, don't you?"

"No."

"Blue . . ."

He reached for her. "I want to go to bed."

Twenty

With a hum of desperation, of need, running through his blood, Blue placed Emily at the foot of the bed and started to undress her. He felt on edge, a little insane . . . Everything she'd just said had been too close to the mark. It made sense, and right now he didn't want sense. Refused it. Because sense called for him to leave this apartment and go back to the Triple, continue treating his mother like shit and turn his back on everything that was once so important to him.

Her eyes, those huge pools of lust and confusion, searched his for answers, for assurance. *Everything's going to be okay, darlin'. Promise.* He lifted her gray tank over her head and let it fall to the floor. Then he unclipped her bra and tossed that away too. Christ, she was beautiful, perfect. Too perfect. Thoughts ripped through his mind. He hadn't wanted to argue with her. Hadn't wanted to hear her opinions of him. Her truth. Even her assurance that she was different, that she wouldn't hurt him.

Off came her black pj bottoms. She wasn't wearing underwear, and his chest tightened as he eased her back on the bed. The bed he'd made for her today. A real bed—forget the futon. Though, shit, they'd had fun on that too. His gaze moved over her, hungrily, covetously. "You are one beautiful woman, Emily Shiver."

Her eyes glistened, but not with appreciation. "And you make my heart hurt."

He groaned. "Don't say that."

"You're holding on to so much, Blue. You don't have to. You really don't." She came up on her elbows, completely at ease with herself, her stunning nudity. Or maybe it was just that she was so focused on him. "None of what's happened has to control you or define you. Or decide your present. Only you can do that."

His chest was so tight it ached. He shook his head.

"I know you want me to stop talking," she continued. "I know you want to push it all away and pretend it doesn't exist—"

"Just for an hour or two," he cut in with a bitter edge.

She looked up at him, and behind her eyes he saw her grappling with what he'd said. How she wanted to respond to it. Continue to push him or just let it be, let him work out his demons his way.

"I want you, Blue," she said with a strange melancholy to her tone.

He shrugged out of his shirt, then knelt down, his hands cupping her knees. He knew what she meant. His heart and guts knew too. He hungered for that closeness. It was nearly unbearable to him, and yet as he eased her thighs apart and settled himself between them, he shook his head. Fuck, what was wrong with him? After all they'd done, experienced—everything he'd touched and tasted, everything she'd explored—it seemed nonsensical to keep sex out of the equation. But he knew that if he took her again, this time would be different. So different. This time, he'd want to claim her, keep her.

This time, she would be inside him as much as he was inside her.

"I need this, Emily," he said, hating how harsh and desperate his voice sounded. "I need you. This way." He ran his hands up her thighs. "Can I shut down, turn off my brain . . . Christ, my heart . . . and just have you the way I want to have you?"

Her eyes, so conflicted yet so turned on, searched his, probed his, and then Blue dropped his head and kissed her sex. Just one, sweet, soft kiss. When he glanced back up, her lips were parting, her chest was rising and falling rapidly, and she nodded.

Hunger seized him. The kind that couldn't be satiated. He wondered if it ever could as he looked at her, his hands pressed inward across her hips.

She was so soft, so warm. He could barely wait to taste her. Gently, he opened her, his thumbs splaying her wide. His gaze dropped. Pink, wet, and so ready.

He licked her. One slow swipe from sex to clit.

"Oh, Blue," she groaned.

He grinned. She was truly his heaven. His place to get lost for days. His place to forget and just be . . .

For just a few seconds, just to make himself wait, make himself crazy with lust, he let his mouth trail over her lower abdomen. The scent of her skin made every inch of him hard. He let his head drop and he nuzzled her hot pussy. He was so hungry, so desperate for her.

As he circled his tongue over her clit, she cried out and let her head fall back. There was nothing better than tasting, scenting, and feeling her desire. She arched her back, canted her hips, and bucked hard against his mouth. Blue slipped his hands under her backside and took the opportunity to tug and suckle on her clit. The action made her wild. Moaning, rocking, she was hard to control.

But, Christ Almighty, he loved it.

He moved down an inch and thrust his tongue inside her.

"Oh yes," she cried. "You inside me. Any way I can get it."

Her words shot into him, straight to his heart. But he pushed the feeling of loss away. She was his. Right now, she belonged to him.

Her hands found his shoulders and she dug her

nails into his skin. And then he spread her wide with his thumbs and ate her. His tongue lapping at her juices, his lips sucking, his teeth gently scraping.

With a hard thrust against his mouth, she came. Her fingernails dug deeper and her head thrashed from side to side. And yet, Blue kept on tasting her. Taking her climax, claiming her pleasure.

And when she started to come down, easily rocking against his mouth, he didn't release her. No. He wasn't about to let her descend. He was still so thirsty.

He thrust two fingers inside her and uttered hoarsely, hungrily against her pussy, "Again."

"It's my day off," Emily grumbled good-naturedly as Blue led her down the stairs. She was exhausted. But in this strange, unfulfilled way. Even after Blue had given her climax after climax, her body still wanted more.

It wanted him.

And he was refusing her.

No. He was refusing himself.

She'd always wondered what guys meant when they talked about blue balls. Well, now she knew.

He lifted her hand to his lips as they hit the bottom stair, his eyes heavy-lidded. "That's why I want to take you to breakfast, darlin'."

"We could have breakfast here," she suggested with a saucy wink.

He opened the door for her and cold morning air rushed at them. "Leftover soup?"

She smiled knowingly at him. "Does a body good."

Before she could take another breath, she was in his arms, pressed hard against him, and he was kissing her—smack dab in the middle of the sidewalk. Lord, she could kiss him for days, weeks. A straight month if work wasn't a factor.

When he finally released her, she tried hard to catch her breath. "That does a body good too."

He laughed.

"Fine, fine, breakfast at Mirabelle's," she said, trying to slow her heart as they moved down the sidewalk. "Besides, I need to stop by the real estate agency anyway and get Aubrey Perdue going on some new rental spaces."

"The flower shop?"

"Mm-hmm."

"How long have you been wanting to do that?"

She sighed thoughtfully. "A few years. I've always loved flowers. How they can change a person's mood in an instant. How each flower, each color, means something different to each person. Their memories, their traditions. When I was little, I used to insist we have fresh flowers, which were mostly wild flowers, mind you, on the kitchen table every day." She looked over at him. Expecting a reaction, a smile of understanding, of camaraderie. But he was staring past her.

"What is it?" she asked.

He stopped at the corner just a few feet away from Mirabelle's, his eyes darkening with fury.

When she turned to see what he was looking at, her heart lurched. Releasing his hand, she walked over to the light pole and yanked down the bright pink flyer that had been taped there.

"What the hell is this?" she ground out. Her eyes narrowed. It was a picture of her from a few years ago with the caption PREGNANT over her head. And underneath: BY WHOM?

Blue was beside her, radiating anger. "I'm going to kill them."

"Them?" she repeated, stunned, shocked, sickened, still staring at the flyer.

"The Cavanaughs."

This time, she turned to look at him. "You don't believe they did this."

"They're the only ones who—"

"No way," she interrupted, shaking her head. "It's not them."

"Then who?"

A slow, startling revelation crept over her. It made bile rise in her throat. Blue had been right. The girl was dangerous. More than dangerous. Diabolical. "This is something a woman does. Out of spite, immaturity, and the perceived belief that I took her man."

"Natalie?" he breathed.

She nodded. "Best guess. I can't image who else would feel the need to humiliate me."

"But how would she know you're pregnant?"

"It's not as much of a secret anymore, is it? My family, your family." She cursed. "Someone must've blabbed or forgotten they were in earshot when they talked about it. And that girl is a lurker."

"Jesus, Em," he whispered. "Fuck. I'm so sorry."

"For what? You didn't do this."

" 'Course I did. She and I—"

"Had an online relationship built on lies."

"Yes, but it was more than that. Granted, we never even met in person. But, Christ, maybe what I did share was the most intimate part of me. I was hurting. Pissed. And she was everything I needed . . . the best listener . . . so kind. She knew me, my feelings, my fears . . . I believed, and I fell."

Emily shook her head. "Jesus. No wonder you can't trust me."

"Don't say that." He dragged a hand through his hair. "At first I thought she was just a liar, but clearly she's got a major screw loose. She thinks there's a bond that's been built between us. She thinks I need saving from you."

"Don't you?" She couldn't help herself. In all the madness, she would reach for humor. Perspective.

Blue's eyes blazed down into hers. "Absolutely not." Then he took her hand. "Come on. Let's forget about this and go eat."

" 'K." She followed him. "How many people do you figure saw this? Do you think there are more?"

He never got the chance to answer, because the second they walked into the diner, the question was answered for them. Granted, there were only ten or so customers in Mirabelle's, but every single one of them not only looked up when she and

Blue entered, but looked directly at Emily's stomach.

"Guess maybe I should skip breakfast and go find the other flyers that are most assuredly posted up around town," she said dryly.

"What are you all gaping at?" Blue called out. He sounded about as fierce as he looked. "Nothing to see here."

"Don't, Blue," she told him. "I don't care."

"I care." He pointed at a couple of men at the counter. "Jerry Duffy, Earl Waverly, you got food in front of you. I suggest you get back to it if you know what's good for you. Same goes for the rest of you."

While she appreciated Blue's strength, championing her the way he was, she felt embarrassed and confused, and honestly a little scared. Her appetite was definitely gone, and she just wanted to get out of there and try to figure out what to do next.

"You stay," she whispered to him before leaving the diner. "I've got work to do."

Twenty-one

He didn't give a shit about food. After giving the occupants of Mirabelle's a death stare, he followed Emily out the door. He couldn't imagine how she was feeling, what this would mean for her in such a small town. Granted, River Black wasn't over-the-top provincial, but it had its unspoken moral-ity clauses. Just to be outed this way—so brutal and hostile. As if she'd done something wrong.

He spotted her right off. She was moving down Main with purpose, her gaze shifting from one side of the street to the next. Christ Almighty, it was worse than he'd even imagined. Bright pink flyers were affixed to every surface. Some blowing in the wind, not as tightly fastened to their surfaces as others. He even saw a teenage kid holding one as he skateboarded down the middle of the street.

Anger rippled through him. He was going to take care of this. Make it right. After he took care of Emily, of course.

Blue caught up with her pretty easily. She'd already pulled off one flyer, and when she reached for another, he did it for her.

Emily jerked out in front of him, her eyes a little wild, her nostrils flared. "No," she told him. "I want to do it."

"I'm just trying to help you," he began.

"No." She was rigid, furious, her face a mask of vitriolic determination. Not that he blamed her one damn bit. He was pretty much there himself. Natalie Palmer was going to feel his wrath.

"Emily," he said, pushing the gentle tone, "I want to help, be by your side through this. It's about us, for crissakes."

"That's where you're wrong," she ground out. "There's nothing on this piece of paper that says us or you."

His guts twisted a fraction. "What I mean is that it's our baby they're talking—"

"Not they," she cut him off. "Her. And right now, it's my baby."

Her words startled him, filled him with a cold dread. Made his chest ache. "What are you talking about?"

She looked away, breathed a couple of heavy breaths. "Just that in this situation, I'm on my own." She caught sight of something, and her eyes narrowed. "Goddammit!" Then she took off, barely looking both ways before she hurried across the street toward the market.

A rumble of fear moved through Blue. *Right now, it's my baby*? Shit, she couldn't say stuff like that to him. Not now. Not ever. He knew she was upset, lashing out, confused, and he didn't blame her. But this was cruelty. Tossing this in his face. Warning, threatening . . . On her own—just her and the child. She didn't need him, didn't want him.

Blue stood there on the street, a couple of pink flyers tumbling past in the wind. Sure it was cruel. Her lashing out this way. But he'd set it up for her to believe that, think that way—feel alone. Right? Hadn't he? Yes, he'd been hanging around, staying the night, showing a fierce interest in the child, making soup—yet he'd refused to make love, refused to get as close as two people could.

Pain laced through him. This was his doing. The whole goddamn thing. Natalie had thought she could get away with this because he hadn't shown her, or anyone else, for that matter—including the woman he was falling for—that Emily was important to him.

That she was who he wanted.

Fuck . . . What an idiot he was. A stupid, stubborn idiot. With a growl of frustration, he took off down the street, following her, watching as she pulled a flyer off the window of the market. What the hell had he done? He'd let down his defenses and allowed that crazy woman inside his mind and heart. And yet he couldn't allow Emily in there?

No wonder she was so pissed.

No wonder she'd just pushed him away.

No. Given up on him.

He was just a half a block away when the door to the market opened and out came Elena. At first his mother didn't see him, but when she turned to check traffic to her right, their eyes met. Locked. She opened her mouth; then her gaze went to the glass, then left to Emily—the woman he was clearly pursuing. When she looked back at him, there were so many things playing behind her stunned gaze he wasn't sure what she was feeling. Then she turned away and crossed the street.

Emily was coming back his way. She'd seen Elena, seen the silent exchange. "Go," she said when she reached him.

He shook his head. "No. It's fine."

"Go after her," she pushed. "Go talk to her. That's your mother, isn't?"

"I'm with you right now," he said with a touch of heat.

She looked disappointed. Maybe even a little disgusted. Like she wondered if he was using her as an excuse not to talk to his mother. And shit, maybe he was. Christ, he was messed up.

"I told you I'm not wanting company right now," she said. "I'm going to take care of this on my own."

Wasn't it only an hour ago when they were kissing, flirting. . . . "We should do this together," he insisted.

That sent her over the edge. "Why are you pretending like we're a team?" she demanded, her eyes narrowed on his. "Together? You don't even feel close enough to fuck me."

His jaw tightened. "I hate when you talk like that."

"You need to be talked to like that," she countered. "You need to be told to get over your shit and move on before it's too late and we all walk away from your ass." She inched closer, her nostrils flaring. "I understand now why you won't make love to me. Why you'll touch me, go down on me—all in the name of making me feel good, and in turn that makes you feel good. It's really because you're too afraid to connect with me. Get lost in me the way you so badly want to." Her eyes filled with tears. "I'm tired of this. And, God"—her voice broke—"we haven't even really started."

He stared at her, his chest held by an invisible vise. Everything she'd just said to him was true. One hundred percent.

"I think we need a break from each other," she said, wiping her eyes.

His nostrils flared. "I don't want that."

"I don't care," she said. "I need it. I have a lot to figure out, and I've got to have a clear head to do it. Go home, Blue."

She walked away from him then, and headed down the street. His chest so tight he could barely breathe, Blue stared after her, watching as she stopped whenever she encountered a flyer. Watching as she ripped each one up with vigor and tossed the remains in the trash.

*   *   *

Diary of Cassandra Cavanaugh

Dear Diary,

Sometimes I look at Mom and Dad and wonder how they found each other. I mean, I know how—I know the story. But why they thought they were meant to be together is what I'm thinking about. Don't get me wrong. I'm glad they did. Otherwise I wouldn't be here. Or Cole and James and Deacon. We wouldn't be a family. It's just, I don't know, when they look at each other it's just . . . blah. Not like when Sweet and I look at each other.

Do the fireworks that everyone talks about stop at some point? Do they just go away? Do you give them to someone else?

Eeep!

I hope not. I want to be with Sweet forever.

Can't sleep,
Cass.

Leaning against the ring in the center of his nearly open River Black gym, Cole glanced up from the diary and shrugged. "What do you think she meant by that? Do you think she suspected something? About Dad?"

"I think she was conflicted," Deacon answered, then gave the heavy bag he'd been knocking around for the past twenty minutes three solid punches. He was starting to tire. He didn't know

how Cole did this for hours every day. "About
Sweet. Worried he'd stop liking her."

Cole didn't look convinced. He'd been obsessed
with the diary since Blue had discovered it. Trying
to piece things together. Deacon was taking everything one step at a time, making sure each piece of
the puzzle got to his PI, then on to Deputy Shiver.

He sent his fists into the bag. One, two. One,
two. Right now, he wasn't in the business of convincing his little brother of anything. He just
wanted to get out some aggression, some stress,
and Cole's new gym was near close to perfect. He
was taking the speed bag next. Then the ring. Cole
was lethal, could kick serious ass, but maybe he'd
go easy on his big brother. At least until his big
brother trained enough to return the favor.

"Your jacket's buzzin', Deac," Cole called out,
then grabbed the thing and tossed it at him.
"Think fast."

His hands being all taped up, Deacon had a
hard time catching the leather jacket, and it ended
up with one sleeve between his wrists and the rest
on the ground. He gave Cole a snarl.

Cole grinned. "You want training, I'll give you
training. First lesson—reflexes."

Pulling out his phone, Deacon snorted. "I can't
wait for the day when I'm capable of taking you
down like I did when we were kids."

"You're going to be waiting awhile, brother,"
Cole returned, grabbing the bag Deacon had been
using and giving it a shockingly hard hit.

Cursing, Deacon turned his attention to the text before him. He read it. Then read it again. He must've been taking some time, because Cole started to get antsy, and curious.

"What's up?" Cole asked. "Is it Mac? Everything okay?"

"It's Deputy Shiver. Wants us to come to the station."

Cole was instantly alert. He hugged the bag to make it stop moving. "Why? Does he say why? Did they find something?" He ran a hand through his hair. "Shit, already? I didn't think we'd hear anything—"

"Cole." Deacon gave his brother a look. "Take it easy. Doesn't say what it's about."

He started pacing. "Well, it's gotta be about Cass, right? I mean, what else is there?"

Deacon wasn't going to speculate. Wasn't in his nature. He ripped the tape off his hands, then threw on the leather jacket over his sweaty T-shirt. "Come on," he said, grabbing his keys. "I'll drive."

"What about James?" Cole asked.

"You text him."

"And Mac?"

Mac. He told his beautiful, hardheaded wife everything. Shared everything. It was how they'd gotten so incredibly tight as a couple in the past several months. No secrets, no pretending. But he knew she was taking the evening off. Branding new cattle all morning, she needed some relaxing time. "I'll wait to text Mac until I know what this is about."

"You sure?" Cole asked as they headed out of the gym and into the parking lot.

"'Course I am."

Ever since Deacon had been knee-high to a grasshopper, he'd taken on the role of the protector, the planner. There were times when he'd felt too much like a mini adult. But for the most part, he'd relished the role.

Until Cass had been taken, that is.

After that, he'd wanted nothing to do with family responsibility. Hell, he'd wanted nothing to do with family, period. But lately, things had changed. He'd fallen back—maybe he'd stepped back—into that role. Cole and James, they looked to him for counsel. And he was thinking that maybe someday Blue might, too. Sure they argued and pissed each other off, but that was just the way of men. Of blood.

Blood.

But the closer they got to finding out the truth of what had happened to Cass, the more Deacon was starting to feel like running. Disconnecting again. Not that he'd let the others know about his feelings. After all, he was their leader, their protector. Only Mac would know that stuff. That private stuff.

He grinned to himself. After all, she was *his* leader, wasn't she? *His* protector.

"You sure you don't want to take my truck?" Cole said when they were nearing the vehicles. "It's way faster than yours."

Deacon gave him an imperious look—an older,

wiser, cooler-brother look—and chided, "You keep telling yourself that, little brother. All the way to the station." Then he unlocked the door to his brand-new night-black Ford F-450 with one easy click.

"Dang," Cole drawled. "When'd you get her . . . ?"

Twenty-two

It was sunset by the time Blue could get loose from work and take care of what needed to be taken care of. The slightly suburban-feeling neighborhood, dotted with ten or so small, tidy houses, was quiet, its residents ready for dinner, some television, then off to bed. Too bad they were going to be interrupted, shaken up a bit. Their meals postponed. Because Blue intended to make some damn noise tonight. First telling that woman he wanted nothing more to do with her—then making her understand, crystal clear–like—that if she was to ever bother, threaten, or talk to Emily Shiver again, he wouldn't stop until Natalie was behind bars. As he stalked up the stone pathway, his insides were so tight with anger he felt near to exploding. Right away he saw lights on and smelled something baking. But the sugary stench just turned his stomach. His hard rap on the door echoed through the neighborhood.

"Blue!" Natalie exclaimed the moment she opened the door. She was barefoot, wearing a peach-and-white dress, and her hair was mussed. As he stood there, her gaze moved over him in a covetous yearning way that made his lip curl.

"Come in," she said. "I just made scones."

He ignored the offer. He wanted nothing from her but the assurance that she was never going to do something so stupid and vile ever again. He pulled out ten flyers from inside his jacket, ripped them in half, and let them fall onto the stoop.

Natalie glanced down, then back up at him. "Littering is against the law," she said in an almost playful way.

"So is defaming someone's character," he rebutted with absolute seriousness.

Clearly, she'd expected this. His coming to see her. Shit, maybe she'd even posted those flyers to get him back here. God, the woman was sick.

She was staring at him, feigning a look of confusion. "I'm sorry. I don't understand."

But Blue had zero patience. "Listen to me, and really hear what I have to say," he said very slowly. "You and I are nothing. We will never be anything. Our e-mails and texts were a joke. A game. You were playing me—"

"I wasn't," she cut in, finally dropping the confused coquette act. "I loved you," she said with such passion it made Blue draw back an inch or two. "I still love you," she added.

He shook his head. "Honey, you don't know the meaning of that word." Granted, neither had he.

Not in a romantic way, at any rate. Not until Emily. "It's twisted up inside your mind."

Tears suddenly pricked her eyes and her lower lip quivered. "Blue. You're being unnecessarily cruel."

"I hope you get help," he said. "I really do. For Cass's sake, for Erica Keller—that was her name, right?"

It was as if Natalie's carefully constructed world started to melt right before his eyes. It was a question she hadn't expected him to ask her. Her eyes bulged and she kept opening and closing her mouth like a fish.

He leaned against the doorframe and whispered, "I don't know if you'll ever be held accountable for your actions, but if you touch one hair on Emily Shiver's head, you will find justice from me."

"Oh, Blue." A single tear snaked down her cheek and she shook her head.

"You don't believe me?" he asked.

"No. It's not that. It just . . . well, it makes me sad, that's all." Was that a look of pity in her eyes? A thread of unease moved up his spine. "To see you being taken in again."

Christ, the woman was pathetic as well as insane, and he wasn't going to waste his time on her another second. Not when he could be with Emily. Making it up to Emily.

Making love to Emily.

He pushed back, away from the door. His brows knit together. "Remember what I said, Natalie."

"You're not sure," she said. "Are you, Blue?"

He ignored her, turned around, and headed down the path.

"If the baby is really yours?" she continued.

He kept walking. Sad, pathetic . . .

"It's your pattern," she cried out. "Don't you see that? You've learned nothing! I tried to help you!"

Blue knew he was listening to the ramblings of a crazy person, but her words—that last bit, at any rate—well, that couldn't help but penetrate his damaged armor and sting his newly emerging heart.

A bath had never felt so good.

Emily had seen three properties today. Two in town and one in the next town over. She hadn't liked any of them. Of course, maybe they were all tainted by the memory of those oh-so-special and informative flyers, she thought, sinking deeper beneath the bubbles. Flyers that had been seen not only by her brothers, but by her mom and dad as well.

Embarrassed, humiliated? Maybe. Probably. Not by the fact that she was pregnant. I mean, this was 2015, for goodness' sake. But by having it plastered around town in such an ugly, malicious way.

Blue had been trying to reach her all day. Text, e-mail, phone. In that order. He was worried about her. Hated what Natalie had done—if it was indeed her—though Emily was convinced of it. Finally, she'd told him by text that she was serious when she'd said she was taking her time. She needed it. Deserved it.

No visitors.

No bed partners.

'Course, she hadn't said that last bit. But it was sure implied. And he'd had the respect to leave it alone.

There was a part of her, however . . . well, many parts, in fact . . . that would've loved seeing him tonight. Having him over. Sharing this large claw-foot tub, then her bed afterward. But that was dangerous. She'd learned something as she'd ripped down a good fifty flyers today. She wasn't okay with being just Blue Cavanaugh's baby mama. Or Blue Cavanaugh's quasi booty call. If this was going to go any further, she wanted him to snap out of it—the malaise, the self-pity party. She wanted him to forgive his family and himself, grow up, and be the boyfriend and partner they both wanted him to be. Hell, if he really wanted to be a good father, as he'd claimed, then this was the first step.

Her hands went to her belly beneath the warm water. Flat, but with promise. She smiled at that. It reminded her of something her mother often said when Emily had come home from school angry or frustrated. A promise doesn't come from wishing and hoping, but from an unapologetic demand.

Maybe that was it. With Blue. If she wanted a promise, she had to demand it.

Without apology, of course.

Twenty-three

He didn't want to go in the house. This house that both tormented him as well as welcomed and soothed him. This house that he'd wanted more than anything to stake claim to; yet he couldn't seem to push out the three men who truly belonged there. This house that had seen nearly every damn milestone of his young life.

Leaning back in the same wicker chair he'd sat in as a boy, Blue stretched his legs out. Nothing felt right anymore. Not since Everett had passed. Not since he'd found out the truth. Not since crazy Natalie had sought him out online. And definitely not since Emily.

His gut ached. That night—that incredible night that had changed the course of his future in ways he'd never imagined. And in ways that made him indescribably happy.

Emily's face swam before him. He missed her. Missed her humor, her smile, her strength, the smell of flowers that always seemed to cling to her skin. Goddammit. Had he screwed this thing up between them? Irrevocably? She didn't want to see him. Wanted time. Whatever that meant. Maybe it was just code for—we're done. You're an ass who couldn't see the amazing beauty and possibility that was standing right in front of him.

He heard the screen door open, then his mother's voice call to him, "Cold out here."

"Yup," he answered.

She didn't say anything for a minute. Just walked over to stand in front of him. He'd been waiting to see if she was going to approach him after what had happened today—what she'd seen and assumed coming out of the market.

Her gaze tried real hard to connect with his. And when it finally did, she said, "You're going to have a baby?"

His heart squeezed. "Yes."

Her eyes searched his; then she looked away and cursed. "Oh, Blue, I'm so disappointed in you."

"Is that so?"

"I had to find out in town, from a ridiculous flyer. Well, first I heard it from Kemp inside the market. Didn't know it was you who'd . . ." She inhaled deeply, shook her head again.

Blue's jaw tightened. "Doesn't feel too good, does it? Hearing the truth from the wrong person?"

Her eyes came back to him then and narrowed. "You did this on purpose. Didn't you? You wanted me to find out this way."

Truth was, he hadn't planned a damn thing. He hadn't wanted her to find out like that. In fact, in the deep recesses of his heart, he'd been hoping that someday soon they'd reconcile and he could give her the good news himself. Over a cup of coffee at the kitchen table.

But he didn't deny her accusation, so she took it as confirmation.

Her eyes glittered with sadness. A deep, long-held sadness that he'd never seen on her face before. It worried him—made him want to pull it back. Let this whole fucking thing go. Forgive. Finally. Or ignore. Maybe move on.

But she didn't give him the chance.

"Okay," she said softly, nodding. "Okay, Blue. You've hurt me. Like you wanted to. A knife slicing deep. But guess what. I'm done now. I can't keep apologizing or trying to explain or make amends to someone who wants none of it." She gave him a hard, pointed look. "You have what you want."

"And what is that?" he asked, his voice no longer edged with heat or anger or bitterness. He was tired too.

She shrugged and said very simply, "I'm out of your life."

And with that, she walked past him, down the drive, and toward the stream, leaving him alone in the cold night air, his gut aching like someone had gone and punched the hell out of him.

And maybe they had.

And maybe he deserved it.

*   *   *

"Evenin', Deputy," Cole called as he and Deacon entered the lockup.

Deacon said nothing. He wasn't in the mood. Not for small talk. Not for light banter or friendly conversation. His heart was heavy, his guts ached a little. And as soon as they were seated in Deputy Shiver's office, he got right to the point.

"Why are we here, Shiver?"

The deputy looked like he wasn't up for any *How you doing tonight*s either. He glanced down at the open folder on his desk. "We spoke with the authorities in New Orleans about Natalie Palmer."

Every muscle in Deac's body went tight. Christ, was this what they'd been waiting for? For so damn long? "And?"

The deputy's eyes lifted to meet his. They were coated in shadow. "Seems she had an alibi the night Erica Keller went missing."

"Fucking unbelievable," Cole ground out.

"Impossible's more like it," Deacon said, his tone darker, harsher than he intended. But goddammit, how many times were they going to run headfirst into this same brick wall? "My PI would've found information like that."

Shiver shrugged. "You'd think."

"What is this alibi?" Deacon demanded, leaning forward in his chair. "I want to check it out."

"A guy who says they were at a museum together. Strangely, that person left the country a year ago. The authorities told me they had no way of contacting him."

It felt like a white-hot poker was slowly pressing into Deacon's chest now. Cass . . . Fuck, she deserved this. Deserved the truth. Deserved to rest in peace.

"This is bullshit," Cole blurted out.

"Not to mention incredibly convenient," Deacon added blackly.

To his surprise, Deputy Shiver agreed. "Does seem that way, doesn't it?" he said.

Cole glanced over at Deacon, brows raised.

"You don't believe it?" Deacon asked Shiver.

The Deputy snorted, crossed his arms over his chest. "I can smell a cover-up from a mile away. Or a couple hundred miles as the case may be."

Deacon was stunned. He'd expected a lecture on pushing for answers that'd never come. But this—

"I'm here." James came blustering into the room. He looked and smelled like he'd been rolling in manure. And he knew it too. "Sorry about that. Having some trouble with Arnie Caborn's new mare. What did I miss?"

"More roadblocks when it comes to Natalie's past," Deacon informed him.

"Total bullshit," Cole put in.

"Hey . . ." Deputy Shiver had his laptop open and was typing furiously. Then he stopped. "This is interesting."

"What?" James asked, coming to stand beside Deac's chair.

"When you check family names. There's a Detective Palmer in the precinct of the next parish over." He looked up—and at each one of them in turn. He shrugged lightly. "Could be a coincidence . . . could be a reason for a cover-up."

"Fuck," Cole ground out. "I swear we're never going to get this resolved. Cass's life—her death . . . she deserves justice."

Steven inhaled deeply and let it out. "It's true that I can't do much with the detective. Big city, out of state, doesn't like to work with a small-town local . . ." His eyes locked with Cole's. "But I'm taking it on anyway."

"You are?" Deacon said, surprised.

Shiver nodded. "Yup."

"Why?" James asked.

The man's brow arched. "She messed with my family. Or so my sister believes."

Deacon didn't know what the man was talking about, but James quickly explained. He'd seen the flyers plastered all over town, had heard the talk. Hadn't known they'd been the product of Natalie though, but clearly Deputy Shiver did.

"She's a menace," Cole said. "Needs to be off the street."

"Unfortunately you can't arrest a person for spreading gossip," James pointed out.

"No," Deputy Shiver agreed. "But it gives me the right to watch her like a goddamned hawk."

Twenty-four

Dean looked at her like she was crazy instead of pregnant. "What are you talking about, Em?" he asked. "'Course you're not fired."

Emily had worked a long day at the Bull's Eye and hadn't had a chance to speak to her boss. So when her shift was nearly up, she'd headed straight for his office. She'd wanted to get everything out on the table, let him express his feelings—let him know she knew her future at the bar wasn't clear.

"I'm sure you've heard," she began, seated across from him, a small desk separating them, ". . . or seen the flyers . . ."

"I have," he confirmed. "Whoever did that was an asshole of the first order. Any idea who it was?"

"Yes, I have an idea," she said loosely. Even though it was more than that, she didn't want to disclose it to her manager. The drama of Natalie Palmer couldn't bleed into her work life. She needed it too much. "I've taken down every flyer I found, so let's hope that's that." But even as she said the words, she wasn't hopeful. Natalie seemed pretty determined to cause trouble. What she thought up next might even be worse.

"But it's true?" he asked, his eyes searching her. "You're going to have a kid?"

She inhaled deeply. "It's true."

He nodded, remained thoughtful for a second, then said, "I know this isn't your ultimate goal, Emily. Working at the Bull's Eye. I remember thinking when you came in with those flowers for every table that your ship was probably set for another port. But I want you to know that you will always have a job here for as long as you want it."

Emily hadn't realized just how tense she'd become until those words wrapped around her, and relief spilled through her. Dean's kindness and his thoughtfulness touched her heart. "Thank you."

"Nothing to thank me for," he said. "You're one of my best employees. Would hate to lose you."

She gave him a grateful smile. "I appreciate that. You have no idea how much."

"Hope they catch that creep with the flyers."

"Me too." She stood up. "I'm going to finish up, then clock out."

"Okeydoke. See you tomorrow?" he asked.

"Bright and early. And by that I mean eleven a.m." She grinned, feeling lighter than she had in days.

Dean laughed as she headed out the door. It

wasn't that she'd expected her boss to can her or look down on her, or even think she wasn't capable of the job as she sported a belly. But she hadn't expected that level of support, and it made her feel good, stronger, ready to tackle what came her way next. And when the time came to put in her notice, she'd be sad to walk away from the family she'd built here.

Out in the house, happy hour had hit in full force, and most of the tables were full and partying up a storm. Rae, Grady, and Kim were on, but Emily just wanted to finish up with a party of twelve, a booth, and one of the two-tops that she'd started. Both for the continuity and for the tips. Ten minutes later, she was just racing by on her way to clock out when she heard someone call out to her.

"I'll have Rae be right with—" she started, then immediately stopped. She knew this older dark-haired woman, sitting alone, with a nervous expression on her beautiful face. She'd seen her in the street with Blue yesterday morning.

She smiled tentatively up at Emily. "Hi."

"Hi."

"I'm Elena Perez."

"Yes, I know. I've just never seen you in here before."

She glanced around. "Never been in here before," she admitted. "No offense. I just do all the cooking at home."

"No offense taken." Emily tried to tamp down the intense curiosity she felt. "Can I get you something? Are you here for dinner or . . ."

"I suppose I could try something." She picked up her menu. "Are you going to be my server?"

"No. Sorry. I'm actually done for the day."

Disappointment registered in the woman's eyes and she put down the menu. The look was so similar to one Emily had seen coming from Elena's son, it unnerved her.

"You didn't stop by to eat, did you?" Emily asked her.

Elena looked a tad sheepish. "I was hoping to see you, actually. Talk to you."

Oh. So she knew. Just like the entire town. *Thank you again, crazy Natalie Palmer.* But Emily was curious about Elena's reaction. Had she spoken to Blue about it? What had been said? No matter what she'd told herself about last night, needing time to process, giving time to Blue to process, she still missed him. Missed his arms around her . . . sleeping beside him, against him . . . talking with him while they ate . . . while they had soup. She smiled to herself. How could one get addicted to the comfort of another person so quickly?

"I'm sorry," Elena said, standing up. "I shouldn't have come. I've done enough damage for three lifetimes—"

"Wait, no," Emily cut in. "Please. I'm glad you're here."

The woman's expression brightened with hope and surprise. "Really?"

Emily nodded. "I'm actually meeting my mom for dinner over at Mirabelle's." She gave the woman a hopeful smile. "Would you like to join us?"

She looked a tad stunned. "Are you sure? Having a stranger around—"

"You're hardly a stranger, Elena." The encouraging smile Emily gave the woman was for herself too. "You're my baby's grandmother."

The woman's lips parted and quick tears pricked her eyes. "Oh my . . ."

"Wait for me," Emily told her with a quick touch to Elena's arm. "Okay? Just going to change; then we can walk over together."

Every damn muscle in his body ached. Shit, he hadn't been thrown from a horse in God only knew how long. He sank deeper into the cold water and cursed up a storm. Legend had it that the stream water on the Triple C land had healing properties. Blue was pretty sure that was bullshit. A joke. A prank. Put forth by one of the Cavanaugh brothers to get back at the others. But he was trying it. His thigh was bruised good, and even though the sun was setting and the water was cold, the pain was receding.

Not that he was going to be thanking those boys anytime soon. Because that would entail him telling them he'd actually taken his clothes off and sat his ass in cold, autumn creek water. And Blue wasn't offering up that bit of comical ammunition. Especially to someone like Cole. That guy—

The sound of a stick cracking up on the hillside stole his attention and he instantly scanned the dirt and trees. For a second, he thought about getting out of the water, getting dressed. But whoever was coming was coming up fast, and he wouldn't have time to throw on anything before they got an up-close-and-personal view of his ass or . . .

Shit, no. Unbelievable. Or maybe not. He sat up. Not in a million goddamned years would he have expected what he saw coming his way. Easy, breezy, not a care in the world. Acting like they hadn't just had a conversation about boundaries and steering clear—acting like she belonged.

"What the hell are you doing here?" he said, his tone as cold as the water he sat in.

Natalie Palmer wore a calm, serene expression and a dark blue dress as she headed down the short incline. "You came to visit me," she called out, the sun setting behind her. But instead of it being a pretty sight, it felt ominous. "And I'm coming to visit you."

The woman was off her fucking rocker. "This is private property."

She shrugged. "Again, you came to see me. On *my* private property."

He hated being naked and ass-deep in river water right now. "What do you want, Natalie?"

"Just to apologize," she said, stopping when she reached the rock with his clothes on it.

Apologize? He sniffed with derision. Hell, no. Didn't buy that for a second. Nor the look of complete normality on her face.

"Here's the thing, Blue," she began, reaching out and ever so gently fingering his jeans. "It's been hard for me. These past weeks. You and I, we had a relationship. One we both treasured. I felt like I could tell you anything—"

"Except who you were," he interrupted harshly.

"We both wanted it that way, didn't we? That was our agreement from the beginning. It allowed us to feel free, safe."

He wanted to tell her he would feel safer around a starving crocodile, but he wanted to see where she was going with all this. Wanted to see if he could glean any information about Cass or the other woman who'd gone missing.

"It felt right," he acquiesced. "At the time."

Her eyes warmed with that little nudge of agreement. She put her hand over her heart. "So then you can't blame me for feeling angry and stupidly spiteful when I see you with another woman."

Off. Her. Rocker.

"What about the flyers?" he said, trying like hell to keep his tone even when what he really wanted to do was throttle her. "Are you still going to pretend you didn't do that?"

She shrugged and looked incredibly vulnerable. "I haven't gotten over you, Blue. I don't work like that. Turn my feelings off so easily and quickly. I gave you my heart, and you wanted to take it. Where does that exchange go?"

When it's all based on a fucking lie? Into the sewer, honey. He stared at her, feeling colder with every breath.

"I know you were with her that night we argued," she continued, her chin lifting slightly. "And I forgive you. We all make mistakes." Her eyes searched his. "Especially in the name of passion."

Calling his night with Emily a mistake was about as idiotic as calling Natalie Palmer sane. Christ. How he had ever thought this woman—"Cowgirl"—was his match was beyond him now. A moment of his own insanity. Or . . . maybe a moment of vulnerability. At that time he'd needed comfort and acceptance—and she'd given it to him.

His gaze connected with hers, and he forced himself to tamp down his own disgust, and go down the path that might lead to answers for so many. "That night was a difficult one," he said carefully. "Finding out you were in River Black, had been all along. Finding Cass's diary . . . what was a man to think?" He left it hanging there. He wanted to see how she'd react, what story she'd concoct.

She shook her head. "That poor girl. You have to believe me, Blue. I didn't do anything to her. I liked her."

"You had her diary, Natalie."

Her face hardened a touch. "You don't want to believe me. You'll never listen to my side."

She sounded like a toddler. "I would listen."

A soft pink blush touched her cheeks. "Really?" He nodded.

"Okay. Well, I'd like that." Her eyes sparkled with happiness and excitement. "We could go up to your house and talk. I've always wanted to see the Triple C. I'm sure I would feel right at home there. Comfortable." She smiled. "With you."

His fucking skin was crawling. As if he was going to take her inside his house. Not a chance. "My mother's there. She wouldn't leave us alone."

"No, she's not," Natalie retorted. Her expression turned suddenly sour. "I just saw your mom in town. She was with . . . *her*."

Blue's chest constricted. "What are you talking about?" Was this more lies?

"Your mother was with Emily Shiver."

"No," he said, shaking his head.

Sensing she'd just poked an already sore subject—one that might be to her advantage if she sharpened the stick a bit—she continued. "They were at Mirabelle's. Emily, her mother, and your mother." She studied him closely. "Does that bother you, Blue? It seems like it does." She pressed her lips together. "Did she go behind your back? Some women can't be trusted. I'm so sorry. But it's good that you found out now. What kind of person she is."

Blue could no longer hold his ire in check. Was he concerned about Emily and his mom having dinner together? Sure. Mostly because Elena was completely and understandably fed up with him right now, and so was Emily. The mutual irritation they must be releasing could probably fuel a jetliner. But that was nothing compared to how Blue felt about the woman in front of him. She was dangerous and manipulative, and she had just insulted the wrong person.

On a curse, he stood up and, naked as a jaybird, waded out of the water and over to Natalie. He grabbed his clothes off the rock and started dressing. "You won't talk about her in front of me ever again," he said. "Understand?"

Natalie's eyes were running up and down his body. Hungrily. Covetously. "Blue," she began breathlessly. "She's—"

"She's the mother of my child," he finished, tugging on his jeans.

His words made Natalie's mouth drop open and her skin turn a ghostly white. "So the baby—"

He nodded. "Is mine." He zipped up his jeans, then grabbed the rest of his clothes. "I'm going now. I suggest you do the same. And if you know what's good for you, stay off this property in the future."

Without another word, he started up the hill toward the big house. What a goddamned mess this was. Maybe Natalie would stay out of it. Maybe she wouldn't. But first thing he needed to deal with was Emily, and the dinner she'd just shared with his mother.

Twenty-five

As the moon's light commingled with the electric ones inside Emily's apartment, she sat at her dining table and stared at the chart she'd created on her laptop. Her budget. Income, expenses, rent. She'd decided to visit River Black Bank tomorrow to see about a small-business loan. Aubrey had left a message on her cell phone earlier, saying she might have found the perfect place for Emily's flower shop. A rental, a little over her budget, but maybe they could get it down?

The screen darkened with lack of use and she ran her fingers over the track pad to bring it back to life again. It was going to be hard to give up the dream of the space downstairs. When you plotted and planned and decorated in your head, it took some time to switch out the image. But then again, she had time.

"Emily?" a voice called outside her door.

She gasped, nearly jumped out of her chair, and

went looking for a knife. Goddamn Blue. What was he thinking? She'd told him she needed time—not a heart attack. And that spare key she'd given him—the one that opened the door downstairs—well, she was going to need that back.

She stalked over to the door and yanked it back with fear-based irritation. "You just scared the hell out of me!"

"We need to talk," was all he said as he walked into the apartment.

"It's late—you could've called me," she suggested, trying not to look directly at him. He was in a red and tan chambray shirt and jeans. His hair was all wet, his skin was tanned, and he was sporting a day's worth of beard stubble.

Damn cowboy.

Damn gorgeous cowboy who made her heart flutter and her panties wet.

She rolled her eyes at herself.

"Yeah, I could have," he answered, glancing around her apartment like he was looking for something or someone.

"Or texted," she suggested.

He turned around, nodded. "Yeah, that's real personal-like."

If she dove at him right now, would he wrap those thick arms around her and just hold her tight? Would he tell her to tip her chin up, maybe do it himself, and kiss her? Because even though she was angry and frustrated with him, at their situation, she missed him.

No. She yearned for him.

"I'm just trying to keep you from investing too much of yourself, Blue," she said, her tone contradictory to what her heart was feeling, what her mind wished for.

His eyes, those incredible blue orbs, drank her in. So fierce, so fraught. "So I see you had a side of sarcasm with your chicken-fried steak tonight." He arched one black brow. "How was dinner, by the way?"

Emily didn't even try to look sheepish. Because she didn't feel that. Didn't buy into that. A woman made her own decisions. Especially this woman. "Good," she said, moving over to where her laptop was open on the dining table. She shut it. "Really nice being with people who are excited and supportive and—"

"Okay. Stop."

His severe tone had her head coming up, her eyes locking with his. Was he really going to be annoyed at her? After how he'd been acting?

He shook his head. "I know you're punishing me."

"That would be incredibly immature of me, wouldn't it?"

A shadow of amusement touched his gaze. "Just listen, okay?"

She sighed, retracted a bit. "Fine."

"I came into this," he began, scrubbing a hand over his jaw, "you and me . . . with a whole helluva lot of baggage. No excuse, just fact. I've been trying ever since to get past my own shit, the distrust I feel, how goddamned painful it was to be lied to again and again." His eyes caught hers and held. "I didn't mean to put that on you, but I have. I did. My instincts are raw, Emily. They make me act or react without involving my heart. I'm going to work on that."

Damn. All sarcasm and imperviousness started to melt within Emily as she listened. Was Blue Perez Cavanaugh actually being vulnerable with her? That was a first. But how long would it last?

"Let's get something straight," he continued, keeping his distance. "I love kissing you, touching you, licking you," his eyes darkened, "but there is nothing I want more than to fuck you."

Emily's mouth dropped open, and breathlessly, she uttered, "So . . . do it."

It was a dare. One he should grab onto if he had any sense.

And yet he hesitated.

"Blue." She shook her head, so tired of this game now. Maybe they both just needed to stop playing. "You need to know if you decide to give your heart to me, I would hold it gently. With great care." She felt emotion building inside her, felt some tears in the back of her throat—but she refused to give in to them. "But if not, that'll be okay too. You and I can be friends. Raise this baby together, as friends."

Horror washed over his face. "Friends."

"Nothing wrong with friends. It's good to have them." And sometimes all you get . . .

"I don't want to be your friend, Emily Shiver,"

he practically growled. "And you damn well know it."

She cocked her head and shrugged. "And I don't want a man's hesitation. I don't want half a man's heart, and none of his trust. I deserve more. Way more. And I intend to get it."

He looked like she'd just slapped him across the face.

And she wasn't stopping there. "You need to let this go, your past, the resentment—every bit of it—once and for all," she said. "Not for me, not for this baby, but for you."

"Those are my mother's words, aren't they?" he said tightly.

"Does it matter?" she pressed.

"Hell, yes, it does."

"It's the truth." She glared at him. "In all your self-righteous anger, have you ever once thought about her?"

"What do you mean?"

"Her struggle? Why she did what she did? Have you ever thought that maybe she kept that secret for you? To keep you safe?"

His expression tightened and his eyes went cold. "Boy, she really did a number on you."

"You're acting like a bastard."

"Fitting then, isn't it?"

He was like a goddamned metal wall. What had happened to him "trying"? "Do you remember how you felt watching me see those flyers today? Watching me tear them down?"

His eyes shuttered.

She nodded. "A single mother. Embarrassed, sure, but never regretting what I carry inside of me. Only protecting it."

Jaw tight, he shook his head. "I didn't always need protecting. She knew that, knew better. She could've told me when I got older—"

"Yes, she could have. But she didn't. Does that one wrong choice really cancel out a lifetime of love?" She cocked her head. "Because if it does, you'd better hope you don't screw up with your own child."

He inhaled sharply. The thoughts going on behind those sky blue eyes were painful and plentiful. But Emily was done for the night. Done trying to reason with the unreasonable.

"You need to go now, Blue," she said.

He released a heavy breath. "No. Dammit, Em. What I need is to stay here, be here—with you . . . fucking sleep with your head on my shoulder again. My arms around you." His eyes clung to hers. "Don't you want that? Don't you miss that?"

Her gut twisted. "I do. More than you can possibly know. But just like you, I don't want to have my heart broken in any more pieces than it already is."

He stared at her for a long time, no doubt trying to decide how hard to push . . . if she was resolute. So Emily went back to her dining table and opened her laptop again. Message sent.

Blue cursed, shook his head. Next to him on the small entry table that had been in Emily's parents'

garage since they'd moved in a few decades before, he spotted one of the many vases of flowers
she'd placed around the apartment. Without a
word, he picked out a red bud and left the apartment.

Feeling as if a part of her had just been stolen,
had its source of sunlight taken away, Emily
dropped into her chair. And with supreme effort,
returned to her budget. And her future.

Twenty-six

Blue sat in his truck in the driveway of the Triple C and stared up at the house. This had been his home for most of his life, and he loved it. But for the past few months, his love had been tainted by secrets and lies. Ones he'd clung to for some strange sense of security.

Emily's words scuttled through him. Had he ever, once, thought about Elena's struggle with her pregnancy, him coming into the world? Sure, he'd thought there was a reason for her lies, but he didn't venture past that. Because he'd been too stubborn, too unwilling to even contemplate forgiveness, and so very entitled.

He scrubbed a hand over his face and exhaled. Then he reached over and grabbed the flower he'd taken from Emily's apartment and headed inside. This needed to end. He found Elena in the sitting room, a book in her hands. It was probably a mystery. She loved a good mystery.

Nerves running around inside his gut, he went over to her and placed the flower on the seat beside her. Then he sat down in the chair opposite and waited for her to look up. "Hey, Mom."

He hadn't called her *Mom* in months, and it startled her. Her gaze shifted to the flower, then back at him. A thousand emotions flickered in those dark depths.

"Please," he said in a tone so gentle it made his own chest ache.

She put her book down on the side table and picked up her mug of coffee. "I wanted to meet her, Blue," she explained. "Make sure she knew that if she needed anything, I was—"

"Mom?"

"What?"

"I'm glad you spent time with her."

Her eyes widened. "You are?"

He nodded. "It made her happy." *Christ.* "I want to make her happy."

"Oh, Blue," she said in the very same voice she'd used when he'd come home from school with a bad grade or a skinned knee. Not pity . . . not anger . . . only love. "I'm so sorry. For everything."

He needed. "Yeah. I know. You've said that so many times. And truly, you only needed to say it once. Now, it's me who needs to apologize." He sat back in his chair and exhaled heavily. "I'm so sorry, for punishing you, for pushing you away, for not even allowing you the opportunity to explain."

Her eyes filled with tears. "It's okay."

"No. It's not. I'm an ass."

She laughed softly. "Oh, I've missed you so much, son."

"I've missed you, too." His eyes caught hers and implored. "Will you tell me now, Mom? I swear I'm ready to hear it."

When what he was asking registered within Elena, she blanched. Obviously, the idea filled her with dread, but even so, she nodded. "You know I grew up in Austin." He nodded. "Pretty much raised by my mother. My father had passed on just days after my third birthday, and I barely remember him. Me and Mom . . . we were all each other had—kind of like you and me used to be—"

Blue felt his insides constrict. With pain, emotion . . . and fuck him, love for this woman.

"And when she got sick," Elena continued, "I had to quit high school to take care of her." She smiled. "She hated that. Nearly forced me to go back. But I was stubborn. She needed me, and I swear I wouldn't have traded that time for anything. Thing is . . ." She sighed. "After she died, finding work wasn't easy. I wanted to go back and finish my education, but I needed to be able to support myself in the meantime. I scoured every Texas newspaper I could get my hands on, and I found a ranch in River Black that needed a housekeeper."

"The Garrisons," Blue put in.

"That's right," she confirmed. "They weren't the nicest folks, but I was able to save some decent money. Which came in handy when the couple broke up and could no longer afford me. After a few other jobs, I landed a real good one as a cook at Pete's . . ." She sighed wistfully. "Oh, I miss that place, miss Pete. He taught me everything. From prep to pastry." She smiled at him. "It was a Saturday afternoon. I'd been experimenting with mole sauce, and I was sure it was the best I'd ever made. A man came back to the kitchen. My kitchen. I never allowed visitors, but this one . . ." Her smile broadened. "Handsomest cowboy I've ever seen. Older than me, but that didn't matter. He told me he'd never tasted anything so good as that mole, and asked if he came back the next Saturday, would I make it again? I said I would."

Blue had seen the way his mother's expression changed as she'd told that last bit of the story. The blush of a woman who still had strong feelings.

"He came back every Saturday for two months," she said. Then her smile faltered. "I knew he was married. I saw the ring. Got no excuse for that. I had fallen in love. And he'd said he wasn't happy. It was a bad, destructive recipe—but so beautifully addictive. Well, things progressed from there and I got pregnant." Her eyes found his and another kind of love glittered in those dark orbs. "He was as thrilled as I was—make no mistake, Blue. But we knew we had to keep it a secret. Too many people would get hurt. And then, Lord, one did . . ."

"Cass?"

She nodded. "And life for everyone went to

hell. Everett wasn't in his right mind. Grieving, angry, desperate. He wanted to blame everyone, including himself for what happened. He'd lost his baby. And when he came to me for comfort, I couldn't turn him away. I could never turn him away."

Blue knew that feeling. He had it for Emily. Couldn't imagine denying her anything. And yet, hell . . . he'd been doing just that since they met. Denying her himself.

"And later?" he pressed. "After Mrs. Cavanaugh passed and the brothers left, why couldn't you be together?"

"Everett actually asked me to marry him." She was watching Blue intently. "But here's the thing, honey: if I said yes, the whole town would suspect our affair, and you . . ." She shook her head. "It was better the way it was."

Oh, Christ . . . so she had been protecting him. Or at least, believed that's what she was doing. They could've waited a year and done it. No one would've known . . . He sighed. So much life wasted. For everyone in this family.

"I was going to tell you after Everett died," she said, blinking back tears. "I was. But the will was read right after the funeral. Lord only knew why Everett would put such a thing in there . . . such a shock . . ." She burst into tears. "Oh, Blue, I'm so desperately sorry."

"It's okay." He stood up and went to her, gathered her in his arms. "Mama, it's okay. We're done with this. All of this. Looking backward, neither one of us can see what's right in front of our faces. All the good."

She clung to him, let him hold her like she'd held him so many times before. "I really like her, Blue," she whispered.

He smiled. "I think I might love her."

Elena Perez released him then and eased back. Her eyes found his and held. "Does she know?"

"Not yet. And it's gonna take more than words for her to believe me."

"Usually does, son. Usually does." She cocked her head to the side and studied him. "But you have a plan, don't you?"

"More like an idea," he admitted.

"Care to run it by me?"

"You got the time?"

Her smile was so bright, so warm as she led him over to the couch. "Always, son. Always."

Three hours. That's all the sleep Emily had managed to get last night. And even the coolish shower she'd taken this morning wasn't managing to wake her tired butt up.

It was all Blue's fault, she reasoned, throwing on a dark gray long-sleeved shirt and a pair of jeans. He'd made her face the truth. About him, about them. About what she wanted, and what she wouldn't allow in her life. Reality was flippin' painful to face sometimes.

She headed into the kitchen and grabbed a banana from the bowl on the counter. There were a few times last night, and even this morning, when

she'd wondered if she'd been too harsh with him—
on him. Had she completely driven him away with
her rant on choice and past and forgiveness—and
his mother? The banana tasted weird. Pregnancy,
maybe? She put it down and drank an entire bottle
of water instead. It was dangerous to involve yourself in someone else's battle, but a mother and
child . . . that could be disastrous. Thing of it was,
she was going to be a mother herself soon, and to
see another mother going through such pain . . .
didn't sit right. Wasn't right. No. Pushing had been
needed. Blue was holding on to the past so tightly,
all the blood was leaving his rational mind and
rushing to his hands. He deserved the peace that
forgiveness brought. She cared that much about
him.

Enough to piss him off.

Enough to push him away.

Speaking of mothers, Emily thought, packing
up her uniform and grabbing her keys. She'd
promised hers that she'd stop by this morning before work. Susie had a couple of boxes of kitchen
supplies she wanted to give to Emily. And there
was nothing Em was loving more than free stuff
and hand-me-downs.

Heading out the door, she was so tired she
nearly tripped over a small square box that had
been placed there. What in the world? She stared
at it. Light green, red ribbon, card. Oh . . . Her
heart lurched in her chest. The good, happy, excited lurching. Without even inspecting it, she
knew it had to be from Blue.

A soft smile touched her mouth as she bent down to pick it up. What could it be? Looked like it would hold half a dozen cookies or a rolled-up scarf. But why would he give her any of those things? After what had happened last night, whatever it was would be an attempt to mend fences or assure her that he was thinking differently. That he understood the gravity of what he'd lose if he didn't forgive—if he kept on clinging to past secrets and lies.

Maybe it was something for the baby, she thought, carrying it inside and over to the counter. She grabbed the scissors out of the drawer and cut off the ribbon. Maybe a onesie or a baby toy. Stuffed animal? Her smile widened as she lifted the lid. A soft little horse would be so adorable—

But it wasn't any of those things. Wasn't anything for the baby. *Oh my God . . .* She looked closer at the thing cushioned inside some white tissue paper. It couldn't be.

Her mind reeled backward. Weeks ago. That night. That incredible first night that started it all. He'd kept it. All this time.

She reached in and lifted out the yellow flower with the burnt-red center—the flower she'd grown herself in the garden at her parents' home—the flower that had been in her hair the night she'd taken him home. The night she'd made love to him. The night they'd conceived their child.

Her breath caught and held in her lungs. Oh, Blue . . . It was dried perfectly, not flattened at all. Preserved. And tied to the stem ever so gently was

a note. Her eyes moved over the text in a ravenous, covetous way.

> *Do you remember? I do. I will never forget.*
> *Come back. I'll be waiting.*

Her heart pounding deliciously, hopefully, Emily didn't think. About his past or their future. She
just wanted to see him. Needed to. It was their
beginning—then and now.

She called and left a hasty message on her
mother's answering machine, then grabbed her
car keys and flew out the door.

Twenty-seven

"You need nails or rope or something?" Deputy Shiver asked.

Deacon wasn't a frequent visitor to RB Hardware, but when Sheriff's Deputy Steven Shiver had called and asked him to meet there, he'd canceled his flight back to Dallas and headed straight into town.

"No nails, no rope," Deacon answered, joining the man near a wall of paint chips. "I only need to know why I'm here."

It was a good thing that Shiver appreciated candor. "Natalie Palmer went to see Blue at the Triple C." His brows knit together. "Know anything about that?"

Deacon regarded the Deputy Sheriff. "Are you suggesting something?"

"Just curious. Triple C land. Your family's land. Thought you might have some awareness of what goes on."

The fact that Natalie Palmer, the woman Deacon believed responsible for his sister's death, had even breathed Triple C air made his insides roll with disgust. And maybe he'd just have a few words with Blue to find out what was behind that. Invitation or no. Deal with it "in the family," so to speak.

"I'm betting that Natalie still thinks there's something between her and Blue," Deacon said. "And she went over to the Triple C to talk to him."

"That's pretty damn brazen," Steven remarked.

"Well, isn't she?" Deacon said with a sniff.

A young woman looking for paint samples sidled up next to them. Shiver gestured for Deacon to follow him over to the front of the store.

"How'd you know she was at the C?" Deacon asked when they got there.

"Told you." He pointed to his eyes with his middle and pointer finger. "Like a hawk."

Deacon sniffed. "Right. So where is she right now, my feathered friend?"

"Right in there." Shiver pointed out the window, across the street to the movie theater. "Went in about ten minutes ago. Seeing the early show."

Deacon's lip curled, the irony of where that woman was not at all lost on him. The very movie theater that Cass had been taken from. No doubt by Natalie Palmer. *I swear to God, that woman is going to live out the rest of her life behind bars if it's the last thing I do.* "Why aren't you in there too?" he pushed. "Watching the movie a few rows behind her?"

Deputy Shiver shrugged. "Didn't like the books, not interested in the movie."

"So you're just going to hang out in the hardware store for two hours?" he said with barely disguised aggression. "That's dedication."

"I think so."

"And the sheriff is okay with this level of commitment?"

"The sheriff is on his way to New Orleans," Shiver revealed, a slow smile spreading across his features.

Deacon stilled. "What?"

Shiver's grin widened. "Yup."

"He's going to talk to the NOLA police?" That's where Deacon's PI was right now too. Deac hadn't expected anyone to really follow up on the new information. This surprised him. Truly.

"That and meeting with people in Palmer's department, in that other parish," Shiver said. "About the alibi."

Again, surprised. And confused. "Why are you doing this?"

Shiver gave him a look like, *What do you think?* "Justice."

"I can't believe that's the only reason," Deacon countered. "Don't misunderstand me, I'm grateful for it. But it's taken a helluva long time, effort, and bitching to bring this case back up in this town. So I'm curious."

Steven glanced out the window, stared at the theater for a few seconds, then turned back. "Listen, I've read everything your man found out about Natalie Palmer. Reread the files from your sister's disappearance. Those diary entries. I'm worried about my sister. You know what I'm saying?"

Deacon's chest constricted again, but he managed a quick, "I do."

The man nodded. "I figured."

"Hell, I'd be standing here too."

The deputy's eyes shuttered as he stared at Deacon. "You know, that wasn't your fault. The movie theater. That was just kids being kids. Could've happened anywhere, anytime—to anyone."

Shit, the guy sounded like Mac. How many times had his wife said those words? And how many times had he struggled to believe them? "I tell myself that all the time, Deputy. But if something happened to Emily that you could've prevented, would you be able to forgive yourself?"

Jaw tight, Shiver blew out a breath. "That's why I'm here, brother. That's why I'm acting the hawk." He turned back to face the window. "We're going to get her. Sooner or later she's going to show her hand. And when she does, we're all going to make sure she never hurts anyone else again."

It was so much easier to navigate her way in the daytime. Last time she was here, it was very much night, and very dark, and drunk Blue was no help at all. She smiled to herself. At least until they'd gotten to the river house. Then he'd scooped her up, tossed her over his shoulder, and carried her inside. She'd laughed at his caveman ways. Hadn't stopped laughing until he set her on her feet, stared into her eyes, then promptly kissed the hell out of her.

The flower, though dried, was tucked behind her ear as she descended the hill. It probably looked ridiculous, but she didn't care. It meant so much that he'd kept it. All this time. It was a very grand gesture. And one she believed was his way of asking for a fresh start.

Her heart beat wildly in her chest as she hurried across the path and up the stairs to the porch. The door was left ajar, ready, waiting for her.

"Blue?" she called out as she walked inside. "It's me." She couldn't stop smiling. She was like a flippin' teenager.

No answer greeted her. She glanced around. It looked exactly the same. Neat, fresh, welcoming.

"I got your note . . . and the flower." She grinned again to herself as she headed into the living room. "You romantic man, you. I can't believe you kept it all this—"

"He didn't," came a woman's voice.

Her heart slamming into her gut, Emily whirled around and came face-to-face with Natalie Palmer. And her gun.

Natalie smiled. "I did."

The breath had left Emily's body, but her mind was zinging with thoughts, fears, questions. Was Blue even here? Had Natalie really been the one who'd sent the flower? And how . . . Goddammit! Why was she thinking any of this when a gun was being pointed at her?

"I'm so sorry," Natalie said, her expression pitying. She looked perfect, like she'd just come out of a salon: makeup lovely, light blue dress, pressed . . . and was that an apron she was wearing . . . ? "I'm sure it's difficult to realize that you don't mean as much to a person as you thought you did," she continued. "One night of drunken sex doesn't make a relationship, Emily. Didn't your mother teach you that?"

Mother. She was going to be a mother. *Think, Emily Elisabeth Shiver. Think and stay calm. How do you get out of this alive? Because you have to.*

"I don't have anything against you, really," Natalie said as she started circling Emily, like a wolf inspecting its prey. "It's just you took something that didn't belong to you."

"I had no idea Blue belonged to you or anyone," Emily began, trying like hell to keep the fear out of her voice. But it was there. How could it not be?

"I think you did," Natalie countered with a tinge of anger. "When I came to that apartment you're renting, you seemed knowledgeable on the subject of Blue and me."

Shit. She wasn't prepared for this. Quick thinking, lifesaving . . . "You're right. I'm sorry. I'll back off."

Natalie laughed softly. It was a terrifyingly mad sound. "You all say that. But you never do."

You all . . . Emily's heart was beating so fiercely in her chest it hurt. *God, how many have there been?*

"I thought the flyers would make Blue see what a whore you are," she continued. "Realize that there's a very good chance he's not the father of whatever you have in there." She gestured to Emily's belly with the gun.

Sick dread flooded Emily and she instinctively wrapped her arms around her stomach. And though fear wanted desperately to claim her, the idea of this bitch hurting her child was enough to force her to stay clear, stay present. She could dive behind the couch, crawl out on her hands and knees. She could make a break for Blue's bedroom—but was there a lock on it? She didn't know. She didn't know.

Natalie shook her head, kept the gun aimed at Emily. "But he's determined to stand by you." She smiled. "That's Blue. Such a good man. Treated so badly by other people. But not me. He relied on me. I was his friend, his rock. I was there for him when he needed someone. And I . . ." Her voice faltered and she stopped moving. Her hand shook a little. "I was supposed to be his lover. Not you."

Think. Think, goddamn you! "You said it yourself, didn't you?" She glanced behind herself. The door was still ajar. Could she make it? How good was this bitch's aim? "It was one drunken night. He'd just come from that fight with you. I'm sure he wanted to be with you."

Her face brightened. "Really? You think so?"

She cocked her head and smiled. "That is so nice of you to admit."

Natalie Palmer was fucking nuts. But keep going. Whatever you can say to stall, do it.

Emily sort of shifted to the right, closer to the door and forced a pout. "You know, he hasn't slept with me since. I'm sure that's because of you. I know he misses you."

Natalie's face fell. "That's not what he says. He doesn't want me anywhere near him." Her eyes narrowed on Emily, and then she started walking toward her.

Emily stepped back.

"He's never going to see me while you're around," Natalie lamented.

Her breath coming shallow now, Emily continued to back up. *What can I use? Pottery on the table . . . Base of a lamp . . .*

Her thoughts, plans, hopes were all cut short. She gasped, cried out as the barrel of Natalie's gun pressed into her stomach. She froze. *No. No. Not there. You're not going to do this to me, to Blue—to our baby.*

"We can't take too long," Natalie whispered as she moved once again, dragging the gun around Emily's side until she was behind her. "Your brother thinks I'm watching a movie." She laughed, her hot breath near Emily's ear as she shoved the gun hard into her lower back. "He's been following me, you know? I think he might like me. Blue won't be happy about that."

Emily's mind fought to register what the woman

was saying. Steven was watching her? How would he know . . . ? Maybe that was a lie, a delusion, too. Even so, she kept Natalie talking. "How did you get out of the movie without him seeing?"

Natalie Palmer leaned in and whispered in her ear, "Same way as before."

Emily stilled as understanding dawned hard and heavy, then tears pricked at her eyes. "With Cass."

"I really liked Cass. We could've been friends. Same with you and me—if you hadn't been such a whore." She inhaled deeply, then pressed the gun even deeper into Emily's back. "Now, walk. Right into the bedroom. I'm sure you know where that is."

Emily didn't move. "Why in there?" she asked, her breathing shallow.

"Because that, my could've-been friend, is where you're going to kill yourself."

Twenty-eight

"Do you want the C?"

Seated in a booth all by himself, James glanced up from his Coke and stared at his half brother. "What are we talking about?" he said loudly. The Bull's Eye was pretty packed.

"Deacon has his land," Blue said impatiently. "Cole has the gym and the house with Grace. You're the only one who's left. You have the mustangs to see to. I know you and Sheridan have been discussing it."

"We have," James admitted, still looking as though he didn't quite understand where they were going here. "Granted, we don't live in River Black in any permanent way. But there are roots we want to plant . . ." He studied Blue for a moment. "You want the Triple. That's no secret. And I'd say probably more so than any of us. More than anything—seems like."

The point stung Blue a little. Not so long ago, he

would've agreed with James. The Triple's belonging to him had been his everything—especially right after Everett's death and the will, and the truth. Shit, it had been all he could cling to. It had been him feeling both close to his father—and his brothers—and like he held something over them too. A punishment of sorts . . . He shook his head. So fucked up. But life can change in an instant. Perspective too. And true love brought about healing, unburdened a weary soul.

He gave James a straight look. "Only thing I want is Emily Shiver."

The man's brows drifted up. "Wow."

"Yep," Blue told him. He glanced around then, looking for her. He thought her shift started at eleven, but he didn't see her anywhere. Must've gotten the time wrong. He turned back to James. "I got a deal for you. You give me the space you just bought, and I'll sign over my share of the Triple to you. With Cole and Deacon doing the same, it'll be yours in an hour."

"Wait," James said, baffled. "Are you talking about the tiny office space? The one with the apartment above it that I rented to Emily?"

"That's the one," Blue confirmed.

"You can't be serious. That's an incredibly bad business choice."

Blue didn't give a good goddamn about business or money. None of that mattered. All that mattered was to show Emily that he wanted her, loved her, had her back, and understood and supported her dreams. He wanted to show her he'd released the past and was ready to embrace the future. With her . . . and their baby.

Blue stuck out his hand. "All I ask is that you keep me on as a cowboy."

James shook Blue's hand, but not enthusiastically. "I don't get this," James said. "What about you? Emily and the baby? Where are you going to live?"

"I thought the river house would suit us just fine. If there's an 'us' to be had," he added dryly. He prayed she'd forgive his bullshit, his pulling away, his fear. He'd do anything to make her believe he'd changed. He saw things different. Maybe Elena could put in a word . . . That made him grin a bit.

James was staring at him. "You're seriously in love with her. Like over the moon, ball and chain—"

"Life and death? Heart and soul?" Blue cut in. "I am." He gave James a questioning look. "So what's your answer?"

James opened his mouth, but before he could say a word, a voice rang out behind them, "She sick or something?"

Both James and Blue turned to see the manager of the Bull's Eye coming toward them.

"Howdy, Dean," James said, giving the man a nod.

He acknowledged James, then turned to Blue, "Emily sick? She usually calls if she's sick."

"What do you mean?"

"She was supposed to be here at eleven."

A thread of unease moved through Blue. He looked at his watch. "It's almost noon."

"Exactly," Dean said. "She's never been late. Never not called. It's not like her."

Unease upgraded to stone-cold fear. Blue turned to James. "You got keys to her apartment? I only have the downstairs one."

Knowing exactly what he meant, James scrambled out of the booth, his face ashen. "Let's go."

The wave after wave of terror running through Emily threatened to steal her mind, her instincts. But she couldn't allow that. Couldn't give in to it. She had to protect the baby. It was the only thought that kept her from breaking, falling to her knees, and begging for her life.

With the butt of the gun pressed between her shoulder blades, Emily kept talking, kept trying to reason with the insane person behind her.

"Blue won't believe I killed myself," she uttered, eyeing an empty vase on the dresser in Blue's bedroom, then a roping trophy on the nightstand. It looked heavy. Probably made of iron.

"He will," Natalie insisted, forcing her toward the bed. "After he reads the note you left him, anyway."

"I didn't leave . . ." She stopped. Exhaled shakily. "What does my note say?"

"That the baby isn't his."

They came up alongside the bed. Near the trophy. Closer. She could do this. God, she prayed she could do this. But one wrong move and a bullet went into her spine, or worse.

"They'll do an autopsy," Emily told her. "The baby is his."

Natalie made a strange sound, like a growl. "All he'll know is that you *thought* it wasn't. That you were fucking several people and were devastated because you had no idea who the father was." She raised the gun suddenly and jammed it into Emily's shoulder. "Now. Lie down on your back. You know how to do that, don't you, whore?"

Now. Do it now. If you get on that mattress, you're dead. Baby is dead.

"Now!" Natalie commanded.

In one quick movement, Emily lunged for the trophy. With a grunt, she whirled around and slammed the thing directly into Natalie's face. The gun went off, a bullet zooming past Emily's shoulder to hit the wall. Someone screamed. Christ, it was probably herself. She didn't know. She didn't care. She didn't stop to think or assess. She raised the trophy and brought it down again—this time on Natalie's hand, then straight back up into her jaw.

Something cracked. Bones maybe?

The gun fell to the floor.

Followed by Natalie herself.

Panic swirled within Emily. She dove for the gun, then stood up and trained it on the woman's unmoving body. Tears were streaming down her face. Her hands were shaking. But she didn't move. This bitch wanted to kill her child. That was fucking never going to happen. And if she even tried to—

"Emily!" someone shouted.

She didn't move. She forced her hands to stay steady. She stared.

"Holy shit!" Another voice.

She didn't listen. She was ready.

"Emily!"

The rush of people in the room didn't faze her. Fine, bring them all. She had this. She had it under control.

"Emily, honey." It was Blue.

Emily's mind started to go fuzzy, her vision unfocused, hazy. Had she killed Natalie Palmer? Had she killed someone to save her baby? Was that okay? Was she okay?

"She killed Cass," Emily hissed, though she wasn't sure it was out loud. "She told me. She took her from the movie theater . . . I won't let her kill my baby . . ."

Suddenly the gun was eased from her shaking hands, and someone was pulling her into their arms. Blue. She recognized him. His scent. His warmth. He was holding her tight and fierce.

"Oh God, darlin'," he uttered. "Are you all right? Are you hurt? Jesus fucking Christ!"

"She's alive."

Was that Steven? Her brother was here too. Oh that was good . . .

"She'll need to go to the hospital to get stitched up," he said. "But damn, Emily did a number on her. She won't be looking pretty for that life sentence in prison."

It was the last thing anyone said that registered. Emily's mind shut down and she just sagged against Blue and let the tears come.

Twenty-nine

"I'm never letting you out of my sight again, Emily Shiver," Blue announced as they walked out of the hospital hand in hand and headed for the car.

"Sounds impractical," she answered, with a trace of her natural humor. She was tired, kind of wrecked, but it felt good to banter again.

"Maybe," he said. "But I'm going to do my best." He stopped in the middle of the parking lot and turned to face her, his hands going to her cheeks. "When James and I found that box, that note in your apartment . . . when I put two and two together . . ." His eyes searched hers. "I've never known that kind of fear, Em. Like my heart had exploded inside my chest. Couldn't breathe. Couldn't bear it . . ." He leaned in and kissed her gently, then pulled back, worry etching his handsome features. "Shit, did I hurt you? I don't know where that maniac touched you . . ."

She smiled. "I'm not hurt. No pain. It was scary as hell. Beyond. But I'm not hurt."

His face taut, he reached for her hand again. "Come on. Let's get out of here."

He led her through the lot. The truck was parked near the back, under a tree. He was so gentle helping her inside. Even made sure her seat belt was buckled.

"Blue," she chided, looking over at him. "I love that you're being so attentive, but—"

"And I love you," he told her.

Emily gasped. This man was constantly taking her by surprise. But this . . .

He sniffed, smiled easily. "You have to know. I mean, hell . . . You have to know how much you mean to me." He put his hand over his heart, like it pained him—or maybe that it had just that very moment switched on. "I'm in love with you. So deeply it aches. I know after what I put you through, how I pushed you away, then pulled you back again, screwed with your feelings and was never straight with mine until this moment, that I don't deserve to hope that you could love me, but . . ."

"Oh, Blue," she said, unclipping her seat belt and turning to face him. They weren't going anywhere for a minute. "Too late."

He deflated instantly, taking her words as a confirmation of what he'd said. He cursed, dropped back in his seat. "Yeah." He nodded. "I figured. And I don't blame you."

Silly boy. Silly, beautiful, soul-crushing boy.

Emily's heart melted as she got out of her seat and crawled up onto his lap. "What I mean, my amazing friend and protector, and baby daddy, and"— she grinned wickedly—"very-soon-to-be lover."

Those surprised, confused blue eyes heated instantly.

"What I mean," she continued, "is that it's too late for you to start hoping I'll love you." She lowered her mouth to his and whispered against his lips. "Because I've loved you for a while now."

As he stared at her—stunned, amazed, excited, hopeful, and happy—she reached down and pressed the seat adjuster. With a hum, his chair moved back, giving her more room.

"My angel," he uttered, his hands coming up to stroke her face and slide into her hair. And then he kissed her. At first with such gentleness, such sweetness, such love, that she wanted to swoon. But there was no space for keeling over. Not in this truck. And plus, she wasn't going to miss this. Kissing this man until he was as breathless and hungry and desperate as she was.

It didn't take long.

After he'd practically devoured her, caused her mind to turn to delicious mush, she eased back and looked at him. Heavy-lidded blue eyes sparkling with hunger . . .

Oh yeah.

Breathing heavily, with her nipples tight and straining against her shirt and her sex wet and so ready, she asked, "Are you going to deny me again, Blue Perez Cavanaugh?"

One dark eyebrow arched and, against her thigh, she felt the hardness of his sex.

"Never," he said with wicked intent. "But here? In my truck?"

Her lips twitched. "No one can see us. You have the tinted windows, and we're all the way back under this lovely tree." She bit her lip. "Unless you can wait until we get home."

"Oh, darlin', I think we've both waited too long." A thread of concern moved across his eyes. "But if you're in any pain—"

"I'm fine," she interrupted. "You heard me and you heard the doctor. All good, baby."

"I don't know if I believe him," he said on a growl.

In response, Emily reached down, grabbed the hem of her sundress and proceeded to pull the entire thing over her head. "Then maybe you need to check me out for yourself." She tossed the dress onto the passenger seat and looked back at him expectantly.

It took under three seconds for Blue to respond. And when he did, it was like an animal had finally been released from its cage. Her bra was off in an instant, and his zipper was down in seconds. She laughed as she clung to him, as she lifted her hips, as he eased her panties to one side. . . . But laughter turned to a groan of utter satisfaction and fulfillment as he entered her.

Finally. God, yes, finally.

For ten seconds, they just remained like that, eyes locked, bodies locked—hearts entwined. And then Emily started to move. The exquisiteness of it, how full and complete she felt as she rode him, was daunting, was so incredibly beautiful.

A fleeting thought entered her head then. They were together. All three of them. In love.

And then the thought drifted from her mind and she gave herself over to him, his hands on her hips as he thrust deeply inside of her.

"Oh God, yes," she moaned, letting her head fall back . . .

"I love you, Emily Shiver," Blue whispered as he found her breasts.

"And I love you, Blue Perez Cavanaugh."

And then his mouth was closing over one hard nipple, and the windows were growing foggy, and Emily's requests were getting dirtier and more brazen by the minute.

It wasn't sweet and gentle and romantic and comfortable. But, hell, they'd have plenty of sweet, comfortable romance in the days and weeks and years to come. What they needed now was a good old-fashioned fuck session in the front seat of Blue's truck. After all, that hot, wonderful sexual bond had started everything. Allowed everything.

Changed everything.

And as they came together, cried out together, with words of love and promises of round two on their lips, that bond became solid, impenetrable.

Unbreakable.

Epilogue

Blue Perez Cavanaugh watched Emily Shiver walk down the aisle toward him. She looked like the angel she was—the angel he'd always thought her to be. That stunning chestnut-colored dress showing off the gentle swell of her belly. His angel. And soon, his wife.

She split off then and went to stand beside Mac, and then the music changed and it was Sheridan's turn to walk down the aisle. Blue turned to look at his brother. James's face told the whole tale. Love, forgiveness, and family. Oh, yes, family.

It was the second wedding at the Triple C. Mac and Deac's had been a lavish affair that had nearly ended in tragedy with Palmer trying to hurt Sheridan. But today's wedding was going to cancel all that out—maybe even renew Deac and Mac's vows. Because, really, this one seemed to belong to them all. Every Cavanaugh who'd come before, and every Cavanaugh who'd come after. They were all there. In their way.

Blue turned to regard his fiancée. She had her eyes on the bride, but Blue would always have his eyes on her. His savior. She'd brought him to a place of peace, and he would spend a lifetime repaying her for that miracle.

Just then she glanced over at him, and her hand went to the gentle swell of her baby. Their baby.

"Will you take each other for a lifetime and beyond?" Reverend McCarron was asking James and Sheridan.

"We will," they answered together.

It was how they'd wanted it. Everything together. Nothing separate. Sheridan and James had decided to buy a house in Dallas and build a smaller house on Triple C land for themselves, for when they came to town. It would be close to where the horses ran. It would be perfect. Family. All three of his brothers had gotten together and decided that they wanted Blue and Emily, and their baby, to have the C. No talking them out of it—hell, Blue had tried. But there was something in them that had wanted life to start fresh here. With a hopeful and happy family. James had even let Blue buy the storefront in town from him. Blue grinned as he remembered. That was where he'd proposed to Emily. Flowers everywhere—flowers to start her shop.

As the reverend pronounced James and Sheridan husband and wife, Blue put his hands together. His applause was met by everyone. His mother, his brothers- and sisters-in-law, and the love of his life. He knew the truth now and it had nothing to do with choices from the past. It was about letting go and allowing himself a happy ending.

For them all.

Including the one who looked down from heaven. For she had finally gotten her truth too.

His sister.

Cass.

Acknowledgments

Thank you to my wonderful readers for embracing and sharing this series. I love you all. And to my amazing editor, Danielle Perez. Your patience, understanding, and incredible skill made these books what they are. Seriously, D. ☺ And to my agent, Maria Carvainis, you're such a tough cookie, and I adore you. Thank you for all you do.

Happiest of reading, my friends.

Laura Wright, out.

Please turn the page for a preview of the
first novel in the Cavanaugh Brothers
series by Laura Wright,

BRANDED

Available from Signet Eclipse.

Diary of Cassandra Cavanaugh

May 12, 2002

Dear Diary,

Today it took five dollars to get the cowboys to look the other way when Mac and I saddled up one of Daddy's prize cow horses. They're so darn mean and greedy. And it's my birthday too! Thirteen years old, people! So, you know, shouldn't I at least get a discount from them boys or something? Jeez. Mac came through, though. She always does. She gave them a piece of her mind, and lots of curse words, too. But they wouldn't budge, so she flipped them her middle finger, paid them off, and told me happy birthday.

She's so funny and crazy.

Mac's been wanting to give Mrs. Lincoln a spin forever. Well, ever since the gray mare came to the Triple C, anyway. Between you and me, I think Mrs. L's a little too much horse for Mac to handle. But o'course Mac doesn't think so. She's as hardheaded as they come. She says what she wants and does what she wants, and she ain't afraid of anything.

I wish I could be like that.
I wish I could be tough.

Mac and me rode out to the Hidey Hole o'course. We had lunch and swam a little bit; then we sunbathed. I'm a total sun worshipper. I wish it were sunshine all day and night and never dark. I don't like the dark. Mac wanted to just wear our underwear and bras while we lay out, but I said no way. The Hidey Hole was always top secret, real hidden down in the gulch, but lately I've been getting the feeling someone might know about it. And I was right!

Not an hour and a half into our fun, my oldest brother, Deacon, found us. He was in a mood, too. He's seventeen and pretty much has his own life. He hates having to come look for me. 'Course, so do James and Cole. But when Mama says move, we all move. Anyway, Deac barked at me to get home and get ready for my birthday party. I told him I'd come along soon. The thing wasn't for another five hours, for goodness' sake! But he wouldn't have any of that. He was in a real snit. Bossy as hell. Which o'course pissed Mac off to no end. She gave it to him good. She sounded like the cowboys when they're working cattle. Definitely R rated! And Deacon hates it. He thinks Mac is a bad influence.

I don't know if I'm right or wrong, but lately, I get the feeling that Mac might have a crush on Deac. Not that she doesn't tell him to take a hike in her colorful way and all, but lately, when she does it, her cheeks go all red. And her blue eyes get all shiny like gemstones. She also plays with her hair,

*wraps it around her finger into a long brown
snake. I don't think she knows she's doing it.*

Maybe I should tell her?

Ugh, I dunno.

*I don't want her to be mad at me. She's my
best friend, but she's also like my sister. And my
family is like her family. All she's got at home is
her pops, and he ain't nothing to sing songs
about in the parenting department, if you know
what I mean.*

*Maybe I can go roundabout with it? Talk
about all the girls who call our house wanting to
speak to Deacon during dinnertime and see how
Mac reacts? Yeah, that sounds good. I'll know if
she's jealous or not. But, Lord, what do I do if
she is?*

*I'll write again tomorrow and let you know
what happens. Wish me luck!*

Cass

One

The glass doors slid open and Deacon Cavanaugh walked out onto the roof of his thirty-story office building. Sunlight blazed down, commingling with the saunalike air to form a potent cocktail of sweat and irritation. The heat of a Texas summer seemed to hit the moment the sky faded from black to gray, and by seven a.m. it was a living thing.

"I've rescheduled your meetings for the rest of the week, sir."

Falling into step beside him, his executive assistant, Sheridan O'Neil, handed off his briefcase, iPad, and business smartphone to the helicopter pilot.

"Good," Deacon told her, heading for the black chopper, the platinum *Cavanaugh Group* painted on the side winking in the shocking light of the sun. "And Angus Breyer?"

"I have no confirmation at this time," she said. Which was code for there was a potential problem, Deacon mused. His assistant was nothing if not meticulously thorough.

Deacon stopped and turned to regard her. Petite, dressed impeccably, sleek auburn hair pulled back in a perfect bun to reveal a stunningly pretty face, Sheridan O'Neil made many of the men in his office forget their names when she walked by. But it was her brains, her guts, her instincts, and her refusal to take any shit that made Deacon respect her. In fact, it had made him hire her right out of business school. When he'd interviewed her, the ink on her diploma had barely dried. But despite her inexperience, her unabashed confidence in proclaiming that she wanted to be him in ten years hit his gut with a *hell yes, this is the one I should hire.* Forget ten years. Deacon was betting she'd achieve her goal in seven.

"What's the problem, Sheridan?" he asked her.

She released a breath. "I attempted to move Mr. Breyer to next week, but he's refused. As you requested, I told no one where you're going or why." Her steely gray gaze grew thoughtful. "Sir, if you would just let me explain to the clients—"

"No."

"Sir."

Deacon's voice turned to ice. "I'll be back on Friday by five, Sheridan."

She nodded. "Of course, sir."

She followed him toward the waiting chopper. "Should I ask Ms. Monroe if she's free to accompany you on Friday?"

Only the mildest strain of interest moved through

him at the mention of Pamela Monroe. Dallas's hottest fashion designer had been his go-to for functions lately. She was beautiful, cultured, and uncomplicated. But in the past few months, he'd been starting to question her loyalty as certain members of the press had begun showing up whenever they went out.

"Not yet," he said.

"Mr. Breyer is bringing his . . . date—" Sheridan stumbled. "And he's more comfortable when you bring one as well."

A slash of a grin hit Deacon's mouth. "What did you wish to call the woman, Sheridan?"

She lifted her chin, her gaze steady. "His daughter, sir."

Deacon chuckled. His assistant could always be counted on for the truth. "I'll let you know in the next few days if I require Pamela."

He stepped into the chopper and nodded at the company's pilot. "I'm taking her, Ty. Bell's been instructed to deliver another if you need it."

The pilot gave him a quick salute. "Very good, sir."

"Mr. Cavanaugh?"

Deacon turned and lifted an eyebrow at his assistant, who was now just outside the chopper's door. "What is it, Sheridan?"

Her normally severe gaze softened imperceptibly. "I'm sorry about your father."

Deacon waited for a whisper of grief to move through him, but there was nothing. "Thank you, Sheridan."

After a quick nod, she turned and headed for the glass doors. Deacon placed his headphones on, stabbed at the starter button, and checked his gauges. Overhead, the rotor blades began to turn.

He'd been to River Black nearly once a month over the past six years. In the first two, he'd attempted to buy the Triple C from his father. When that hadn't worked, he'd tried blackmailing the man. But still Everett Cavanaugh wouldn't sell to him. The idea of buying up land in and around the ranch soon followed. Deacon thought that if he couldn't take down the Triple C through ownership and subsequent neglect and/or bulldozing the property to the ground, then he'd do it the old-fashioned way.

Competition.

His ranch would offer lower prices to the cattle buyers, better wages and benefits to the hands, and the best soil, grass, and grain for the healthiest cattle around. Only problem was, the place wasn't near being done. Even with all the overtime he was paying, his ranch still wasn't going to be up and running for at least a year.

Revenge would have to wait.

Or so he'd thought.

"Tower, this is Deacon Cavanaugh. The *Long Horn* is cleared for departure. Confirm, over."

"Roger that, *Long Horn*. You are clear. Have a good flight, sir."

"Copy, Tower."

As the engine hummed beneath him, Deacon

pulled up on the collective and rose swiftly into the air. For ten years, he'd dreamed of seeing the Triple C Ranch destroyed. And now, with his father's death, he would finally have his goal realized.

Gripping the stick, he sent the chopper forward, leaving the glass-and-metal world of Cavanaugh Towers for the unpredictable, rural beauty of the childhood home he planned to destroy.

Mac thundered across the earth on Gypsy, the black overo gelding who didn't much enjoy working cows but lived for speed. Especially when a mare was snorting at his heels.

"Is the tractor already there?" Mac called over her shoulder to Blue.

Her second in command, best friend, and the one cowboy on the ranch who seemed to share her brain in how things should be run brought his red roan, Barbarella, up beside her.

"Should be," he said, his dusty white Stetson casting a shadow over half his Hollywood-handsome face.

"Any idea how long she's been stuck?" Mac called as the hot wind lashed over her skin.

"Overnight, most like."

"How deep?"

"With the amount of rain we got last night, I can't imagine it's more than a couple feet."

In all the years she'd been doing this ride and rescue, she'd prayed the cow would still be breathing by the time she got there. Never had she prayed for a speedy excavation. Slow and steady was the way to keep an animal calm and intact, but there wasn't a shitload of time.

"Of all the days for this to happen," she called over the wind.

Blue turned and flashed her a broad grin, his striking eyes matching the perfect summer-blue sky. "Ranch life don't stop for a funeral, Mac. Not even for Everett's."

Just the mention of Everett Cavanaugh, her mentor, friend, savior, and damn, Cass's father, made Mac's gut twist painfully. He was gone. From the ranch and from her life. Shoot, they were all without a patriarch now, the Triple C's future in the hands of lawyers. God only knew what that would mean for her and for Blue. For everyone in River Black who loved the Triple C, who called it home, and all those who counted on it for their livelihood.

"Giddyap, Gyps!" she called, giving her horse a kick as she spotted the watering hole in the distance.

She had just two hours to get the cow freed and get herself to the church. And somewhere in there, a shower needed to be had. She wasn't showing up to Everett's funeral stinking to high heaven; that was certain.

With Blue just a fox length behind her, Mac raced toward the hole and the groaning cow. When she got there and reined in her horse next to the promised tractor, she tipped her hat back and eyed the situation. The freshly dug trench was deep and lined with a wood ramp. Frank had done a damn fine job, she thought. And he'd done it fast. Maybe the cowboy had been looking at his watch, too.

She nodded her approval to the muddy eighteen-year-old hand as Blue's horse snorted and jerked her head from the abrupt change of pace. "Leaving us the best part, eh, Frank?" she said, slipping from the saddle with a grin.

The cowboy lifted his head and flashed her some straight white teeth. "I know you appreciate working the hind end, foreman."

"Better than actually being the hind end, Frank," Mac shot back before slipping on her gloves and walking into the thick black muck.

"She got you there, cowboy." Blue chuckled as he grabbed the strap from the cab of the tractor and tossed it to Mac.

"Get up on the Kioti, Frank," Mac called to the cowboy. "This poor girl's looking panicky, and we got a funeral to go to. I'd at least like to change my boots before I head to the church."

As Frank climbed up onto the tractor, Blue and Mac worked with the cargo strap, sliding it down the cow's back to her rump. While Mac held it in place, whispering encouragement to the cow, Blue attached both sides of the strap to the tractor.

"All right," Mac called. "Go slow and gentle, Frank. She's not all that deep, but even so, the suction's going to put a lot of pressure on her legs."

As Blue moved around the cow's rear, Mac joined him. When Frank started the tractor forward, the two of them pushed. A deep wail sounded from the cow, followed by a sucking sound as she tried to pull her feet out of the muck.

"Come on, girl," Mac uttered, leaning in, digging her boots in further, using her shoulder to push the cow's hind end.

Blue grunted beside her. "Give it a little more gas, Frank!" he called out. His eyes connected with Mac's. "On three, Mac, okay?"

She nodded. "Let's do it."

"One. Two. Push fucking hard."

With every ounce of strength she had in her, Mac pushed against heavily muscled cow flesh. Her skin tightened around her muscles, and her breath rushed out of her lungs. She clamped her eyes shut and gritted her teeth, hoping that would give her just a little extra power. It seemed like hours, but truly it was only seconds before the sucking sounds of hooves pulling from mud rent the air. Hot damn! The cow found her purchase, and, groaning, she clambered onto the wood boards. Maybe the old gal darted away too fast and Mac wasn't expecting it. Or maybe Mac's boots were just too deeply embedded in the mud. Or, shit, maybe she was thinking about how she'd never do this with Everett again, this life-and-death moment that both of them had loved so damn much it had bonded them forever.

Whatever the reason, when the cow lurched forward, so did Mac. Knees and palms hitting the wet black earth in a resounding splat.

"She's out!" Frank called from the cab.

"No shit!" Mac called back, laughing in spite of herself, in spite of the thoughts about Everett.

Eyes bright with amusement, Blue extended a muddy hand, and Mac took it and pulled herself up.

"Good thing you have time for a shower," he said, chuckling.

Mac lifted an eyebrow at his clothes caked in mud and sticking to his tall, lean-muscled frame. "Not you. You're all set. Say, why don't you head over to the church right now?"

"Come on, Mac," he drawled, wiping his hands on his jeans as he started out of the mud hole. "I can't go like this."

Mac followed him. "What do you mean? You look downright perfect to me."

"Shit, woman." Standing on high, dry ground now, Blue took off his Stetson, revealing his short black hair. "You know I need a different hat. This one's way too dirty for church."

Mac broke out into another bout of laughter. It felt good to be joking after some hard-won labor. It felt right in this setting, on this day in particular. Everett would have approved. Nothing he'd liked better than the sound of laughter riding on the wind.

Overhead, another sound broke through their laughter and stole their attention. And it wasn't one Everett would have thought kindly on.

Frank glanced up from tending to the exhausted cow and shaded his eyes. "What the hell's that?"

Mac tilted her face to the sky and the gleaming

black helicopter with a name she recognized painted on the side in fancy silver lettering. Instantly, her pulse sped up and her damned heart sank into her shit-caked boots.

"That'd be trouble," she said in a quiet voice.

"With a capital C," Blue agreed, his eyes following the movement of the chopper, too. "Looks like the eldest Cavanaugh has come home to bury his daddy."

"And bury us right along with it," Mac added dryly.

"You think?" Blue asked.

"Hell, yes." As the chopper moved on, heading toward the sizable ranch land Deacon Cavanaugh had bought a few years back, Mac's gaze slid back to Blue. "He's been trying to get his hands on the Triple C since he walked out its gate ten years ago. I'm guessing he thinks this is his big chance."

"But he's got all that property now," Blue observed. "More land than we got here. A house being framed up, the whole thing fenced in for cattle." He shrugged. "Maybe he's over wanting to run the Triple C."

Mac smiled grimly. "I don't think he ever wanted to run this place, Blue."

That had the cowboy looking confused and curious. "Then what? Why would he work so hard and offer so much money for something he didn't want?"

Mac shook her head, dug the tip of her boot into the dirt, into the land she loved. "I don't know. I'm not sure about his reasons. I just know they ain't pure. I tried talking to Everett about it a few times, 'bout why Deacon was pushing him so hard, being such a slick-ass bastard—trying to take over the very home he and James and Cole had all run from as soon as they were able. But he brushed me off, said all his boys had been changed in the head after Cass was taken, and they weren't thinking right." Mac chewed her lip, shook her head. That explanation had never made sense to her, but she didn't push it. Everett had gone through hell, and if he hadn't wanted to talk about it, that had to be respected.

'Course, that didn't mean she hadn't tried to work it out in her head a few times.

"I always wondered if it was just Deacon's way of doing business," she continued. "How he makes his money. Buying and selling off pieces of other people's dreams and sweat." Her eyes lifted to meet Blue's. "But he could do that anywhere. Why the Triple C?"

Blue was silent for a moment. Granted, the cowboy knew some of the history with Deacon, his father, and the ranch, because Mac had filled him in when the former had started his war with Everett six years ago. But Blue didn't know the particulars of the loss the Cavanaugh boys had endured before they'd left home. He didn't know about the day Cass had been taken or the night Sheriff Hunter had come to their door with the news that her body had been found. He didn't know that her killer was never caught, or about the morning they all sat in the very same church Everett Cavanaugh would be eulogized in today, over a beautiful white casket, their lives changed forever.

But Mac knew. And hell's bells, she'd shared that unending grief along with them. Her best friend gone before she'd seen her fourteenth birthday. It wasn't right. For any of them. But neither was taking that grief out on people. Especially family. Especially a man as good-hearted as Everett.

"So you think this is Deacon's big chance?" Blue asked her, his face a mask of seriousness now. "You think he's gonna get his hands on the Triple C?"

"Not if I can help it," Mac uttered tightly.

She watched the helicopter shrink to the size of a dime and then finally disappear behind the mountain. She didn't know what Everett's will was going to say, whom he'd left the Triple C to. But she did know that whoever it was, they'd have her standing over them, watching every move they made. Making sure that this land she'd come to love so damn much was taken care of properly.

"Let's drive this cow home to her friends, boys," she called out. Determination coursing through her, she walked over to Gypsy and shoved her boot in the stirrup. "Let's do the job we've been hired on to do, then go pay our last respects to our boss, our friend, and hand-to-God, one of the best men I've ever known, Everett Cavanaugh."

Also available from
New York Times bestselling author

LAURA WRIGHT

Branded
The Cavanaugh Brothers

When the Cavanaugh brothers return home to River Black,
Texas, for their father's funeral, they discover unexpected
evidence of the old man's surprising double life—a son
named Blue, who wants the Triple C Ranch as much as they
do. The eldest son, Deacon, a wealthy businessman, is
looking to use his powerful connections to stop Blue at any
cost. But he never expected the ranch's forewoman,
Mackenzie Byrd, to get in his way...

Mac knows Deacon means to destroy the ranch and
therefore destroy her livelihood. But as the two battle for
control, their attraction to each other builds. Now Deacon is
faced with the choice of a lifetime: Take down the Triple C
to feed his need for revenge, or embrace the love of the one
person who has broken down every barrier to his heart.

"A sexy hero, a sassy heroine, and a compelling
storyline...I loved it!"
—*New York Times* bestselling author Lorelei James

Available wherever books are sold or at
penguin.com

S0548

Also available from
New York Times bestselling author

LAURA WRIGHT

Broken
The Cavanaugh Brothers

For years, James Cavanaugh has traveled the world as a horse whisperer, but even the millions he's earned haven't healed the pain he hides behind his stoic exterior. Forced to tackle old demons at the ranch, James throws himself into work to avoid his true feelings. Until he meets a woman who shakes the foundations of his well-built walls...

Sheridan O'Neil's quiet confidence has served her well, except when it comes to romance. But after Sheridan is rescued from a horse stampede by the most beautiful cowboy she's ever met, her vow to keep her heart penned wavers.

"Secrets, sins, and spurs—Laura Wright will brand your heart!"
—*New York Times* bestselling author Skye Jordan

Also available from
New York Times bestselling author

LAURA WRIGHT

Brash
The Cavanaugh Brothers

No matter how many fights UFC champion Cole
Cavanaugh wins, he can't rid himself of the guilt of not
having saved his twin sister's life. Now, not only is he facing
his archenemy in the ring, he's fighting to uncover the truth
about Cass's death.

The mystery surrounding Cass's murder also haunts
veterinarian Grace Hunter. Many believe that her father may
hold the key to the truth. As Cole persuades Grace to help
him unlock the elusive clues, her defenses weaken. She finds
the Stetson-wearing fighter irresistible. But while the truth
could free Cole's heart, it could very well end up
shattering hers.

"Saddle up for a sexy and thrilling ride! Laura Wright's
cowboys are sinfully hot."
—*New York Times* bestselling author Elisabeth Naughton

Available wherever books are sold or at
penguin.com

S0601

LOVE
ROMANCE
NOVELS?

For news on all your favorite romance authors,
sneak peeks into the newest releases, book
giveaways, and much more—

"Like" Love Always on Facebook!

 **LoveAlwaysBooks**